THE DEAL GOES DOWN

ALSO BY LARRY BEINHART

FICTION
Zombie Pharm
Salvation Boulevard
The Librarian
Wag the Dog
(originally published as
American Hero)

THE CASSELLA BOOKS
Foreign Exchange
You Get What You Pay For
No One Rides for Free

WITH AND AS GILLIAN FARRELL
Murder and a Muse
Alibi for an Actress
Seven Stages of Deception

NONFICTION
*Fog Facts: Searching for Truth
in the Land of Spin*

THE
DEAL
GOES
DOWN

LARRY
BEINHART

MELVILLE HOUSE
BROOKLYN • LONDON

THE DEAL GOES DOWN

First published in 2022 by Melville House
Copyright © Larry Beinhart, 2021
All rights reserved
First Melville House Printing: July 2022

Melville House Publishing
46 John Street
Brooklyn, NY 11201
and
Melville House UK
Suite 2000
16/18 Woodford Road
London E7 0HA

mhpbooks.com
@melvillehouse

ISBN: 978-1-61219-990-0

ISBN: 978-1-61219-991-7 (eBook)

Library of Congress Control Number: 2022936526

Designed by Emily Considine

Printed in the United States of America
1 3 5 7 9 10 8 6 4 2

This book is dedicated to a rather random group of mostly Woodstock people who make it the place it is. Some of them living. Some dead.

Some show up in this book, real people strolling through fiction, as we all like to do. They're not in the list below, not even the two who just lent their names to a pair of cats.

So, to Julie Beesmer, who runs Bread Alone the way a coffee shop should be run. Joe & Denise Clark at Bearsville Garage. Mikhail Slobodynak with the banya & frozen pond. Gioia Timpanelli, Sicilian-American storyteller & Ken Barricklo, architect. Graham Blackburn, expert in antique woodworking tools.

Dean Schambach, actor, bohemian, ski jumper; Rocky Rosario, person of interest; and Richard Segalman, artist; representing the deceased. But there are videos of them on YouTube, Dean's under his own name, Rocky's is *Rocky Lama*, and Richard's simply and mysteriously called *Winter*.

Plus apologies to the rest of the people I play poker with, play tennis with, ski with, and otherwise know about town, who are not mentioned. How damn long can I make a list like this. All of us with our aspirations & disappointments, achievements & frustrations, what the ancient Greeks called the *agon*.

THE DEAL GOES DOWN

CHAPTER ONE

WOMAN ON A TRAIN

THE WOMAN ON THE TRAIN asked me to kill someone.

I liked the train. I didn't especially like the woman. It was a real train, an Amtrak, not one of the commuter trains like Metro-North, which are more like buses that happen to be stuck on rails. We both got on at Rhinecliff.

The line is called Empire Service. It runs along the east bank of the Hudson River from Albany to New York City. There are about thirteen trains a day, weekdays. Each one has a cafe car. They're the old types with tables that are simple rectangles with badly cushioned bench seats on both sides. You can really sit there and enjoy the ride. The new ones, like they have on the Acela Express, have uncomfortable stools at a counter too skinny for you to even read a newspaper with your coffee, making it clear that what they really want is for you not to be there. Take your sandwich, snack, and whatever you're slurping on, and go back to your seat.

These sit four. Comfortably. In this case it was just the two of us. Me facing south, the direction we were headed, and her facing north, the places we were leaving behind. Our table was on the west side, our windows facing the marvelous and great river that looks different every season, every day, every time, no matter how many times you've seen it.

Some years ago, I don't remember if it was a dozen or two decades by now, they stopped offering cafe *service* on the short hauls, the seven that originated or terminated in Albany. The other six include two for Niagara Falls, two for Rutland, Vermont, one for Toronto and one for Montreal. Those still have cafe service in the cafe cars. They're also the most likely to run late, especially the two that cross the border because fear is mud and it makes for a slow slog.

We were on the Ethan Allen Express out of Rutland. We'd boarded at about 2:50 in the afternoon and it had left the station right on time at 2:54.

I was on my way to a funeral. I headed straight for the cafe car. What was there to do but look out the window, contemplate the river. You think of it as flowing south, water entering it from the mountains on either side, all going down to New York and then to the Atlantic. But actually the ocean pushes back. The whole river will flow north for a hundred and fifty something miles; you can't really see it except in winter if it's cold enough for ice to form and then break up and if you're watching at the right time you see the white slabs moving the wrong way.

On my way to a funeral, another old friend gone. Sitting there, moving south, watching the water flow as it did before I came and will do after I'm gone, and the light and the hills, trying to come to terms with the rhythms of life and death.

I was happy to find an empty table.

She'd gone past me to the service counter. A couple of minutes after we got rolling, she swayed back down the aisle, came to where I sat, and slid in across from me as she was surely entitled to do. She had a cardboard tray with a miniature bottle of Tito's Handmade Vodka, a can of Schweppes Ginger Ale, and a plastic railroad cup with ice. She opened the Tito's, poured it all out into the cup, and then popped the tab on the can and added a measured amount of the Schweppes.

She didn't start out asking me to kill someone.

She started with a simple, "Hi, Tony, how are you?"

We knew each other slightly, vaguely, from running into each other, up and around the Woodstock area, or maybe Saugerties or even Phoenicia or Shandanken. At that point, I couldn't for the life of me remember her name. "Fine, fine," I said. "And yourself?"

"I'm grand, just grand," she said in a tone that said all things opposite, miserable, bitter, and disappointed in life. I tried my best to take her at her word and ignore her manner, because I had no desire to know.

"Good, good," I mumbled and turned to watch the winds making small waves on the river and the illusion created by the turning of the Earth on which we ride that it's the sun that's moving, to the west and sinking, on its way to hiding below the horizon.

She was a reasonably attractive woman, as these things go, and had probably been an almost beautiful one ten or twenty years earlier. What the hell was her name? And where exactly did I know her from? I guessed her to be staring at forty and hoping it wasn't staring back at her. Well dressed. Expensively dressed to the degree that I could judge. The manner with which she raised her glass and put her lips to it was trying very hard to say I'm just sipping at this for the flavor and because it's refreshingly cool. She was good at it, having practiced it a lot I guessed, and it was convincing if you didn't put an odometer on the speed with which it went down, which told another story, that her natural state was a place she wanted to leave behind and the 80 proof was rolling her away from it as surely as the steel wheels on the steel rails below us. She said this and that, I was listening just enough to make polite noises and I don't recall what. If I'd had computer in front of me or even a bunch of paper or a serious looking book, I would have said "Pardon me, I don't mean to be rude, I'd love to chat, but I have to get this done." Instead I just hoped I could keep her nattering at a sufficient psychological distance that it wouldn't build to the point where I blurted out a strident command to shut up.

Madelaine, that was her name. Maddie.

Right, right, she was going on about a son-of-a-bitch husband who was ruining her, cheating, of course, with secretaries and what not, of course, the nanny, that ex-nanny, two nannies back, maybe the housekeeper even if she had fat thighs, alienating her children from her, Leslie and Sandra.

They had a lot of money. Or he had a lot of money. Maybe not by New York City standards, hedge fund *billions* and such. Certainly, by upstate standards. Maybe millions? This was from vague, passing gossip, about people I barely knew, from people I slightly knew and didn't listen to very much. There was money there and there was little or no money here—meaning with me—and I felt its tug. I don't know when it happened or if it was always that way and I was just blind to it, money has gravitational force. The bigger the mass of it, the closer you get to it, the more it pulls you.

Maddie finished that drink and went back for another. I was grateful for the silence when she was gone. Then she was back. She poured again, mixed again, and drank again, faster this time. She said I was looking good, was I going into the city on business. I said no. She said, jacket and tie, fresh shave, being inquisitive, but friendly.

"A funeral," I said.

"Oh, death," she said. "I'm sorry. Were you close?"

None of your fucking business is what I wanted to say. "Close enough" is what I said. It didn't quite shut her up. Of course not.

"You're a detective," she said.

I twisted my head, half a shake, half a denial. I raised one shoulder, shrugging it off.

"You used to be a detective," she said.

I made one of those noises. Yes, it was true. I acknowledge it. Don't have any interest in discussing it. She wanted to know if it was exciting. Did I do any famous cases? Did I carry a gun? Did I ever shoot anyone? Things like that. What kind of people did I work for? It was all long ago, and far away, is what I said, in several different ways. Retired now, living on social security and a little of this and a little of that.

Maddie said that I didn't look that old. I'm vain enough to want that to be true. I still have hair on my head, I haven't gone to fat, and I'm as fit for my age as I'm likely to be short of being fanatical, medicated, and on a regimen of human growth hormone.

We'd passed Croton-Harmon. That was her third drink. On the train. I expect she'd started before she'd boarded. She got the fourth just after Yonkers. We'd be seeing the Palisades across the river soon. The fragments in her mind were mixing and matching without the normal controls and separations of sobriety. "Millions," she said. "The pig has millions. And he is a pig. He's cruel and plotting and vicious and mean. I have bruises. I could show you bruises. Not to mention the emotional abuse. Plus, if Me Too catches up with him. The problem is everyone is scared of him. And his money, of course. I should have a big, big piece of that money. He wouldn't have made it without me. Will I get it? No. I told you some of the things he's manufactured and faked to cut me out. Plus, he will spend on lawyers. Lying, mean, despicable lawyers.

"A funeral," she said, in a quick gear shift. "Death. That's what has me thinking this way."

Yes, that and alcohol.

"Death is the only way out for me," she said, like it was a well thought out conclusion after much study. "Really, I'm ruined. I'll have nothing. Unless he dies. Soon. Now, I guess. Then . . . and I deserve it . . . it's what's right. I want to have him killed."

"No, you don't mean that."

"Yes, yes, I totally do."

"You're asking for trouble."

"I would pay," she said.

"Look . . ."

"Really," she said. "You must know people like that. Right? You must."

"Come on, you should maybe have some coffee."

"A hundred thousand," she said.

"Do you have money like that?"

"After," she said. "After he's dead. Easily."

"You want someone to do it on spec?" I knew enough literary and movie types to know the difference between working on commission and speculation.

"I could . . . I have some . . . I could come up with like ten . . . ten K up front. The rest after."

"That's not enough, not nearly enough," I said, trying to shut her down.

"I could do twenty," she said. "Twenty thousand. Cash. Untraceable. I could do that."

"Really?"

"Yes, yes, I can," she said, with what appeared to be utter sincerity and conviction.

I was very broke. That's not an excuse. Maybe it's an explanation. Maybe it's not. My home was thirty-six hours from going into foreclosure. Maybe it was one of those moments where you're saying to yourself, I have to do something new and different with my life, though that's not something you expect when you've recently turned seventy, and then something just comes along and presents itself. I'd never done anything like that. Not remotely like that.

I said, "Yes."

"Yes?"

"Yes. I think I can help you."

CHAPTER TWO
DARK AND DAWN

"I have outlasted all desire,
  My dreams and I have grown apart."

ALEXANDER PUSHKIN

THERE IS A TIME THAT is neither dark nor dawn as there is a time between sleep and waking.

Sleep is the time of dreams, the real kind, that are run by a part of our mind that might as well be a different person, with its own drives, desires, and needs, that uses us the way that writers use the stories of strangers, snatching and stealing parts and pieces, kibbles and bits, putting them out of order, into other arrangements, for different made-up tales, loose in logic, ungrounded by space-time, using our synapses like fiber-optic cables to play them IMAX-style against the curved inside walls of our skulls as if they'd been already cleaned and polished white by death. That particular dream time, on the way to morning after the mourning of the funeral, was filled with corpses and cadavers.

It started with reality, Winston C. Walker, centerpiece in an open casket.

A big man in his prime. A black man—so the music at least was good—though it may be incorrect to say, to even notice—African

Americans have much better music for death than white people do. He'd been a cop. Starting in the sixties. Then bookended by scandals. The one in the seventies opened the gold shield door for him. The second, in the nineties, prompted his exit.

They were the crazy years.

I know the man been to the wall, I know the wall was rough. I don't know how many men he killed. I know he killed enough. Their ghosts seemed to form themselves from the thick, heavy, urban air, into sad, dim things, coming toward the casket, maybe drawn by the burnished bronze, silver handles, plush champagne satin liner, glittering like a fishing lure. Maybe to waft his ghost away. Maybe to be sure he was really dead. Once they'd bushwhacked a route from the impalpable to the corporeal, other haunts sensed the opportunity, or just got pulled along by the draft. I surmised that the ones that followed immediately behind, based on whom they gazed at and whom they attempted to address, belonged to Owen Cohen, who had been Winston's partner in the NYPD.

I'd done business with both of them. While they were still on the job, they'd moonlighted for me. When I wanted to get out of the PI racket, they turned up to buy me out and paid in cash. Whatever that suggests is far more likely to be true than not.

I meanwhile had an ordinary, pleasant, live person's conversation with Owen. He said business was good, but not as good as it had been, big companies largely created through national security money were moving in and everything was going digital. By then, some of my own ghosts were sneaking in, some to taunt, some to make me mourn . . . my wife and my son . . . to tear my heart out if I'd still had one.

Back home, the scrambling of my two cats intent on a kill woke me from my memories and dreams. Carl Sandberg had conned us all . . . "the fog comes on little cat feet. It sits looking over the harbor and city on silent haunches and then moves on" . . . into thinking that cats move with no more sound than drifting mist . . . but given the right surface they thump and thud, they skid, and even knock things over. I have two. Scotty's the cute, sociable one. Huba's the killer. His little face actually looks somewhat like Elisha Cook, Jr.'s, the little gangster in *The Maltese Falcon*, but when he kills, he's as straightforward and ruthless as Richard Widmark pushing the old lady in the wheelchair down the stairs in *Kiss of Death*. Scotty's starting to learn from Huba. I praised them both for the mouse they'd caught sneaking into the kitchen. It's their job.

I picked up the corpse with a paper towel and took it outside. There was mist in the air. I tossed the little carcass into the trees. Other creatures would find it and eat it quick enough.

Later, when I went into Woodstock, I saw that the fog around my house was part of a layer of clouds caught between the peaks, hanging around, halfway down the hills, and it was clear down in the valleys and up above them. I understood quite clearly that it was beautiful. Once it would have moved me. I felt nothing.

The air had a definite chill in it. Distinct enough to say that snow would be coming soon, a matter of weeks, even days. Once that would have filled me with eagerness. Now it didn't.

I was on the verge of losing my house. I couldn't bring myself to care.

Inertia. My choice of choices. I could have been a TV ad with an elephant sitting on my head representing depression or some other mental disorder so as to sell a medication that would knock a pachyderm off a person.

The only thing I could bring myself to care about was the cats. They would need a new home.

I went into Bread Alone, automatically, because it's what I always do. There were a couple of writers there that I knew. Shalom Auslander, sat at his usual spot toward the back. I asked him if he'd like two cats, excellent mousers, dedicated killers. He said, "I'm moving to L.A." Larry Beinhart was sitting in his usual spot, at the other end, just opposite the Geezers. I told him I might be moving away and my two excellent cats needed a home. "If all a *man*'s got left to care about is a dog," he said, with emphasis on man, "that's one thing. But if all a *man*'s got to care about is a couple of cats, then he's in big trouble." It was snarky, but I think I agreed with him. The Geezers shook their various heads before I even said anything.

Was Madelaine still asleep? When she woke, what would she remember? What would she think? Would she still want her husband dead? Would she think she—we—would actually go ahead with it?

I could already make a long list of the problems, the dangers, and the clear why nots. What I couldn't understand, at all, was why I'd said yes. I had never killed anyone for money. I had never killed anyone out of anger, hatred, jealousy, or greed. Never for revenge, for pleasure, as an alternative to divorce, or as the fifty-first way to leave a lover. The problem was that it had launched the mechanism inside me that insists that if I've said I'm going to do something, then, like kid that's taken a dare or a gangster that's made a stand, I must do it. Once I thought that was a virtue. Maybe, I somehow lived in a world, back then, in which it was, and the world had changed around me. Maybe it was always a fool's cap. The sensible, grown-up mechanism that should say forget about it—it was a mistake, a foolishness, a lie, if that's what you want to call it—is not as self-propelled and not nearly as strong. How could I know—how could anyone know—if they were an insane person in a sane world or a sane person in an insane world. I may have blurted that question out loud—or maybe just thought it forcefully. In any case there was no reply. Just some blank gazes.

Hopefully, fortunately, *surely*, all that was moot.

Madelaine would wake up to the realization that she'd discussed murder-for-hire with someone she barely knew. She'd desperately hope that it would be forgotten by both of us. I'd never hear another word about it. That was far more likely, and frankly, much to be preferred.

CHAPTER THREE

AT THE END OF
THE ROAD

I HEADED HOME, TRYING TO figure out how to explain things to the cats.

I turned off the county road onto Shanty Road, heading up into Hellmenn Hollow, where I lived, tucked between Round Bear Hill and Slate Mountain. The air had turned crisp and clear. The low-hanging clouds had blown out, but they'd left their mist on the last of the autumn colors, making them vivid in the sun. I knew it was beautiful. I knew any of us who lived here were blessed to do so, but I only knew it like the answer to questions on a civil service exam.

After the first four miles the pavement ends, and then there's another five of dirt road to my house, the last one, sitting up there by its lonesome. As I came around the wide, eighty-year-old oak on the final curve that hides the house from sight, I saw a car there.

It was unmistakable.

Ford Interceptor. One of the new ones. Shaped like something between an SUV and a station wagon. This one was white with a super-bumper up front, *Sheriff* in big letters written on the side, *Ulster County* in much smaller letters above it, and the image of their seven-pointed badge in front of it. Plus, a small American flag over the front wheel.

I pulled up. Stopped. Got out.

He opened his door. He got out. Dark gray shirt, lighter gray pants with a darker stripe, leaving his trooper hat in the car. He was about 6 foot, maybe more, probably 220 pounds, the bulletproof vest making him look even chunkier. Hard to stay slim when mostly what you do is ride around in a cushiony car all day. He was going bald. What hair he had on his head was cut to a quarter inch. I knew him slightly.

"Hey, Rollie." Short for Roland, last name Robidoux.

"Hey, Tony."

"What's up?"

"I gotta give you some papers."

"They sent a deputy?" I assumed it was the bank. One of the required steps to seize my home from me. Any process server, any person for that matter, could do it. They could even just mail it. Though that meant they'd have to give me more time to respond.

"Well, what I heard," Rollie said, "is that the guy they sent before was a little lost. Then he ran into someone down by the fork and asked that person where your address was. And whoever that helpful local was, he said, 'Oh don't go up that way, there's a bear's den up there. A momma with three cubs and you know how bears get if they think the cubs are threatened. And the guy who lives up there has a whole bunch of guns . . . because of the bears . . . but he's a little paranoid and trigger happy so I wouldn't go up there if I were you.'"

"Who would say such a thing?" I said, though the way he told it made it clear he knew it had been me.

"Not a problem," Rollie said. "We all thought it was kind of funny.

Anyway, the guy didn't want to get chewed up or shot, so he left. He was conscientious, though, I'll say that for him. He could have given you sewer service."

"We don't have sewers up here," I said.

"I know that," Rollie said, getting irritated. He was quite willing to be amused about messing with a process server but not with him. The foundation stone of police psychology is that anything short of 'Yes, sir,' 'No, sir' is a rattle that warns them that their very life is at stake. "He could have tossed it and said you were served, but he didn't. So here I am, and here you are." He handed the papers to me.

"OK," I said. "I wasn't giving you a hard time."

That was enough to flip his switch back to your-policeman-is-a-good-neighbor. "Hey, losing your home is hard. It's fucked, is what it is. You know there are services and appeals and they have to inform you about them."

"I know," I said. I did. I should have had the energy, the will, the caring, to fight. The process could be stretched out for years if you tried hard and got a little bit lucky. But it hadn't been in me to do it. And still wasn't. I said, "Thanks."

"Yeah." He nodded. He turned around. He got back into his car. Maneuvered it so he was facing the descent and began heading down into the valley. Almost as soon as he started, he slowed, then eased over, trying to make room on the narrow way. There was the sound of another car coming up the hill. That car slowed. Then they squeezed past each other.

It was Madelaine in her shiny new Lexus. They inched past each other at about three miles an hour. They looked at each other. They were both pleased that they'd accomplished it without a thump, a thunk, or a scratch. Rollie was hardly Super-Cop, but I could see that he was looking at her with automatic cop's eyes—*Who's this? What's she doing here?* He wasn't suspicious, not at all, just a bit of information into the mental file. If it came to pass that Madelaine became a widow through violence, Rollie would likely flip through his memory and find the image of her driving up to the home of Tony Cassella, a man who had been in documented desperate financial straits at the moment he saw them together but who had subsequently saved his abode by delivering a healthy chunk of cash to the bank.

CHAPTER FOUR

WHAT A DEAL

"That which starts fucked, stays fucked."

HENRY SHEINKOPF, POLITICAL CONSULTANT

MADELAINE HAD THE TOP-END LEXUS SUV, the LX. It was big.
It had a V-8. The exterior was "atomic silver." The company described
the interior as "parchment semi-aniline leather with Open-Pore Brown
Walnut trim." It cost upwards of $90,000. She stopped right in the
middle of the drive, blocking my way if I wanted to get out and anyone
else if they wanted in. Your subjective, personal impression that it's always a Mercedes or a Beemer or such that cuts you off is accurate. There
are studies that prove that people with expensive cars have a sense of
entitlement, expectations of impunity, and less regard for others.

Madelaine climbed out. She wore a hip-length shearling jacket
over light brown slacks and stylish boots, all so in tune with the Lexus'
upholstery it was hard to tell if she was accessorizing herself to the
car or the car was accessorized to her. She was also wearing a smile
and sunglasses. They were meant to convey that she was competent,
optimistic, and unperturbed by a conspiracy to commit murder. The
smile, however, seemed thin and strained, and there was just a trace

of twitch at one corner of her lips. The sunglasses, I was willing to bet, covered slightly bloodshot eyes, and if she took them off in the full daylight her eyes would scrunch up in a squint.

Not only had she been seen arriving by the sheriff's deputy, the big car had a GPS and her cell phone was tracking and recording her every move. If her husband died—or survived some nearly fatal accident—even if I had nothing to do with it—and nothing further to do with Madelaine in any manner—a trail had been laid that would wend its way back to this moment and to me.

"Get back in your car," I said.

"What?"

"Back. In. Now."

She looked as hurt and bewildered as she would be if the maître d' at her favorite restaurant had suddenly denied her reservation. In front of others . . . who knew her!

"Now," I said. "Do it."

"Don't order me about."

"Why not?"

"I will not . . . will not . . . I won't let men push me around. You're not my husband. Times have changed."

"Fuck it. Do what I say or just get gone." I was either going to establish control or offend her sufficiently that she went back down the hill and back across the river where she lived and I would simply continue my slow floating fall from nothing to nowhere at all. Both options were fine with me. When you got nothing, you got nothing to lose.

She paused, confused, bewildered.

I walked past her and around to the passenger side of her hulking SUV and tugged on the door handle. She'd locked it. Which was pointless. Not even the racoons had figured out how to open a car door. "Come on," I said.

"What?"

I said, "Click," accompanied by a gesture of pushing the unlock button on an e-key.

She did as I'd ordered. An excessively patriarchal command structure was being established. Oh, dear. But in this case, it was a good thing.

I pulled the door open, got in. I pointed at her and then to the driver's seat.

She got in.

"Down the hill," I said.

She started to say something.

I put my finger to my lips, the universal silence sign, and shook my head from side to side to add "no" to it. Then I pointed. Down the hill.

The Lexus purred. It had a better purr than my two cats. It purred in dollars and yen. So smooth. It rolled down the rough dirt track like an old-time Cadillac on a freshly paved Eisenhower interstate. About a half mile on, I gestured her to go slow. As we neared the next driveway on her left, I pointed to the turn. She turned. Two hundred yards in we got to a good-sized house, relatively new, with a wide deck off the second floor, facing the downhill side, higher than the nearest trees so it had a vast view across the valley and off to the western hills. I used a gesture again, to tell her to stop. When she did, I got out and indicated that she should also.

She got out, not sure if she should be angry, obedient, resentful, or just confused.

I held my hand up to the side of my face like I was making a call. Then held out my hand for her phone. She was extremely reluctant to hand it over.

I shrugged and starting walking away back up the mountain.

"OK," she called out.

I turned around. Walked up to her. Held out my hand again. She put her phone in it, watching me like my cats watch a large dog.

Nervous and ready to jump or to make their scariest snarl. I turned away from her. She gasped. I opened her car door, put the phone inside, and closed the door again.

She stared at me.

"OK," I said in a normal, conversational tone of voice. "Tell me what you want."

"What we said, what we said, yesterday. On the train."

"You're sure?"

She swallowed and nodded.

"Say it. Say it out loud," I said. "You're sober, right?"

"That's got nothing to do with it. I don't have a problem with drinking."

"Of course not. It's what? About 11:00 in the morning?"

"I don't know, I'd have to look at my phone."

"Oh, for God's sake, look at the sun. See where it is in the sky. It's 11:00, maybe ten minutes after. Have you had a drink yet today?"

"No. No, I haven't."

I thought she was telling the truth. But I wasn't going to get close enough to smell her breath right then. Maybe later, just to run a truthometer.

"So tell me."

"I want . . . I need . . . my husband to be dead. He's a monster. He really, truly is."

"Alright."

"And I'll pay."

"Twenty thousand up front," I said. "Plus, if there are expenses. Expenses."

"OK, yes," she said.

"I'm not going to invoice you or give you receipts. Whatever I say they are, they are, and you cover them."

"Sure, yes, of course."

"Then $100,000 afterward."

"As soon as the estate is settled."

"How long will that be?"

"I don't know. The normal time. Weeks, a couple of months, if there are no complications."

"Do you inherit? Or has he cut you out of his will? Willed it to your kids or his mistress or your dogs or the Committee to Sanctify Donald Trump?"

"I inherit. I do. At least half. Half, I think, in trust for the children."

"Are you sure?"

"Yes, yes, I'm sure. It's part of the prenup."

"If we do this, we do it my way, every step."

"I guess. Sure. Can I ask you something?"

"What?"

"Why are we here? At this house?"

"Your car, your phone, your everything, tracks you. And leaves that trail. Let's say you husband dies. In a suspicious way. You're carefully somewhere else and you can prove it. Oh, boy, you have an iron-clad alibi. But the spouse is always the first and primary suspect and, you being a well-off, well-bred, upper-crust woman, nobody expects you to soil your hands. Not directly. You'd find help. Like for everything else, your gardener, housekeeper, nanny, whatever. The cops start looking at your car. At your phone. Also, there's already a sheriff's deputy, Rollie Robidoux, who's seen you drive up to my house. Well, what the fuck are you doing at my house? Talking to me? Are we friends? Not that anyone remembers. Lovers? I'm what, forty years older than you. But if I were, that wouldn't make it better, it would make it worse. Everyone knows the plot of *Body Heat* even if they haven't seen it. It's your basic *noir* story. A little hot sex, man gets besotted, woman gets besotted man to kill for her.

"So, what the hell are we going to do about all this information that you've already created that—should we do this insanity—that will lead to a connection between us that has no acceptable explanation?"

She shook her head. She didn't know.

"I do know. Which is why you're going to do things my way.

"See this house. It's number 46. I'm 135, at the top of the hill. But remember 46. It's for sale. It was listed a while ago, then the owners stopped showing it because they have some other things going on. You saw it a month, five weeks ago. It looked interesting. Four bedrooms, three full bathrooms, two-story living room with a beautiful fireplace, seven acres, a hot tub, spectacular views, and so on. You decided you wanted to take a look. You couldn't find the listing, but somehow remembered the address. You came looking. There was no for sale sign and you can easily miss the 46 hammered onto a tree, which you did, so you drove right on past it, until you got to the very end of the road. Up at 135. You saw someone and, logically, stopped—which your GPS will testify to—and got out—which your phone probably knows and will remember. But then you did something they can neither know nor deny, you asked me a question. 'Excuse me, sir, do you know where number 46 is?' And I said, 'Oh, it's right down the hill.' I added how far it was and the stand of white birch that helped you spot the driveway.

"Your car and your phone will show you weren't at my place long enough to plan a murder. Just long enough to get directions. No one was here. But you looked around a bit. You were enthralled with the location and the view.

"Does that make sense to you?"

"Yes, yes, thank you," she said. "That's very good."

"Here's how we proceed. We'll get burner phones. I'll do that. But it will take a few days. In the meantime, you can say you asked for my phone number, in case there was any more information about number

46. You can text me, to ask if the owners are around and say you'd like to see it and say when. If I say yes, come here. Not to my place. Just here. I know the people who own the place. They're in Portugal at the moment. I'll actually contact them. As if there really is an interested buyer. If you don't buy it, that's more normal than not. Are we clear on that?"

"Yes. Yes, we are."

I made her tell it back to me. It's your basic check for understanding. People forget things. I made her do it twice.

"A few more things," I said. "You tell no one else about this. Just the two of us. That's it."

"Yes, of course," she said.

"You said you had the money, the up-front money, on hand."

"Yes, I do."

"Good," I said. "Tomorrow. By three in the afternoon."

"But does it have to be that soon? I do have plans tomorrow. I have a school thing for my children . . ."

"Yes," I said. "It has to be tomorrow."

First, I had hoped that she wouldn't ever call. Then, when she came, that it would be to say please forget what was said on the train. It had so many ways to go wrong. I wasn't a killer for hire, I didn't want to be a killer for hire, I even understood the standard definitions of the difference between right and wrong. Yet here I was, playing it out, drawn to it somehow, and instead of doing the simple thing, walking away, I was trying to come up with a gimmick that would make it stop. When someone has to cough up the cash, things turn to smoke, mist, a puff of dust, to be scattered on the wind. That was what I really wanted to happen.

I said, "If you want to make it earlier, you can text me, the way I told you. Otherwise, I'll see you here at three. With the money." Very matter-of-fact about it. "Or I walk away." See how sane that was?

CHAPTER FIVE

DUKKHA, BABY. IT LEADS TO KARMA

"I should fancy, however, that murder is always a mistake. One should never do anything that one cannot talk about after dinner."

OSCAR WILDE, *THE PICTURE OF DORIAN GRAY*

I DIDN'T HEAR FROM HER. But I wasn't supposed to.

From the second-story window of my house I can see a bit of the county road. At around 2:00, I started watching. I told myself that I was doing it so I could be sure no one was following her and also so that I could go down to #46 and be there to stop her from getting nervous and driving up to my house or calling me or texting me. But I suspected it was because I was impatient, meaning that I had started to want this to happen, that desire had entered the playing field. Woodstock probably has more Buddhists per capita than anyplace else on the East Coast. There's the Karma Triyana Dharmachakra, the Tibetan Buddhist Center, straight up above the town, on the saddle between Guardian Mountain and Lookout Mountain, the North American seat of the 17th Karmapa.

Then there's the Zen Mountain Monastery, a few miles to the west in Mount Tremper.

You can't be around Buddhism very much and not know that desire is problematic.

The essence of the Buddha's teaching is the Four Noble Truths.
The Second Noble Truth is that the root of all suffering is desire.
This comes in three forms, which he described as the Three Roots of
Evil, or the Three Fires, or the Three Poisons. The first of these is
Greed and Desire.

It has been my own personal experience and observation, that Truth is easy to see, unless Desire clouds your mind. Lies succeed by speaking to Desire. The most successful lies are the ones we tell to ourselves. Thus speaketh my inner bodhisattva when it sits beneath the bodhi tree.

At around 2:40 I spotted the atomic silver-gray Lexus LX rolling toward me. The afternoon sun glinted off it.

The road wound and twisted more than a slithering snake. If you were following someone, you'd have to be right behind or their car would be constantly disappearing, and one of those moments of invisibility could be the point where they turned off into a side road or a long driveway and it would be many miles before you knew for sure that was what had happened. It was a solid four minutes before another vehicle appeared going in the same direction as the Lexus. It was a pickup with a load of firewood in the cargo bed.

I felt an internal chemical tick of pleasure. Money. Action. On offer. I told myself, "Let warnings warn you. Right now, the only enemy you have is yourself."

I headed down to #46, cutting through the woods on foot. I had to pass a few other houses. I circled wide enough around them and sufficiently deep into the trees that I could be sure that none of my neighbors would see or hear me. Even the three dogs in #87, who loved to yelp and howl at everything, remained silent.

I got to the property before Maddie arrived. I waited where the woods met the cleared grounds above the house. The driveway ran from the west, curving uphill, making it west by northwest. The Lexus pulled in. It came to a stop. It looked very clean, as it had yesterday, as if it never ran on dirt roads, even though it just had. Madelaine got out. This time her outfit didn't match the car's interior. She wore a very spiffy, and costly, Moncler jacket, tight designer jeans, and lightweight hiking boots, as if a few steps across the lawn called for special equipment. She looked around. When she didn't see me right away she took out her phone. Of course.

"Don't," I said. "I'm here."

"Oh," she said, seeing me.

Then the passenger side door opened. Between the angle of the car and the angle of the sun, bright behind it, and the way it threw a glare off the shiny paint, I hadn't seen that there'd been two people inside, let alone who the second person might be. I was furious. At Madelaine for bringing someone else in. Even more at myself for picking a spot from which I couldn't see what was coming. I barked out, "What have you done?" full of fury.

It was another woman.

I assessed her as somewhat older than Madelaine. Not from her physical features alone. I estimated that Madelaine had some age added due to the stresses of living a life of total leisure. She'd started as a creature of genetically created beauty, more than sufficient for her to live on. Then there'd been two pregnancies, giving birth, raising children, keeping up appearances as a mother and a loving spouse, and all through that needing to remain an object of sufficient desire to get the Lexus, the homes, the vacations, and the Moncler jacket. A plain white T-shirt from Moncler was more than $200.

This second woman was, at first glance, a creature more of her own self. Someone who made money. Which, somehow, had aged her less. Her clothes were expensive, but in a different way. They were more assured, less needy, like the woman herself.

All these estimations and valuations were secondary, conducted as autonomic background computations, no matter what was playing on the front screen.

What I was aware of was rage.

And great pleasure in feeling it. I was aroused. I was alive. In a way that I hadn't felt for years. Energy and power pumping through my arteries. I thought it felt better than love. Maybe because I didn't imagine love as an available option. Roll on, roll on.

Dealing with these people was dangerous. It was stupid. It was producing rage, justified, valid, well-founded rage. I liked it. So, I displayed it. I offered it up. I ignored the new woman. I addressed Maddie. "How stupid can you be? Every person you add to this mess doubles the risk. You're gonna do this? With this idiot? Whoever the fuck she is? You're going to end up doing life without parole. And I'm not. Because I'm not going to have anything to do with you or with it. I'm done. I'm out of here."

I turned away. I headed back into the woods. Disappearing into the trees.

"Wait," the other woman called.

I kept going.

"Wait," she said again. "I have your money."

CHAPTER SIX

MONEY, HONEY. IF YOU WANT TO GET ALONG WITH ME

"MONEY (THAT'S WHAT I WANT)."

Motown's first hit. Back in 1959.

The original writing credits went to Berry Gordy, the founder of Motown, Janie Bradford, a songwriter, and Barrett Strong, who sang the first version.

One of the oddities of the music business is that the strongest claim on money, frequently the only claim on money, comes from the copyright, called the publishing rights.

Three years later, Strong's name was taken off the copyright. Without telling him.

Meanwhile, "Money (That's What I Want)" was recorded by the Beatles, the Rolling Stones, the Kingsmen, Jr. Walker & the All Stars, Jerry Lee Lewis, Freddie and the Dreamers, John Lee Hooker, and the Flying Lizards. Berry Gordy and Janie Bradford got royalties from all those recordings. Barrett Strong didn't.

Berry Gordy is a hell of a businessman. His net worth is said to be $400 million.

Barrett Strong also wrote "I Heard It Through the Grapevine," "Papa Was a Rollin' Stone," "War," "Smiling Faces Sometimes," "Cloud Nine." He's a hell of a songwriter. He's living in a retirement home.

Money—cheat, steal, or kill—"What it don't get, I can't use."

I walked back. Like an amiable bear shambling out of the shadows.

The unknown woman reached into her pocketbook and took out an envelope.

I made my way to her. I suspect that if tourists were watching from an observation deck it would look like some sort of wild animal cautiously making its way to a trainer holding out a tasty tidbit. I took the envelope. It had the feel of a stack of U.S. greenbacks. Possibly a little light. Maybe. Maybe not. I was going to count it anyway.

"Who are you?"

"Elizabeth Bloom Carter," she said. "Most people call me Liz." She held out her hand to shake. I didn't take it.

"I meant *what* are you?"

"I'm Madelaine's backer."

"You're what?"

"I'm providing her financing."

"Is that what you finance? People who want other people killed?"

"No. No. Not at all."

"What do you normally do?"

"Madelaine's situation . . . I'd say it's almost uniquely bad." She spoke like she was presenting a report at a management meeting in a corporate conference room furnished in a spare Scandinavian style. "Her husband has done very despicable things. And it's not just the things he's done. He is a very dangerous person."

Which hadn't answered my question at all. "I mean what do you normally do?"

"What are you asking?"

"I'm asking you what you do," I said, opening the envelope with my finger. "Where does the money come from?" I started counting the money, looking down at it, not at her. "Do you have a real profession? What is it? Did you inherent millions? Are you a widow, killed your husband, got rich that way, and now you think it's such a great way to go, you're convincing your friends to do it too?" I looked at her. "What do you do?"

"I'm in litigation finance."

"You invest in lawsuits."

"Yes. Of all sorts. It's a vibrantly growing business. We back plaintiffs with good causes, with a high likelihood of success, but without the means to achieve equity." I bet that was in their PowerPoint presentation on their website. "It is also of great benefit to corporate clients. The larger and better capitalized they are, the more likely they are to use legal financing. Those involved with large litigations are able to offload cost and risk. It's a fast-growing multibillion-dollar industry."

"How does that take you to your friend over there?"

"I understand that you were in the investigative area for quite some time."

"I was."

"You know how expensive such services are. More often than not, investigators are employed by law firms, not directly by clients. That mandates additional overhead and administrative costs, let alone a mark-up for a reasonable level of profit. That's just one small element of the legal system. It's expensive. The more that's at stake, generally, the more expensive it gets."

"Yeah, yeah, and yada yada yada warden, how does that get us to Madelaine, you, and me, here, now." There was, without doubt, a madness to this conversation. Outdoors, high on a hill, next to a house in which nobody was living at the moment. It was a little bit chilly, but comfortable if you stood in the sun. I wanted it to rain. Not a Catskill storm that drenches you in a minute with the thunder rolling down the mountains and up again like the magic men playing ninepins in the legend of Rip Van Winkle. It called for a British rain, just a tad heavier than a drizzle, and the women could put up umbrellas and I could let the water drip from my hair down my collar, so the absurdity would manifest itself in images. For the motion picture version.

"Our firm is actively expanding the utility and range of litigation finance," Elizabeth continued in her PR pitch person voice. "The imbalance of financial resources is very common in divorce situations. There is a clear need for our services and the employment of our services is a virtual guarantee, based on actual statistical data, of improved outcomes."

By then I'd counted the money in the envelope. "So why don't you simply invest in Madelaine's divorce? If her husband is as vile and reprehensible and disgusting as you say he is, Madelaine and her lawyers should be able to take him for a bundle, and then you just rake off your piece."

"Sometimes the worse they are," Elizabeth replied patiently, with just a tick of disapproval that crude power so often gets its way, "the more difficult the situation. Mick McMunchun, her husband, comes from the Roy Cohn school of litigation. Hide, lose, and destroy records. Attack, threaten, and smear. They've promised to go after Madelaine's father as an embezzler, which he is not, but since he's in the financial services industry it would do him great harm. They have photoshopped her mother into photographs having an affair with an African American busboy at an Applebee's. Madelaine has two sisters and they've been targeted, too.

"As many rich people do, especially in divorce situations, he has hidden his money away. We have a sense of how much he has . . ."

"Which is?"

" . . . I have client confidentiality . . ."

"You're not her fucking attorney. You're a speculator. Betting on her husband dying so she can get money that she can then share with you. How much?"

She stumbled and stalled.

I turned to Madelaine. "How much?"

"Ten. . . maybe twelve . . . we think. Maybe more."

"Ten, twelve, what?"

"Million," Madelaine said.

"I've seen divorces where they dig that stuff out."

Elizabeth stepped in. "In this case, even if it were successful, it would take years, maybe decades."

"If he dies, how does that improve things?"

"We've made the assumption," Elizabeth said, "based on certain evidence, as well as reason, that he doesn't want his money to disappear into whatever banks and shell companies that are hiding it. If he were to die, it would reappear."

"Magically," I said.

"Relatively speaking, yes. Then there's the other issue. He's threatened to kill Madelaine. We . . . she and I, at least . . . regard those threats as genuine."

"Interesting. Fascinating," I said, sounding amiable.

Liz nodded. She presumably had made many pitches in her time. She judged this one to have been successful. She glanced over at Maddie, who nodded, and looked relieved.

I took the money out of the envelope. I stuffed it into the inside pocket of my jacket.

"You're short," I said.

"Well . . ."

"There's only ten in here. The deal was twenty."

"It's reasonable to negotiate," she said, as if there was absolutely nothing wrong. "Besides, I wanted to meet you before being fully committed."

I stuck my finger in her face.

The moment I'd taken the envelope, I'd guessed from its size and weight that the amount would be wrong. The rage began to cook in my center. It surprised me. That I actually cared about something. As I became certain, it rose up. Like nausea does. But it wasn't sour and acrid like evil, it tasted of being alive, smooth and sweet, and now it gave me pleasure to let it release. "I don't know what kind of weird, privileged world you come from, lady, but the two of you are stupid and double down stupid. You make a deal with a man that you actually believe will kill people for money, then you stiff him. You stiff him for ten grand on his up-front money. You think I'll do business with you? Fuck you. Fuck her. Do you have any understanding of what deep shit you're in? I call Rollie, the deputy who was here yesterday and saw Maddie, or Detective John Amoroso, or Chief Keefe, in Woodstock, or the new DA, and tell them what the two of you asked me to do, show them the money, and you're going to prison. Have you ever been in a prison? I don't expect either you have done time, but have you ever even visited or toured one? I was once in the New York corrections department. I've been arrested a few times. It's not a fucking TV show. It's humiliation, abuse, being ripped off for everything from toothpaste to tampons to your phone calls. It's degradation. Every day. It's why Jeffrey Epstein hanged himself.

"As for this ten thousand, which doesn't seem to be in sequential bills, which is good, and they're used, which is good, and I don't think they're marked, but I'll check, what this bought you is the opportunity to have spoken with me. And, at least temporarily, my not talking about it to anyone else. And that's all you get. For trying to fuck with me.

"Goodbye," I said. "Don't come back. Don't call. Don't text. And don't even ride a train I'm on." I turned and began to walk away.

"You will not take our money," Liz said.

I ignored her.

"I was prepared for this," she said. "I have a gun."

I looked back. She was actually taking one out of her purse. It was a Glock 43, their subcompact 9mm. It was black and hot pink. Mostly hot pink. I didn't laugh. A bullet is a bullet. But maybe it made me stupider than I should have been. Instead of stopping or running from her, I began walking toward her. "I don't think you'll shoot."

"I will shoot you. I want my money back."

"If you could kill someone, what do you need me for?" I kept moving toward her, but slowly. "Why make it all complicated, add another person, make it more likely to go wrong?"

"Stop. Or I'll shoot. I will."

"If you kill me, what are you going to do with the body? If you don't kill me, you're really fucked."

"I will shoot. I won't miss. I have been trained. I've practiced at the range. I will hit you."

"Oh, come on," I said. I was about three feet from her. "You don't even have the safety off. You pushed it the wrong way. Take a look."

She could have laughed and shot me, since the Glock doesn't have that kind of safety. It just has a little thingamajig on the trigger. Simply squeezing the trigger in the normal way releases it. But she glanced down. I launched myself at her. Lord, God, I was old and slow. Once I probably would have disarmed her with some efficiency, even elegance. From the moment I started my move, I realized how much was gone. I just flung myself at her in a full body tackle. I hit her like we were ten-year-olds trying to play football like we'd seen on TV, headfirst into her belly, arms around her, taking her down to the ground. Either by reflex or the sudden recollection of her gun range training, she squeezed the trigger. The Glock went off.

The bullet certainly hit something because there was a loud sound and Madelaine screamed. Liz went flying onto her back. Her body hit the ground with a thud and with my weight on top of her. She grunted. Then she gasped and swallowed, trying not to vomit. Fortunately, she succeeded, otherwise she would have spewed on me.

She was still holding on to the nifty little handgun with her outstretched right hand. She was trying to lift it up. I grabbed her wrist with my left hand. She swore. I shoved it down on the dirt. I think her arm hit a rock, because her "motherfucker" was punctuated with a yelp. I sat up as she tried to claw at my face with her left hand and twisted away from it, mostly because I wanted to get my right hand on her right arm. I seized her behind her elbow. I pulled up, while my left hand still held her wrist down. I was folding her arm backward toward the snapping point. She screeched. I felt her hand open, and the gun fell out.

I released her, rolled off, and snatched up the Glock.

CHAPTER SEVEN

LISTEN

"... the stick-up kids know how I roll,
I'll shoot you if I like
I'm a gun slinging rambler
and I live a rambler's life."

"GUNSLINGING RAMBLER,"
GANGSTAGRASS

MADELAINE WAS ON HER KNEES, bent over, practically in a fetal position, sort of sobbing, sort of gasping.

Liz was on the ground, staring up at me, doing her best to give me a hard, mean look. She said, "You won't get away with this," dressing it up with standard swear words front and back.

In return, I just gave her a look that said, *Don't you get it?*

She swore at me again. I raised her pink-and-black Glock 43 and pointed it at her. She stopped threatening and swearing. Her pocketbook was on the ground. I picked it up, opened it, and took her phone.

I walked over toward Madelaine. She backed away from me, still in her crouching huddle. Under normal circumstances I would have done my best to be reassuring, telling her she was safe, be calm, everything was going to be alright. But it didn't seem appropriate. I went right up to her, reached down, felt around her jacket—it was really quite stylish and very well made—until I found the pocket with her phone. I reached in and took it.

Then I headed up the hill on foot. This is stony country. About five yards off the lawn and into the trees, there was a large outcropping of bluestone, higher than my waist as I climbed past it. The adrenaline pump had turned itself off. The vibrations of energy, rage, and the urge to action, were slowing, thoughts were returning and one of them was about the way our phones track us all.

Liz was calling to Maddie, "Are you alright? Are you alright?"

I guessed that I was already out of their sight. I could stop, slink down behind the rhino-sized hunk of rock, turn off their phones and, for good measure, remove the batteries and SIM cards.

There had been no reply. Liz tried again. "Are you hurt?"

"No."

"Oh, thank God. I didn't know where the shot went."

"You shot Bruno!"

"Bruno?"

"Bruno! My LX. My big beautiful LX."

"Look, I'm sorry."

"Bruno was perfect. Not a scratch. Not a dent. Like fresh from the showroom. Not a stain on the seats!"

"I'm sorry. It was *his* fault. His fault. *He* grabbed me and made the shot go wild."

"You shot my car. You shot my car."

"Where? Where did I shoot it?"

"In his side, like in his shoulder, right by the wheel."

"Is the wheel alright? I mean, are we going to have change the tire?" I could hear real alarm from Elizabeth over that possibility.

"I think it's OK, but there's a bullet hole."

"It can be repaired. I promise you it can be repaired. It will be like new. Better than new. Cars are repaired all the time. That's what insurance is for."

"It's a bullet hole. How am I going to explain a bullet hole? Tell them you shot it when you were really trying to shoot the guy that we were trying to hire to kill my husband?"

"It's not my fault. It's *his* fault. Men. Fucking men are always like that. Throwing their weight around. Taking over. They can't stand having a woman running things. That's what this is about." Liz took a breath. It powered her switch from complaining to blaming. "I told you to find a *woman*. Why didn't you find a woman? And stand up already. He's gone. It's over. Stop . . . whatever . . . and stand up. Why not a woman?"

"I couldn't find one," Maddie said. "I tried. I mean mostly you have to just hint around things and there was no response. I tried . . . you know . . . like *Strangers on a Train* . . . *oh, you hate your husband, I hate mine* . . . *what if we swapped* . . . then they'd say *I'm not into swapping* and I'd say *I mean to get rid of them* . . . then it was like 'ha-ha.' Or no response. I even tried some black women, they're more . . . physical and radical . . . right?"

"That's ridiculous. There must be women assassins all over the place. Like Villanelle. Like Nikita. I mean Nikita was just one of a whole school of trained female assassins. Elizabeth in *The Americans*. And *Red Sparrow*."

"They're Russian, all Russian. I don't know any Russians. Well, maybe two, but that counts a grandmother. Oh, and I once met Yul Brynner's son."

"It's not just Russians. What about what's her name, *Queen of the South*?"

"I don't know. I never watch it. It's too violent."

"It's a woman who's beating men," Liz said. "There are American women, *FBI*, *Quantico*, and *Covert Affairs*. What about *Kill Bill* . . . Uma Thurman lives right here in Woodstock."

"Well, sometimes," Maddie said. "Not all the time. It depends on who she's married to. Besides . . ." She made a sudden return to sanity. "Besides, those are movies. Just movies."

"I know that. But Hollywood wouldn't make so many movies about female assassins . . . and female law enforcement people who kill . . . if they weren't around. Those are signals that they're around."

"Hollywood makes movies about women having vaginal orgasms. Every time, while some guy is holding them in the air. You think that's a signal that vaginal orgasms are around?"

"That's different."

"Well, I couldn't find them. I'm sorry. So there, I'm sorry. Now, what are you going to do about the bullet hole in my car? From *your* gun."

Liz said, "I don't know."

Then Maddie said, "I bet Tony would figure it out."

That was very gratifying to hear.

This had all taken much longer than I had anticipated. I had to get to the bank. I got up, slowly and quietly from my hiding spot, and continued the trek up the hill. Once I could have sprinted up, now just putting one foot in front of the other left me breathing hard.

CHAPTER EIGHT
FU**IN' BANKS

"There ain't no clean way to make a hundred million
bucks . . . Somewhere along the line guys got pushed to the
wall, nice little businesses got the ground cut
out from under them . . . Decent people lost their
jobs . . . Big money is big power and big power gets
used wrong. It's the system."

RAYMOND CHANDLER, *THE LONG GOODBYE*

YEARS AGO, WHEN I WAS still in business, and sometimes had things
or held on to things that I wouldn't want found in my possession, I
got a substantial metal container about the size of three shoe boxes. I
buried it just over the property line, putting it beyond the reach of any
warrant that failed to specify my neighbor's land in addition to my own.

If you're visualizing quarter-acre, suburban properties, with
nicely groomed lawns, perhaps some hedges, and a few trees that
stand decorously alone, don't. He has fifty-four acres. I have fifteen
and a half, almost all of it untended. There's only a thin layer of soil
over rock and stone. It's what's called a "dirty forest." Trees can spread
their roots wide, but not deep. Strong winds, heavy snow, even a lot of
rain that loosens the dirt, will bring them down. Many stand tall, but
many fall, the ground is littered with broken branches and entire trees.
The only way to tell where my land ends and my neighbor's begins is
with a property map and a surveyor who has to work from old iron
stakes pounded into the ground decades ago.

My woodland safety deposit box is covered with a large flat rock. It's one among many, that look like they were tossed about by God, or nature, in a moment of dishevelment.

I put Liz's gun and the phones and their parts in the box and replaced the rock. I drove into Kingston to the bank. It had been a local operation when I signed on, but it had recently been take over by Bank of America. I parked, entered, and went up to a teller. I said, "I'm $7,800 in arrears on my mortgage. Here it is," and I put the cash on the counter.

She asked for the account number. I gave it to her. She typed the numbers into the machine in front of her, waited a moment, read something I couldn't see, then said, "Just a moment, sir," and went away.

I waited. The clock ticked. Waited and waited. So as not to grow irritated I thought about how much better it was than being on hold on a telephone and forced to listen to obnoxious music.

Eventually she returned. She said, "I can't accept it."

"Why not?" A genuine question, politely asked.

"I was told not to. You'd have to speak to someone in our mortgage department."

"OK," I said, feeling patient, pleasant, and tolerant. Why not, it was like God had intervened, and He'd said, *Hey, wake up, Tony, don't look a divinity's gift in the mouth*, and here I was with the money to save my home. "Where are they?"

"No one's here right now. You would have to come back tomorrow. Or call for an appointment."

"Hmph," I said, still more thoughtful than annoyed. "Hmph, can I get something notarized?"

"I'm sure we can do that."

She turned and walked along behind the counter until she was close to a small office cubicle with another woman inside. Well-dressed, middle-aged, overweight. Most women who work in banks tend to be all three, but not as heavy as the women who work in doctor's offices and medical facilities. She was polite and waved me in. She took out her stamp and asked for ID. I gave it to her and asked for a pen and paper. She supplied them. I put the date on top, then wrote down that I had appeared at the bank with cash to pay my arrears but the teller had refused to take it without explanation.

She looked at it. Read it. Then said, "Oh, I can't notarize this."

Phone. I took mine out. I took a picture of the paper, then tapped the photo app to switch to video recording. I then verbally repeated the sequence of events, repeated the request, and moved the lens to go with the dialogue, "I just want a formal record, could you please notarize this."

She said she couldn't. I asked why not. She said it was past closing time and I would have to leave and I would have to delete the recording, which was still going.

"Why would I do that?" I asked.

"I'll call security," she said, but she'd already buzzed for assistance. A fellow in a uniform appeared behind me. The woman said, "He has to leave. But first he has to delete that recording or give us his phone."

"I'm afraid you'll have to," the security guard said, holding out his hand as if he expected obedience. "You don't want me to call the police."

"Actually, I have a better idea, I'll call them."

He started moving toward me. I was going to tap 911, but then decided to call the sheriff's department and while I did, I told the guard, "Back off, you don't want to do this. I'm the one calling the cops. If there's an altercation, you will look like the person committing"—the sheriff's department answered, I covered the little microphone hole to finish—"the assault." I took my thumb away, said "Hello," gave my name, and asked if Rollie Robidoux was still on duty. The dispatcher said he was. I said, "Look, I'm at BoA, corner of Shwenk Drive and

Washington Avenue. We have a conflict here and I feel a law enforcement officer would help straighten things out . . . No, no, no. Not a bank robbery. Nothing that serious. There's a bank officer attempting to take a customer's property . . . No, it's not a joke. Of course, I know that's what banks do. . . . OK . . . thank you."

We all stood. Frozen. Staring at each other. It was after five. They wanted to go home. I said, "I should have brought a book." They looked at me blankly as if they'd never heard of such things.

It was only ten or fifteen minutes before Rollie rolled up in his sheriff's car. Security had to leave me, quite sullenly, to unlock the door to let him in. They came back together. Rollie and I greeted each other by name.

"I didn't expect to see you so soon," he said.

"You motivated me," I told him.

"I did?"

"You made me realize I should take control of my life again. Not let it slip-slide away, which is what I was doing."

"That's good. But is there a problem here?"

"Not with me. With them."

"That's not true," the woman behind the desk said.

"He's the problem," the security guy said.

"Quiet," Rollie said. "One at a time."

"He was taking unauthorized pictures," the woman said.

"This is private property," the security guy said. "He has to do what he's told."

Rollie looked at me. I went through the whole sequence, trying to pay, being refused, trying to get proof that I tried. Rollie asked the woman if that was reasonably correct. Faced with an officer of the law, in uniform, with a badge, she admitted that it was. She insisted, however, that it was private property and they had a right to forbid people from taking pictures and making recordings. How were they to know it was not for some nefarious purpose like planning a robbery or a terrorist attack?

I started a rant about how every time we called the bank, or just about anything else, they recorded us, "'for training purposes.' Ha! Who believes that? Now, when I want to record them . . ."

"Quiet, would ya." Rollie looked at each of us in turn. "This here, this is a very complex matter. Honestly, it's beyond me to sort it out and be sure I'm correct about it. I think it's a matter for a judge."

That didn't sound good.

"Here's what I'm going to do," he continued. "For now, I think Mr. Cassella should retain his cell phone and whatever is on it. The bank, which has an extensive and experienced legal staff, can then file legal proceedings. If a judge finds for the bank, I'm sure Mr. Cassella here will be happy to remit the material. Won't you? If a court says to?"

"Of course, I will," I said, compliant, upright, and true.

"See," Rollie said. "For now, let's all go about our business."

The security guard escorted us to the front door. He unlocked it. Rollie and I left together. When we were outside, I said, "That was very well done. I'm impressed. Thank you, Rollie."

He said, "Fuckin' banks. Taking homes from people. You drive around the county and you see empty homes all over. They're falling down. Falling into ruin. You can bet, most of them, somebody came up short, got foreclosed. We got houses falling down and people with no place to live. Fuckin' banks."

"Fuckin' banks," I said, the choir echoing the preacher.

"I won't even ask you where you came up with the money, in cash, from yesterday to today."

CHAPTER NINE

ON FEEDING CATS

"No one here gets out alive."

JIM MORRISON, "FIVE TO ONE."
Also the title of his biography.

I TREATED MYSELF TO DINNER in a trendy restaurant. My starter had the title "Tomato and Tuna," and the ingredients ran like movie credits: *heirloom tomato, tomato-tamarind chutney, mint, sweet chile, shaved bonito.*

For the main course, I contemplated the cassoulet. I thought about it. I lingered over it. But I knew that if it wasn't particularly good I would be angry. If it was good, well, then I would probably weep. Cassoulet was the peculiar tagline of a private joke about death and love. No, change that. From love, about death, and what is there to say. Remembering her would make me weep there at my table, in a place that was nothing but bare, clean rectangles and right angles, hardly a place for tears, in sight of the young, bald, bearded chef with tats running up his arms from his knuckles into his short sleeves, and the pert, hipster-looking waitperson, as well as the various other customers around me. An old man, dining alone, silently crying would remind them that this could be their endgame, too, and ruin their dinners.

Instead, I ordered the pork sugo, slow-cooked pork jowl, tomato-vinegar broth, green peas, barley, summer vegetables, garlic creme, pesto, herbs, $24.00, oh what charming details. Both courses were good and made me feel indulged. To feel. Feel. Anything. Was good.

On the way home, I got the cats their preferred cat food. In Rome, the feral cats eat pasta. But cats are cunning. Once they know some human wants to feed them, they become manipulative. They turn down spaghetti and wait for chicken. Then not just any chicken, their favorite brand. Certain people are like that, too.

The message light on my landline was blinking.

An old friend had died in Paris. I had neglected her as I'd neglected so much else. Her children had called to tell me. I felt that the world was made less by her absence. I felt faint tremors of guilt that I hadn't done more to stay in touch. I felt death creeping 'round.

Aden Elwood had called. He often got teased that he should have been a Blues Brother because of his name. He worked ski patrol at Hunter, part time, and I taught there part time, and he lived pretty close, so we shared rides in a semi-regular way. His message was that he couldn't commit to it this year, for medical reasons. I called him back. It was cancer. What kind? Pancreatic. He was going to have an operation. Then chemo. I said that since they'd caught it early, his chances were good. I was lying.

Aden was thirty-one years younger than me. Likely we'd never ski together again.

Madelaine McMunchun had called. "I really, really need my telephone. Everything is on my phone. All my numbers." As she spoke, she got more and more intense. "My schedule. I really need my phone back. I do not want to tell my husband I lost it and need a new one. They're quite expensive. Give me my phone back. It's mine. It's mine."

She took a deep breath, bringing herself under control, but the record time had run out and whatever her next word was going to be, it was cut off at half syllable.

She called again in order to continue her expression of her desperation and need. Also, to say whatever the problem was, it had been Elizabeth's fault, not her own. On her third call, she left her home number, and the times that would be best to call so some wrong person wouldn't pick up.

There are no spaghetti trees in Italy. Nor do rigatonis sprout among the ruins. The people of Rome obviously put out the pasta. They don't let the cats starve, but nor do they indulge them. I felt sympathy for Madelaine's plights, but she was hardly about to die of malnutrition, and since she was not mine, I didn't feel like allowing her to manipulate anything more out of me.

Elizabeth Bloom Carter had also called. She sounded much calmer than Maddie. She was quite businesslike: "We appear to have gotten off on the wrong foot. I'm sure that can be rectified. Why don't we meet for lunch?" No point in calling her cell phone, it was in a box, under a rock, in the woods. She left her office number and her extension.

She'd tried to stiff me. She'd pulled a gun on me. And been stupid enough to fire it. She had defined herself as someone not to do business with. Let alone business as full of risk—to both our souls, to whatever degree we have such things, and to our liberties—as contract murder.

I decided, sensibly, not to respond.

CHAPTER TEN

MY LAWYER IS SMALLER THAN THEIR LAWYER

"That's the difference between crime and business.
For business you gotta have capital.
Sometimes I think it's the only difference."

RAYMOND CHANDLER, *THE LONG GOODBYE*

"THEY STARTED FORECLOSURE. THIS IS not the first time you got behind. It's not even the first time they tried to foreclose."

"My place is worth five, maybe ten times, what I owe," I protested.

The lawyer was Kenny Rosenbaum, a perfectly adequate local practitioner, in an area where perfectly adequate was about as good as it gets. There's a small legal district in the City of Kingston, around the Ulster County Courthouse. Kenny and his three partners occupied a place that had been built as a three-story home, back around 1870, charming, a bit run down, and fairly typical of our local firms.

His response was, "Right, fine! You have the option of selling it, paying them off, and keeping anything over what you owe. If they foreclose, it goes to auction. Anything above what you owe, including fees and charges and the like, goes to you."

"What I'm saying is, I want to keep the place. It's my place. Mine."

"Look, if you want me to fight them, I can. What will most likely happen is that the foreclosure proceedings will be put on hold . . ."

"What about the video? Them refusing to take my money? Trying to prevent me from proving it?"

"It'll help, but it won't . . ."

"The reason I'm in this fix is because of Bank of America." We'd already agreed that I would leave off the obscenities I routinely attached to their name, fore and aft. "I had a homeowner's loan from Onbank more than twenty-five years ago. That kind of loan was great for me. When I was flush, I could pay it, but I still had access to the money. When I was short, all I had to do was pay the interest."

"Yes, I understand."

"They got bought by Norstar. No problem. The loan had a time limit. Ten years or something like that. When it was up, we just rolled it over. Norstar got bought by Fleet. No problem. When it was time to roll it over, we just did it. Then they were taken over by BoA. Everything was fine for about five years, then came rollover time. I go in, they suggest I increase the amount, even double it, that way they'll give me a cheaper interest rate. Great. So, I put in the application.

"They reject me.

"I point out that the property is worth vastly more than they're loaning me. 'Oh,' says the bank officer, who hadn't been there when I put in the application two weeks earlier. Nobody seems to stay there more than a few months. She puts me on the phone with a 'mortgage expert,' who will help me. I start talking to this person, and she doesn't quite know where Woodstock, New York, is. She tries to look it up on her computer and can't find it. I ask her where she is, and she's in Plant City, Florida, or someplace like that.

"Suddenly, I no longer have the setup that I've had for twenty-five years. Suddenly I have to pay off over $100,000. And I have to do it fast. How the hell am I going to come up with that?

"I start putting in applications. But I don't have a job. The last time I had a job, I think it was 1972. Since then I've been self-employed. I owned half of a detective agency. I owned a Laundromat in Austria. Then a detective agency again. Sold it. Owned half a logging company and a B&B with a French bistro. Sold them, too. With the new federal guidelines that came in after 2008, self-employment has no more validity than vagrancy.

"But there was a VP, that I knew personally over at Bank of the Mountains and the River, a local bank. I did some work for him. He makes a genuine personal effort, and accesses a fund made up of the bank's own money, which makes it truly discretionary. He can't give me a homeowner's loan, but he can do me a mortgage. OK, fine. I'm out from under Bank of America and I'm saved. It's not a great loan, but I'm saved.

"Then, one year ago, the Bank of the Mountains and the River gets taken over. Guess who by? Bank of America. Plus, my buddy retired. To Costa Rica. Yes, sure, I've been late a bunch of times, but it's because these motherfuckers forced me into this."

"Let me ask you, did you ever have a mortgage on the property before that?"

"No," I said.

"You bought it outright? For cash?"

"There was a guy named Seymour Herschkowitz. In 1984, he was suddenly charged with a murder from twenty years earlier. Supposedly part of an extortion scheme to take over this string of dry cleaners that he owns down in Weehawken, Union City, Jersey City, Hoboken, all through there."

"That's like Soprano country," Kenny says, happy to identify with it in terms of TV gangsters.

"They wouldn't give him bail. He's inside for over a year. His wife comes to see him only once in all that time, mainly to say, 'a shanda far die goyim,' and 'How do I access the money?' And that's it. Never,

'I believe in you,' 'I'll be here when you get out.' The kids don't come. Nobody comes.

"I keep working the case. It's twenty years old. There's enough this and that to fill a legal encyclopedia with reasons for doubt. At last, he gets off. He gets out of prison.

"Meantime, I've racked up a whole lot more hours than I've been paid for. He owes me a bit more than $24,000. He says he's going to pay, but the stress and whatever has left him with high blood pressure and heart problems. In addition to me, he's got legal bills, and he's paying to not live at home because he's so angry at the wife and she's so angry at him.

"Sixteen months after he's released, he keels over and dies. Still owing me most of it.

"Come probate, I'm there because I figure I have some sort of claim. The lawyer's reading out the will and it says, 'To Tony Cassella, he stood by me when my own family wouldn't. They should go to hell. He should go to my beautiful piece of property near Woodstock, New York, which is closer to heaven than anyplace I'm likely to go now that I'm gone. Therefore, I leave it to him. Along with money for any taxes and fees attached to the transfer.'"

"Hey, that must feel good, really good," Kenny said. "Saving an innocent man. Even if he only had a short time of freedom afterward."

I barked or sighed or laughed or something. "Innocent? Nah. He not only did that one, he did at least two more."

Kenny looked at me. More confused and appalled than a lawyer should be.

"That's what we do, counselor, that's what we do."

He took a breath. He centered himself. Patted his thinning hair down, where he had some, along the sides. "Let me ask you a question," he said.

"Sure."

"Are you going to be able to make the coming months? And pay regularly after that?"

"Chissà." He didn't know the word. "Who knows."

"If you don't make it, they're right back at you. Here's what I recommend. I can stretch this out. I can make it take another three months, six months, even a year. If you can't afford me, I'll tell you the moves you should make to do it yourself. That will give you time to sell your place for a good price."

"No," I said. "I don't know. I don't want to give it up."

"You seemed like you would. You didn't fight it until after the last minute. My job is to tell you what the choices appear to be. Your job is to make them. Either reorganize your life so you make all the payments, all the time, on time, and even have some way to demonstrate that you'll be able to keep it up . . ."

"Like what?"

"Like a job with a paycheck. Or an annuity."

"Oh, sure."

"Or, you figure out how to pay it off. All of it. Or you lose."

I surprised myself. I said, "I'm not going to lose." And I sounded to myself like I meant it.

CHAPTER ELEVEN
ROAD KILL

"What did it matter where you lay once you were dead?
In a dirty sump or in a marble tower on top of a high hill?
You were dead, you were sleeping the big sleep . . ."

RAYMOND CHANDLER, *THE BIG SLEEP*

I'D HAD THREE MORE CALLS from Maddie. None of which I answered. She told me of her woes again and again. On my answering machine.

Once, long ago, when I was young, in love, full of lust, and casually adulterous, with a lovely Puerto Rican girl with liquid eyes, the kind of eyes you could fall into, like Homer's wine-dark sea, I got death threats on my answering machine from her husband. My assessment was that if he was actually going to kill me, he wouldn't go out of his way to establish a record of it before the fact. It seemed a good rule of thumb to doubt the accuracy of what people say when they know they're being recorded.

That reflexive restraint, like so much else, seems to be fading in the age of social media, selfies, Tumblr, tattle, Twitter, uberhorny, and maturesforfuck. Yet with Maddie, I had the expectation that certain veneers of dishonest civility would have remained.

I still didn't call her back.

———————

I went to breakfast. I read my *New York Times*. Two obituaries caught my attention. Jimmy Johnson had been one of the Swampers. Back in 1969, they'd opened Muscle Shoals Sound Studio in an old coffin warehouse. He'd played with Aretha Franklin, Wilson Pickett, Lynyrd Skynyrd, Bob Dylan, Duane Allman, Leon Russell, the Rolling Stones, and Willie Nelson.

Robert Mugabe, the president for life of Zimbabwe, was the other.

The white man had made great soul music. The black man had run his country into the ground. It seemed like a significant racial reversal. But no one said so.

I finished my coffee and headed back home.

A car pulled out behind me and followed. There's only one street that runs all the way through town, and if you're headed west to Mount Tremper, Phoenicia, Margaretville, Big Indian, or any of those places, there aren't a whole lot of ways to go, so it didn't necessarily mean anything. But it was a large silver Lexus.

About four miles along, a guy had pulled off to the side and was standing by his car. He waved his hand to flag me down.

I stopped and rolled down my window. I noticed the car behind me had stopped, too. But not in the natural manner of someone who was just headed in the same direction, coming up, and not stopping until they were right behind me.

"There's a deer that was hit by a car up ahead," the guy said. He was clearly distraught. "He won't make it. I've called the police to put it out of its misery."

"Alright," I said, "thanks," though I wasn't sure for what, and started moving again, slowly. When I did, the Lexus did, too. Silly game.

Around the bend, there it was. It kept lifting its head, trying to rise, to run off and live, even though it couldn't. It had big eyes and a desperate look. More expressive, even, than the man who'd flagged me down. "Put it out of its misery." Euthanasia. Kill it. Murder. Whatever you need to call it.

Trees fight for life. If you climb to the high, rocky places, where the soil's been stripped by the beating of the winds, day and night, you'll see the pines hanging on, their roots crawling into the splits between the stones and wrapping tight around them, like the crew of a ghost sailing ship, desperately clinging forever to the lines as they ride through an eternal storm.

This love of life that we go on about, how precious it is and such, is just a mechanism. Spiders and flies, blades of grass, and bacteria have it. Any form of life that doesn't have it gets wiped out. Ipso facto, it's built in, like spark plugs in an internal combustion engine. We spend endless hours wondering if our life will be short or long, good or bad, worthwhile or worthless, then death comes, and we have no idea at all.

The Lexus stayed behind me. Sure enough, when I turned off the county road, onto Shanty Road, up into the hollow, she followed.

I stopped at #46, got out, and waited, blocking the way.

It was Maddie. She stopped. I pointed at the driveway. She started to get out of her car, her mouth moving in full yelp. I shook my head, "No," and pointed again. She started to yell, with outrage, that I had her phone and I had to give it back. I said, "If you want to talk to me at all, you'll go in there, and you'll wait."

"But you have my property!"

"If you follow me up, I'll shoot you with Miz Bloom Carter's gun.

With her prints all over it and all over the cartridges. I'll shoot out your windshield, I'll shoot out your headlights."

She pouted. Got back. Turned on the engine and started to go where she'd been told.

"Wait," I called. I walked up to her window.

"You want your phone back?"

"Yes, yes I do."

"What's the password?"

"What? No. I can't."

"Based on our exchanges to date, I need to know if you've done anything more to put me in danger. And yourself, for that matter. You can tell me or you can wait until I get my hacker to do it. Which might take a couple of weeks."

She wanted that phone back. She told me the password.

I told her to wait where she was. Then I drove up to my house. I went to the rock, lifted it, opened the box, got her phone and its vital parts. I went to the house, hooked it up to my laptop, and did a back-up of everything except her music, which was not to my taste. If it left a trace, a blip for the eighty seconds or so that it took, so be it. I'd seen my own phone be confused for longer than that, frequently thinking it was at its ancestral home in Cupertino before it registered it was in the Catskills. When the transfer was done, I took the phone apart, and walked down the hill.

After I gave her the phone, she started in about her car. She didn't blame me. Which was good. But she was intensely distraught. She was parking and even driving so that the bullet hole would be hidden from others, like a girl with a particularly embarrassing stain on her dress trying to face away from the world so that it couldn't be seen. She didn't know what to do about it.

"Ask Liz," I said.

"I did."

"And?"

"She didn't have an answer."

"She's the one who shot it."

"She said she'd pay, but how do I explain it?"

"You can either not explain it, like if your car got hit in a parking lot, and you found it."

"Or?"

"Or you drive somewhere like the South Bronx. Or Newburgh or Albany for that matter. Anyplace with a high crime rate. You go at night, when people can't see that much, and when you get to a bad area . . ."

"How do I judge?"

"When you get scared. Then call 911. Say you heard shots fired and you think, 'oh God, one hit my car. I'm getting out of here.' Then you report it to your insurance and get it fixed. And have a reason you were in that area, a concert, a women's march, good cannoli."

"Thank you, thank you," she said. "That's so simple."

"OK," I said. I turned to walk away.

"Wait," she said.

"What?"

"My husband."

We were getting back to that. Kenny Rosenbaum, the perfectly adequate legal practitioner had laid out the case for why I needed Maddie's money. It was interesting, and very perverse, that the idea of murder for money had made me come alive again and made it more likely that I'd actually do it. I was determined not to let that show. My fatalistic indifference and cantankerous reluctance seemed to work well with her.

"I didn't tell you this before . . . because . . . it's so humiliating . . . embarrassing. So horrible."

"Go on."

"He likes young girls."

"Like six or seven?"

"No. More . . . after puberty . . . thirteen, fourteen . . . my daughter's eleven and starting to develop, and the way he looks at her . . ."

My, how cynical I've become. Was she bringing up Jeffrey Epstein Syndrome, call it *middle pedophilia*, which comes between *early pedophilia*—sex with children before puberty—and *late pedophilia*—when many normal teens are sexually active but calendar-designated as being below the age of legal consent—because it was certain to come draped with adjectives like "horrible," "heinous," "odious," and "abhorrent," which the listener was required to echo, and we could all agree that it was bad, really, really bad, and it must be stopped.

Or was it a real concern?

I shook my head in sad agreement. I said, "Why not just report him to the police? Get a protection order. Keep him away from your daughter. And it will help with your divorce."

"It's not that simple," she said.

It should have been. I wondered why it wasn't.

"Talk to Liz," she said. "Please. She admits she made a mistake. Talk to her."

"I'll think about it," I said in my old-fashioned, stern, and manly way. Then I began walking back up the hill, doing my damnedest to disguise how hard it made me breathe.

CHAPTER TWELVE

LET US REASON TOGETHER

"Women who seek to be
equal with men lack ambition."

TIMOTHY LEARY

ELIZABETH BLOOM CARTER'S OPENING MOVE, after greetings and some this and that, had been to let me know that she knew about my problems with my property and the bank and exactly how much was involved. It didn't need to be said that this business would fix all that. If I cared. She clearly thought I did—that anyone would—that I was desperate—and therefore she had me hooked. I left that alone. Neither confirmed nor denied.

"The one problem that must be solved," I said, "is the back end."

"We're good for it," Liz said. She sounded very certain and deeply sincere. "And we will pay."

"You know Larry Beinhart?"

"I do. Well, actually, Maddie knows him better than I do. I only met him once, briefly."

It was three o'clock in the afternoon. In Manhattan. She'd made the invitation. She'd picked the time. I'd picked the place. A nondescript hotel room.

"Would you like a drink?" I asked. "It's a very well-stocked minibar."

She looked thoughtful. This wasn't a conversation. It was a game. A contest. A set of maneuvers. Every little thing, looking for an edge. We were in Midtown. The place was modern. Clean. Innocuous. $565, including taxes and fees. On my tab. For the moment. I pulled the little refrigerator open. "I wouldn't trust the wine, maybe a gin and tonic, both generic enough that the brand hardly matters." I selected them for her, knowing that men were no longer supposed to make choices for women, even in such small matters. Let her make a quarrel over something that small. I opened the tiny gin bottle and the pocket-sized tonic, found the glasses and the small ice bucket, and made the drink for her while I talked.

"There's a story he loves to tell. About Art Buchwald. Buchwald had written a bunch of film treatments. He handed them in, got paid, and forgot about them. Then, one day, a friend of his, all excited, says, 'Art, I saw your movie!' Art doesn't have a clue what the guy is talking about. His friend tells him the name of it. Art goes to see it, and sure enough, it looks like it came from his treatment. It's *Coming to America*, with Eddie Murphy.

"Art tries to make a claim. The company, Paramount, says that it's based on an original idea from Eddie Murphy, who has a 'story' credit in the film, and has nothing to with Buchwald's treatment."

I put her drink on the blond wood table beside her. Next to our two cell phones, both shut off, and the batteries out, just to be sure about it.

"Art can afford some top-notch lawyers and he doesn't care 'that you'll never work in this town again.' He sues. Eddie's so-called original story is, in fact, a lot like Art's story. That wouldn't mean anything, but Art's very lucky because he's able to prove a direct line from his treatment to Eddie Murphy, even that Murphy read it, talked about it, saw multiple screenplays based on it.

"Art wins. This is near the peak of Murphy's career. The film has grossed over $200 million, back when that was a lot of money. He goes to Paramount to get his percentage of the net profits. They laugh. There is no net. Art sues again. Eddie, testifying in court, explains that net points are 'monkey points.'

"The judge says, 'I want to look at the books.' At that point, Paramount settles. Out of court. They are not going to let anyone look at their books."

"And the point of that story is?"

"For me or for Beinhart?"

"What the hell," she said with a sigh, halfway through her gin and tonic, "for both."

"He wrote a book, originally called *American Hero*. Which became the movie *Wag the Dog*, with Hoffman, De Niro, and a bunch of other cool people, including Willie Nelson. The movie was low budget by Hollywood standards; twenty million. In the first quarter it grossed forty million. Beinhart, who has monkey points, gets his first statement. Do you want to guess?"

"Zero? They claim it made no money?"

"Please. You have no respect for Hollywood creativity. It was twenty million in the hole. A few years later, as it continued to play around the world, it got to forty million in the hole. He claims that the last time he asked, which was about eighteen years after it was released, it had reached sixty million in the hole.

"Beinhart was unlucky. He couldn't afford a few hundred thousand for lawyers and forensic accountants. But he was lucky. He'd read the book . . . *Fatal Subtraction* . . . about Buchwald, Murphy, and Paramount, as part of his research for the novel, and knew he had to be satisfied with the up-front money, which he was, and not to be surprised or disappointed that they were liars and thieves and there was no back end."

"What does that have to do with you and me?"

"And Maddie," I said. "After all, we're acting on her behalf."

"And Maddie."

"How do we enforce the back end? I certainly can't do what Buchwald did, hire hot-shit lawyers, take you into court, and have the judge force you to pay me for an illegal action."

"You have my word . . ."

"Please," I said. "Even if Maddie had showed up alone, as agreed, with twenty thousand, as agreed, instead of you with half that amount, I would want to find some way to insure the back end."

"I simply wanted to meet you, have a better sense, and establish a working relationship," she said. "I thought it reasonable to break things into a couple of extra steps."

"Don't be defensive," I said, adding with an offensive sneer, "You are what you are," and then switched back to my let-us-reason-together voice. "The other solution would be to raise the front end high enough that I'd accept the fact that you were unlikely to pay the back end."

"How much would that be?"

"Originally the back end was going to be a hundred, on top of the twenty, up front. Since then, we've had some problems. Also, Maddie said her husband was worth ten or twelve million . . . and the sense I got from her voice and her manner was that she was coming up with the lowest number she thought she could get away with . . . but even if she was being honest and accurate and even if you're getting 30 percent for your litigation finance . . . there's more than enough at stake for me to raise my price."

"How much?"

"Let's say two-fifty," I said.

"To be clear, two hundred and fifty thousand?"

"Sounds a decent number."

"It's an indecent number," she said, sharpish. "And besides, I would never pay it up front. What's to stop you from taking the money and walking away? How do I make sure you do *your* job?"

"That's always the problem with contracts for illegal acts," I said patiently, quite pleased that I'd spoken rather like an academic conversing with colleagues at a seminar. "Their enforcement."

"If you manage to do this . . . this thing . . . in a timely fashion, I . . . Maddie and I . . . are certainly going to pay you. Not to pay a hitman, if you don't mind the expression, would be the height of foolishness. It's obvious what your response would be."

"Response is not a solution." So logical. "Dead people don't pay." So dry. "Also, killing people is a dangerous, messy business. Especially rich, white people. And there'd be no point to it, unless it was my regular business, then, maybe, *pour encourager les autres.*" I continued, sounding nothing but reasonable, and offered the problem up to her. "Do you have a solution? That ensures that whomever goes last, the person who acts or the person who pays, comes through."

"We're going to have to trust each other," she said. She gave it a really good reading. It was right up there with Mary Astor telling lies to Humphrey Bogart in the *Maltese Falcon*. If they did a remake I'd call the casting director on her behalf.

"You want me to do this? You want me to kill Mick McMunchun for Maddie and you?"

"Yes. Yes, it has to be done."

"Then don't be fuckin' ridiculous," I said, all nasty and mean, but low so no one in the hall or the next rooms could hear. "I don't do this without insurance."

"What, what insurance?"

"Stand up," I said, taking her by the hand and pulling her up.

"Get your hands off me."

"Here's what we're going to do," I said. "You're going to take off all your clothes."

"The hell I will."

"This is not about sex. This is about recordings. Yeah, we have our phones on the table. But I have another one in my back pocket. You could have another stashed somewhere. Or a wire. A microphone. If you want to make this happen, you'll get naked.

"There's a robe laid out on the bed there—nice, thick terry cloth thing—you can put it on to preserve your modesty, since you seem to care. Then you will read from this script, and I will record us.

"We'll have a conversation. You will ask me to kill McMunchun. You will offer money. I will turn you down. I'll be emphatic and say that's crazy, don't do it.

"Then I will stop recording. If we come to an agreement and I do my part and you two don't pay, then I'll go to the local DA or PD or whatever, and say, 'Hey, they approached me about this thing. I didn't report it at the time, because, oh hell officer, who would've actually believed it, but now that he's dead in that dreadful way—whatever it turns out to have been—I had to come forward. I had the phone on by accident and it was even recorded. You'll go down, I'll be fine. In prison when they have you strip down you also bend over, spread your cheeks, and they do a cavity search. It's up to you. You do it or you don't, but it's the only way this works."

She shrugged out of her jacket and began to unbutton her blouse. "The art of the deal," she said.

CHAPTER THIRTEEN

NOW WHAT?

"It'd be a hell of a note if somebody was
being murdered during all this comedy we're having."

COFFIN ED JOHNSON
THE HEAT'S ON, CHESTER HIMES

I GOT MOST OF WHAT I wanted.

I was keeping the $10,000 I'd taken. I was getting another $20,000 up front. With $170,000 when it was done. Most importantly, I had the taped conversation as my insurance policy.

She wanted it done in two weeks. I wanted to know why the rush. She gave me quite reasonable answers but not necessarily the whole truth. Or any of the truth. I explained that I wasn't going to walk up and shoot the guy. Killing a rich white man was the only thing in America that would attract more attention than killing a young white woman. To make it worse, those Hudson Valley counties, Ulster, Greene, Dutchess, Columbia, Putnam, even Orange and Westchester, were practically No Murder zones. Each of them had between five and zero—*zero*—killings per year. All of them had lots of cops. Town police, county sheriffs, and state police. The first might be bumpkins, the second concerned with serving papers and running jails, but the staties had the BCI, Bureau of Criminal Investigation, with all the resources, experience, and expertise of a truly large force.

Liz said, like we were happily cooperative colleagues, "That's why I wanted to work with you in spite of getting off to a bad start. You've been around. You understand these things."

I said, "You don't want it to look like murder. Certainly, Madelaine shouldn't. The spouse is the number one suspect. We all know that. Plus, they're in the middle of a divorce . . ."

"No one's filed . . ."

"In a cop's mind, that's a technicality. They've said it to each other. They've said it to lawyers."

"We'll have her back off. It will look like she's seeking peace and reconciliation."

"The cops won't believe it. Sure, it'll help if it gets to trial. Throw sand in the jury's eyes. But we don't want it to get that far. It has to go down one of two ways. Either, it's a setup, so someone else is in the frame. For good and certain. Or it doesn't look like murder at all, it looks like an accident or natural causes."

"You're right," she said. "You're absolutely right. How are you going to do it?"

That was a great question. That was *the* question. I had no idea. "I have to get to know the target," I said.

"I can tell you a lot about him. Maddie can tell you more. Naturally."

"No. I want to meet him. Observe him. Watch him in action."

"Seriously, do you think you have a special Spider Sense to figure him out?"

"You know that old story about the blind men and the elephant? Each grabs a different part. One thinks he's like a tree trunk, another like a rope, another like a hose, and so on. Perspective, point of view, determines what you see. Maddie knows him like a wife. Once she loved him, now she hates him. You know him as someone to sue. I need to know him as someone that I'm going to kill. And get away with it.

"Arrange it," I said. "Arrange it so I can get close to him."

CHAPTER FOURTEEN

PARTY TIME

"My husband and I have never considered divorce . . . murder sometimes, but never divorce."

—JOYCE BROTHERS
Once an advice columnist, psychologist,
TV personality, and she answered
The $64,000 Question, which was once
America's #1 quiz show . . .

THERE WAS GOING TO BE a party. A fundraiser for Hudson Valley Libraries. A worthy cause. One that I could actually support.

Madelaine and Mick McMunchun were the hosts. Rich people had been invited to consort with writers. Several of them were mystery, detective, and crime writers. Madelaine came up with an immensely clever idea. Writers would be allowed—encouraged—to bring along as their guests, actual detectives, or even criminals. That would make the whole thing ever so much more scintillating and dramatic and would let me be there in a way that seemed totally natural.

Where would my invitation come from?

I knew the answer even before I asked the question. Beinhart. I would be his accessory. He'd probably have two. His wife had once been a detective. Good at it, too. She was attractive, gracious, and very likable. Many people wondered how they were still together.

It was Maddie's thing. Even though she and her husband were

batting and slapping each other back and forth, collecting allies, mar-shaling forces, they had not yet gotten to a declaration of war, the actual filing for divorce, they still shared real estate and minor public performances of amity. He had little interest in this particular one, but was willing to go along with it for some domestic tranquility and some local good guy credits. The problem remained, how to really make use of it. Most people who have a lot of money truly believe that money is the measure of all things. Unless a writer—or a detective—was raking in millions, he'd give them about as much time and attention as he gave the gardener or the kids' grade school teachers. He'd shake my hand, nod at me, turn away, and shortly thereafter find a way to excuse himself from the room entirely.

If Maddie was telling the truth, I knew what would hold his attention. If I was a hot fourteen-year-old girl, he'd chat with me all night.

Owen Cohen.

West Forty-Sixth Street, between Ninth and Tenth Avenues. Up on the third floor. It was a good space with high ceilings. When the space was mine, I'd called it TCI—my name, plus *Investigations*—Ltd. Not very imaginative. Owen kept that, so he could use the statio-nery, the logo, the name on the door, but used it to represent Total Confidentiality Investigations, Ltd.

He didn't make me wait. He came right out to the reception area to greet me. We traded a long and caring handshake. I offered con-dolences and commiseration over the death of his partner, Winston, whom I'd liked quite a lot. Owen accepted them with a shrug. Then we walked into his private office, which had once been my private office.

"What can I do for you?" he said. Cordial. And down to business.

Who Owen was, was hung on the office walls for all to see, provided that you brought some knowledge to what you were looking at. The cover of *New York* magazine from December 8, 1986, had been blown up about four times its real size and encased in a clear laminate. The banner headline was "COP STORY: In Black & White." It was above a photo of Winston and Owen—standing proud—and together—looking right at you—amid a dystopian urban landscape.

It was both true and false, real and fake.

The backstory is a novella of The City in the Eighties. Mayor Ed Koch was planning to run for a fourth term. He was going to be challenged by an African American candidate. It was *their turn*.

In February 1985, *New York*'s cover story had been "Blacks and Jews: How Wide the Rift?"

The mayor's people were looking for good Blacks-and-Jews-together stories. Desperately.

Owen and Winston had made a couple of solid murder cases up in the Two-Five, the 25th Precinct, the northern half of East Harlem, which had once been Italian Harlem and then had become Spanish Harlem, the place with a Rose, who had eyes as black as coal, that Ben E. King sang about.

Owen and Winston got plucked from the sea of blue by Koch's PR team. Owen loved to claim that he told the magazine people that the title should be "The Nig and The Yid." In more recent years, he's been framing that anecdote by bemoaning the rise of political correctness, so he can't tell it anymore, except to *you*, 'cause you're a special person, and you understand. Owen is very sharp and knows when he can pull that off and when he can't.

In November 1986, a police scandal erupted in Brooklyn.

That made the mayor's people push even harder because Owen

and Winston were not just a Jew and a Black, they were Good Cops. Whether they knew it or not, they were in a race with staff writer Michael Daly, who was digging to get the in-depth goodies on the dark doings down in the 77th Precinct.

Daly delivered. It was a much juicier tale. Owen and Winston were bumped.

The actual cover story of the actual December 8, 1986, edition of *New York* magazine, turned out to be *The Crack in the Shield: the Fall of the Seven-Seven.*

Owen managed to get the artwork that had been prepped but never published. After they bought me out, he had it printed up, and hung it on the wall. It looked good.

"I'm looking for a girl," I said.

"Searching?"

"No, to go to an event, a party, with me."

"Like an escort?"

"Good description," I said.

"You back in this game?"

"No," I said. "More like doing a favor for a friend."

"For free?" It was hard to tell if that was suspicion or revulsion in his voice.

"Not for free," I said, but added reassuringly, "It's a one-off. Only because it's for a friend. I'm not making a business of it." That was also meant to be reassuring.

"Should you want to," he said, gesturing at the offices to say that he might be open to doing something together. "With Winston gone." A void. A place to be filled. "If you bring any business with you, we'd make that work so it's good for both of us, you know that."

"I'm too old," I said. "Forget about the knock-around stuff, I wouldn't even want to do a stakeout. What if it went past eleven? That's after my bedtime."

He gave that as much of a laugh as it deserved. Then back to business. "A girl, you're looking for a girl?"

"Escort was a good word."

There was a pause. A flicker. Something very brief.

Why come to Owen with this?

He and Winston had spent most of their career in the Two-Five. They'd done well for themselves there.

Look closely at the cover shot from *New York*. Winston's wearing a black cashmere coat from Barney's over an Armani suit. Owen has an Ermenegildo Zegna suit and an Ermenegildo Zegna tie, with a Hugo Boss shirt. When they bought me out, they paid in cash. In real estate, "cash sale" is often used to describe a purchase without a mortgage. The usage here refers to an attaché case with stacks of greenbacks.

But it wasn't those years, the ones in Spanish Harlem, that had given Owen the special expertise that had me sitting across from him right then.

The ripples outward from the Seven-Seven to other "active" precincts did not come immediately. But Owen had been sure they would come inevitably. The wild, crack-crazed eighties could not last. Not for the meat-eaters, the term that cops used for those of their tribe who sat down at the banquet of crime and carved off prime beef for themselves. He and Winston were not ready to leave the NYPD, but they did want to get out from the most likely lines of fire. They both reached out for their rabbis. Why "rabbi" became the preferred term for hook, patron, guardian, in a police department dominated by Irish, Germans, and Italians, is unknown, but it is, and it was Winston's rabbi who came through and got them transferred to the perfect place.

The One-Nine. The 19th Precinct. The Upper East Side. Fifth Avenue to the East River, Fifty-Ninth Street to Ninety-Sixth Street. The richest, quietest, best-behaved principality in all of Manhattan. There was but one kind of crime indigenous to the region, high-end prostitution. It was the land of *The Happy Hooker*, Xaviera Hollander, who ran the Vertical Brothel on East Seventy-Third and had an advice column in *Penthouse*; Utopia on East Seventieth; Anna Gristina, the "Soccer Mom Madam," on East Seventy-Eighth Street, aka "The Millionaire Madam," operating on East Seventy-Fourth.

Owen and Winston adapted well to their new environment, forming all the appropriate and inappropriate relationships.

If I was looking for a runaway and there was reason to think she might have *Pretty Woman* fantasies, turning $1,000 tricks for millionaires who looked like Richard Gere, and a fair number of teenyboppers did, Owen and Winston were the go-to guys.

They left the force in 1994.

The Mollen Commission Report was coming out. Rudy Giuliani was coming in.

Rudy had run for mayor as the White, Right, Return-to-Law-and-Order guy. He was going to crack down. It was going to be a very awkward time for the usual police corruption. Yet the need for cooperation between the sex industry and law enforcement, street cops up through prosecutors to the judges, remained. Owen recognized the gap. He realized it could best be filled by a nongovernmental intermediary. Someone who could collect funds from one side for "security and investigative services," and then dispense funds on the other side to cops for legal moonlighting assignments, to ADAs for legal opinions, and to judges as campaign contributions.

Owen's knowledge base of New York's finer prostitutes, madams, and escorts was still the best around.

He was looking at me. I guessed that his antenna had gone up, but then he'd reviewed what he knew of me and I knew of him and decided I wasn't there to harm him or wearing a wire or anything stupid like that. The flicker was gone. The pause was over. He said, "Yeah, OK, something specific?"

"I want to find a girl who could pass for fourteen or so."

"Why not a real fourteen-year-old?"

Good question. On a lot of levels. If I was willing to commit murder for money, why would the morality of employing a fourteen-year-old be an issue? I wasn't even planning to have whomever it was commit actual sex acts. Just to entice, arouse, and see how the target would act. And yet . . . I said, "I want someone smart. Someone who knows people and can evaluate them. And can stay out of trouble."

"You mean more like an investigation, not a fuck 'n' suck?"

"Not a fuck 'n' suck," I said, "Not even a fuck or suck."

"And you'd be more comfortable not using a real fourteen-year-old." Saying it to confirm that was one of my personal limitations.

I had to acknowledge that was true and did so with a gesture.

That settled, it was time to fill out my order form. "What would you like, style-wise?" He threw in a little accent and attitude, lending a little color and character to every choice. "Joisy shore? A little loud and a lot slutty." Very reality show. "Hot LaaaTina?" almost had a salsa beat. "Upper East Side, private school . . ."

Bingo. "That."

"You sure?" I obviously hadn't heard all the selections. "Russky girl. Ludmilla, blonde, Slavic. Ve could do orthodox Jew, even. Real forbidden fruit."

"Upper East Side," I said. "Dalton, Spence, Horace Mann, like that."

"Good choice," he said. "Have I got a girl for you."

"I have to meet her."

"Of course. You have to know the price, too."

"Fine."

"This gathering, this whatever, how many hours are we talking about?"

"The whole evening, probably pick her up at seven, have her home by curfew."

"Like midnight?"

"Yeah, or sooner or a couple of hours later. In that range."

"Figure seven."

"Seven what?"

"Seven K."

"What? To dress nice and go to a party. No fuck 'n' suck, remember."

"She's special, she's spectacular, she's exactly what you want. She's seven K. Plus one for me."

"If I meet her and don't want her?"

"I'll find you a second choice, even a second *and* a third choice. Included. Because of our prior relationship. I only ask one thing. If you don't have the money . . . and you're looking for a hundred an hour tart, like that, let me know now, so we don't fuck around and waste time."

"I have the money," I said.

"I have the girl," he said, sounding more certain of his product than any car salesman I've ever met. "Isn't life fun? You want a meet, I'll call, or she'll call, and set it up."

"Soon," I said.

"Soon," he said, "tonight or tomarra."

As I turned to leave I noticed a new set of pictures on the wall. It was a sort of series, going from left to right, the way we read. It started with the cover of Charley Rosen's book, *The Chosen Game: A Jewish*

Basketball History. It was followed by five black-and-white photos of basketball players from the 1920s and '30s, white, mostly short, and presumably Jewish.

Owen was right behind me. "You like that?"

"Interesting," I said.

"My grandfather, who was all of five foot six, was on the City College championship team"—he pointed at one of the photos—"back in the 1920s."

The little exhibit reached its conclusion with a quote from *Farewell to Sport*, by Paul Gallico, who'd been a sports writer and the sports editor for the *New York Daily News* during that period. It said basketball "is a game that above all others . . . appeals to the Hebrew with his Oriental background . . . the game places a premium on an alert, scheming mind and flashy trickiness, artful dodging, and general smart-aleckness."

"I take it it's a dig at racial and ethnic stereotyping."

"Nah," he said. "I think that's an accurate description of my people."

Both of us keeping straight faces, neither of us sure if the other was mocking or utterly sincere.

CHAPTER FIFTEEN
MERETRICIOUS

"The martinis tasted like rubbing alcohol."
BUSINESS INSIDER, REVIEW OF TRUMP GRILL

WE MET IN THE TRUMP Grill in Trump Tower.

I was there first. A girl walked in and I said to myself, "That, that girl would be perfect." She looked to be fourteen, possibly a little younger even, less possibly a little older. She was pretty, slender, almost skinny and a little bit gawky, like fawns that haven't grown into their own bodies yet. The clothes, the grooming, the hair styling, you'd figure her for an expensive prep school and wealthy parents. So perfect that she couldn't possibly be the hooker I was seeking.

Until the hostess brought her to my table.

I stood up to introduce myself, enthralled by the look, but terrified that when she opened her mouth it would be like that moment in *Singin' In the Rain* when the beautiful silent movie actress has to speak and caterwauling sounds come out. She smiled, seeming a little bit awkward and shy, told me her name—Allison Leslie Scott—her voice was fine, just fine—and shook my hand. We sat down. I asked her if she'd like something to eat or drink.

"A sparkling water."

"Nothing to eat?"

"Oh, I wouldn't eat a thing here," she said.

"So why did you pick it?"

"Oh," she clasped her hands together right between her modest, but high and firm breasts, looked briefly down at her hands, sort of biting her lips, then looked back up and said, "It was the most meretricious place I could think of."

"And by that you mean?"

She cocked her head a little. Who was testing whom? Was I ignorant of what it meant, or did I suspect that she was using a word that was too big for her? She said, "Garish, glitzy, ornate yet phony. Tinsel and tawdry."

"Alright, but why would you want to go someplace like that?"

"To give me the opportunity to say 'meretricious.' It's such a gorgeous and underutilized word in a world that's growing more meretricious every day."

"You like using ostentatious words in a pretentious way," I said.

"I thought," she said, "it would make me seem precocious and eager to appear older than I am."

"How old are you? Really."

"I meant in terms of the scenario. A precocious fourteen-year-old, who's read too many books and would like to know more of real life but trembles before it." Which was pretty much how she sounded.

"I think this is going to work," I said.

"Where are we going for this party?" she asked. "And how should I dress?"

"It's actually a fundraiser," I said.

"For?"

"For the libraries of the Hudson Valley."

"That's so . . . laudable," she said. "I majored in literature. Briefly. But I still have a great admiration for it. And where is it?"

"About an hour and a half upstate. Near Rhinebeck."

"Oh, how perfect," she said. "How wonderful to be back there."

CHAPTER SIXTEEN

PRAYERS?

"**A JOURNEY OF A THOUSAND** miles begins with a single step."

That comes from *Tao Te Ching*, by Lao Tzu, the father of Taoism. All such things are open to multiple interpretations, even if they aren't translations from an archaic version of a distant language and credited to a person whose very existence is disputed. Nonetheless, this aphorism seems to have a certain clarity to it. However long the journey, it must start with that first step. If you try to look 1,000 miles ahead and think about how long it will take and how much effort is needed, you will be overwhelmed. Instead, take the single step. Next, all you need to do is take one step. Not one more step, there is no past to weary you, no endless future to intimidate you, only the present, with one single step.

Murdering Mick McMunchun—so it wouldn't look like murder, getting away with it, making sure I got paid the promised amount— was a journey of 1,000 miles. Too great a distance, too many mountains to climb, rivers to cross, people who might try to stop me on purpose or by accident, too many possible accidents to anticipate, too many mistakes I might make.

Finding the girl, having her seem so right—it felt like that first step. The first step that I was certain was going forward on that journey. I'd been a half-dead thing. Saying yes to this beyond-the-bounds project into precarious and treacherous territory had made me feel like I was coming back to life. Looking at myself from an imaginary distance, as we often do, I was watching a sci-fi film, and I was an automaton taken out of storage, experiencing reactivation.

Of course, I'd felt good about that, because in sci-fi films automatons have consciousness, self-awareness, and feelings. It had also awakened tension and stress. Pulled my nervous system so tight that it created its own vibrations. I only realized that part now. Because it had stopped. I'd taken the first step. It brought me calm. Great calm. Even though I could discern that both ends were . . . could well be described as . . . Did not sane . . . clinically speaking . . . mean insane? Oh well, this end seemed more pleasing than the other.

I woke rested. Having slept deeply and well. I rose to go about my extraordinarily ordinary, bland, and trouble-free routines. Wake, feed the cats, shower, make the bed, go to town, coffee and something, read the paper, in print, not online. Go back home, pick up whatever needed picking up. Turn on the television, realize that I didn't really want to watch anything that was on TV. Turn off the television.

There was a good, clean, touch of cold. Now that I was going to keep the place, I should be cutting and splitting firewood.

Suddenly I knew that the unknowns vastly outnumbered the knowns. The calm was a delusion. The eye of a hurricane. A trick. Mongol warriors on their ponies coming across the steppe, barbarians circling around a village, Viking longboats landing on the beach. After that first step, the second, or the third, or fourth, would take me back out where the winds were blowing, faster and stronger, faster and stronger, until they were howling.

I was alone.

Normally, not an issue. Accepted. Like I accepted the age in my body, that some summer days were heavy with heat and some winter days could be viciously cold, that *The New York Times* had obituaries in every issue because death never skipped a day. Now, I had a need, a forlorn craving, for someone to talk to, a destitute man holding out one hand for your spare change.

I went back into the house. I picked up the phone. I took a deep breath. I dialed my daughter, in Couzon-au-Mont-d'Or, a village along the Rhône, near Lyon. When she answered, I said, "Hello."

She said, "Oh, it's you." Sounding totally U.S.A., both in accent and attitude. It's what she'd grown up with. The years away hadn't erased them.

"I just wanted to talk to you," I said.

"Is it something terribly urgent?"

"It's . . . it's complicated . . ." My words found themselves stuck in the muck of family history and tangled in a thicket of waist-high weeds. ". . . I'm trying to reach out and . . ."

"Are you calling to say you have cancer, you're on the verge of death, something like that?" Her voice was dry, flipping through various subjects, on little stiff paper cards, the sort they used in old-fashioned library catalogues.

"Nothing like that. Physically, physically, at least, I'm healthy, very healthy for my age."

"Well, good for you."

"Spiritually . . ." I said, not entirely sure if I was saying it because that's what I actually thought was at issue, or because spirituality was something she'd always believed in to such a degree that we'd constantly quarreled about it. Nor was I entirely sure if that was meant as a genuine gesture toward reconciliation or an attempt at being manipulative. "I guess that would be the word . . ."

In any case, it didn't work. "Don't talk to me about that," she dismissed it. "Spiritually you were always a disaster. That's you. Don't worry about it. I have some things to do."

"I'm sorry," I said.

"I'm sure," she said. "Goodbye."

I stood outside. It was a moment—and they are few—when I wished I could pray—to some hard-core version of a monotheistic top-of-it-all deity who had all the answers.

I began walking up the mountain. There are no houses, roads, or structures above me. I was going deeper into the forest land. Strangely, walking up hill required no extra effort. It didn't drain my breathing or make my thighs begin to ache.

The sun was low but bright. There was a daytime moon, three-quarters, simple and white, at an angle across from it. There was a wind, it made the trees rustle and murmur. Leaves were yellow, red, gold, and a lot of brown. They were dropping off the trees with their own subtle noises. I heard squirrels racing around, spotted some chipmunks, geese flew overhead, and a woodpecker rat-a-tat-tatted into a tree. Farther away, I heard some deer moving, at first slowly, just walking, browsing, then suddenly running and leaping, three or four of them.

In the forest lands, the winds, the heat of the sun, the cold of the night, all the things that grow, the animals and birds and even the insects are driven by forces, inhabited by spirits, have souls and their own demigods, in competition, going in different directions, speaking so many distant languages, it won't lead you to imagine that there must be no gods but the One.

Monotheism was born in the deserts, where it's empty and quiet and dead.

I was told that by Beinhart.

He got it from one of his fictional characters. "That's no reason not to listen," he told me. "There can be great wisdom in your hallucinations." It came with a proviso, a stipulation. "But keep some part of yourself awake and aware that you're hallucinating. That's the key to not letting it become a bad trip."

If you've made up the character that's talking to you, and you know it, it's fairly easy to stay aware that it's you talking to yourself.

It's more difficult when it's a common-usage character. One that an entire group believes exists, that everyone and anyone can use, are even encouraged to use, for hallucinations. Where's the hook on which you can hang the certainty that it's imaginary? If multitudes believe in its existence, and many claim to have conversed with it, how do you not believe that such imaginary characters are alive, real, animate, and chatty. How do you not believe that their messages are to be trusted? Obeyed.

There are some who will say that all perceptions are made up, that all our visions of the world are fictions. That is true in certain very abstract ways. But it is also absolutely false if you happen to have the perception that you, yourself, possess the wings of an angel, and they're as reliable as the wings of an Airbus A320, and you attempt to make the flight from Buenos Aires to Berlin.

That was the gibberish—abstract and useless?—steel pinballs bouncing off skull walls, as my feet moved me through the woods. I passed the stand of white birch. They like the cold, so the higher it is, the more likely they'll grow. They can be tapped, like maples, their sap about a third as sweet. It can even be fermented. Birch, ash, and oak are the sacred trees of the Druids, Celts, and the Norse. My feet knew where I was going.

There's a great oak that lives above me.

These lands were clear-cut back in the nineteenth century. It's rare to find a tree much older than one hundred or so. Somehow, for some reason, the landowner or the lumberjacks left this one. It's lived to grow bigger than anything around it. I would guess, without much science to substantiate it, that it's perhaps 250 years old.

I knelt there. In the dirt. Against the roots. I reached out to put my hands on its bark, rougher and harder than a boxer's knuckles. I wanted to connect through it to life, to the sacred, if there is such a thing, to the each in all, to the all in each. I opened my senses and myself to all the things moving around me.

I knew who I wanted to speak to. I called out to my wife. I called out to my son. I knew that in order to speak to them I would have to hallucinate their deaths away. Summon their avatars in the way that some say they summon saints. "Help me. Talk to me," I said. "You're only body dead. My soul is deader than either one of yours."

My wife said, "Je connais la tristesse, la douleur . . . the pain, the sadness, of losing life. When death came to eat me away, knowing that I was leaving those I love and would no longer be able to give the gifts I wish to give . . ."

My son said, "I wanted to save lives, heal bodies, prolong lives. I wanted to be a hero . . . a hero to life . . ."

I so wanted it to be true that they somehow still lived and were talking to me.

Ravens and crows cawed to announce that another voice would speak, my voices should be silent, and I should attend.

The weather came over the ridge and the wind began to blow. It grabbed at the weariest leaves, pulling them off their branches. An owl flew out of the oak. It cruised in a circle, wings spread wide, then swooped fast and low, caught something in its talons and disappeared.

I knew that if a spirit lived in the oak, if there was such a thing, it would be a deity of the woodlands, pre-Christian, the kind of god that fights, fucks, lies, and feasts. With its very first words, that is what it revealed itself to be. "Only warriors that die in battle go on to fight and to feast in the afterlife." Then another voice, a woman's voice, more playful, sultry, and teasing, said, "He picks half, I pick half, wandering through the battlefield, from the corpses." Then she answered a question I hadn't spoken. "Yes, in the place we're from, sex and death are united with beauty, with grace, honor." Then, laughing, "With trickery, treachery, longing, and lechery." I knew her. Her chariot, it was said, was pulled by cats. The part of my mind that was able to still hang on to our standard earthly sphere, the modern one, of science, secularism, and rationality, knew there was humor and wonderful puns in there, but also knew that if I said anything about being pulled by pussy power, the hallucinations would be offended and leave.

The ravens called and pulled my focus back.

The wind was growing stronger, blowing harder, and melded its power into His voice, giving it more gravitas and it came out lower, deeper, and stronger all at once. He said, "Thus spake Zarathustra." Perhaps it was a joke, because he laughed, and his laugh was so large and rumbling that it rolled like thunder rolls in the Catskills, all the way down the mountain, into the valley, and up the other side, bouncing off it as an echo. "Nietzsche," he said, "was a humbug asshole. Did you ever hear anything dumber than 'What does not kill us, makes us stronger'? That from a man who went mad from syphilis. But from time to time his aphorisms are instructive. Try this one on for size. 'True man wants two things, danger and play.'" I stood up. Everything was spinning around, but I was not dizzy.

The ravens were cawing. Squirrels chattering. The wind was making the trees bend and bow, snap and moan. Leaves were falling all around. The gods in the oak were chortling.

I was mad—not angry, ha-ha, no-no, not at all, I thought it was quite gracious of my hallucinations to be so open and conversational with me—I mean, insane. I'd clung on to enough realism to at least know that.

It was necessary to walk away from the hallucinatory part of myself, toward where my more normal self was known to live, while that was still possible. I attempted to do so. As I took the first steps down the hill, away from the great oak, I did become dizzy. I felt that all the chattering and chortling and the wind-driven noises were affecting my inner ear, making me lose my ability to balance myself.

One step at a time.

One foot in front of the other.

Don't trip or get caught by a fallen branch or an uprising root.

Don't let loose stones roll your feet out from under you and twist your ankle.

Slowly. And step and step.

Breathe. And breathe.

CHAPTER SEVENTEEN

A GYPSY QUEEN IN A FAIRY TALE

"They used to race ice yachts on the Hudson River. The Roosevelts, the Rockefellers, the Astors, the Livingstons. Not ice boats. Ice yachts. Sixty-eight-foot-long. A thousand feet of sail. Eighty miles an hour. The fastest vehicles on Earth back in the nineteenth century."

LARRY BEINHART, *WHERE WE'VE BEEN*

THE EAST BANK OF THE Hudson River was a gold coast as rich as the North Shore of Long Island where F. Scott Fitzgerald set *The Great Gatsby*. A low ridge runs parallel to the water. The Astors, Rockefellers, Vanderbilts, Roosevelts, and Livingstons built mansion after mansion from Westchester to Albany along that highline. They were landscaped in emulation of England's stately homes. The trees were cleared for the view, except, always, for a few that would stand in isolated grandeur. The forests were replaced with vast lawns, immaculately groomed green carpets covering the slopes down to the water. Often formal gardens, large and small, were added. With gardeners to keep the shrubs and flowers as watered, fed, trimmed, and primped as their owners.

That Gilded Age is gone, but their side of the river still seems tidier, more kempt, better mannered, than our side.

I picked up Allison from Rhinecliff station.

She asked me if we could stop by Bard, for fifteen minutes or so, on the way.

Bard is about eight miles straight north from the station, on Route 103, a two-lane local road.

Almost everything you'd see on your left, toward the river, is the land of the great estates. You pass Ferncliff. Now a nursing home. You cross 199, which would take you to the bridge over to Kingston. Poet's Walk is next. Then Rokeby Mansion, owned by the Astors and Livingstons, and still occupied by their heirs, but shabby with the paint peeling from the walls. Then there's Union Theological Seminary, completely hidden away, originally owned by the Livingstons, who sold it to John D. Rockefeller so he could build a monastery for the Christian Brothers. Then it went to Rev. Sun Myung Moon for his Unification Church. It's currently on the market for $17,000,000 or so. Edgewater, another Livingston mansion is nearby. It belonged to Gore Vidal from 1950 to 1969. A smaller mansion, Sylvania is the next property to the north.

Then there's Montgomery Place, which Bard had recently purchased, to add to the next two, Ward Manor and Blithewood, which make up the college campus. Blithewood Mansion is now the Levy Economics Institute.

"You said you were on the verge of graduation."

"Yes, about a semester to go."

"I have a question . . ."

"Of course you do. 'Why quit so close to the finish line and take up the still disreputable—and possibly dangerous—trade of sex worker?'"

"About age . . ."

"I know I seem excessively grown up for my chronological age," Allison said, cutting me off. "Or look very young for my whatever . . . my precocity. Did you ever look up that word? I did once, and the first definition up there—this was a web search . . . so take it for what it's worth . . . but still, the first example of the use of the word was: 'You'll be proud of your puppy's precocity if he is perfectly trained by the age of four months.' That's frequently what I felt like, a paper-trained puppy for others to be proud of. Being precocious is weirder than people understand, sometimes I think it should be classified as a disorder. Maybe that's why I stopped, and what's a nice girl like me doing something like this?"

"I wasn't going to ask that."

"Really?"

"Really. I just couldn't make it compute. There don't seem to be enough years in there." Not that I needed to make the age and educational claims work, but I did want to get a sense of how much truth she was telling me.

She said, "Leon Botstein and Ronan Farrow."

"Which means?"

"Botstein is the president of Bard College. He gets that high school is humdrum, stupid, horseshit. At least for bright children. They can handle what's called college-level material. He set up several high schools to do that. I skipped eighth grade, then got into the one in Cleveland. I'm actually from Ohio. I was done there at sixteen with two years of college credits. Then I came here, to Bard, and if I hadn't changed my major three times I probably could have graduated last spring, when I turned eighteen."

"And Ronan Farrow?"

"A cherished Bard legend. He graduated from Bard at fourteen. Bard's youngest ever. Son of Mia Farrow and Woody Allen. There's a rumor that Frank Sinatra is his biological father. Actually, it was Mia Farrow who pushed that story. *He* did not go into the sex trade. He got more degrees, then became a journalist. He's credited with exposing

Harvey Weinstein. If you think about it, maybe making a living from exposing someone else's sexual activities is part of the sex trade."

We were in the middle of the campus. She pointed and said, "Park there." I pulled over. She jumped out. "I won't be more than fifteen minutes. Promise." She reached in back and grabbed her suitcase. "I'll change, too. I know just what to wear for this. It'll be perfect, you'll see." She scrambled away with that quickness and liveliness of youth.

I sat back to wait and watch the rain come down.

The raving madness had left me. I expect it was because I had made the decision not to commit murder. I felt good. Even cleansed. The way you do after a fever has passed through you, the sweat pulling the poisons out, and you've woken up the next morning and showered them away.

I wasn't going to walk away either.

Microchips are binary. People aren't. There's lots of room between yes and no, either and or. There had to be ways to divert a significant portion of Mick's mega-millions to Madelaine even if he stayed alive, and there had to be some point at which Madelaine and Elizabeth would be satisfied short of his demise. I had several ideas circling round as the drops splashed on the car's roof and windows. It was a chilly night out there. The leaves were coming down. Over on my side of the river and up in the hills they were almost all gone, the trees gone stark and bare. The weather report was warning of freezing rain at higher elevations.

Allison came back in about the time she'd promised, holding a jacket over her head to shield herself from the rain. She'd changed from her jeans, hoodie, and cross-trainers. She had a short skirt. Not sluttishly short, but one that looked short because her legs were so long. She had a nice white blouse. It wasn't tight, but whatever the fabric it was made from, it draped to her shape. It, too, was short. Not so short that there was a gap between it and the top of her skirt, but just short enough that you'd be certain that if she moved a certain way, stretched, reached for something on a high shelf, twisted, then, yes, there would a gap and flesh would be revealed. I had to give her credit. She was very good, so far, at what she did. She could tell that I thought so.

"Do you want to be an actor?" I asked her.

"No," she said, quite definitively.

"You seem to like being a character, the details, the costumes." I pointed at her girlish backpack. "Even the props."

"I love acting," she said. "But not as a made-up character in a movie. In reality. Not like reality TV, which is bullshit. In real reality. Isn't it weird that we have to say that now? In a life. Like whatever it is I'm doing tonight."

"His wife says this guy is dangerous," I said, though I didn't think there would be much of an occasion for worry. It was a fundraiser for *libraries*. I added, "I want you to be careful," sort of a disclaimer. In addition to disparagements and denunciations from Maddie, I had a dossier on Mick from Liz. It was more than what I could find on the internet. But none of the above provided the handle, the hook, the something that I'd need to turn the guy. It's the questions you don't know to ask that have important answers. My inarticulate instruction was, "We need to get a sense of the guy."

"People are acting all the time," she said, moving her hands as if that would show me the ideas that were happening so vividly for her, dancing in front of her mind. "Like what politicians do. Businesspeople sometimes. They put on acts. They perform. But it's real actions into real worlds with real consequences. Most people have their work act, their married act, maybe their parent act. Most people, once they develop a role, they get stuck in it, nearly forever. Typecasting in life. Right now, I'm doing short-term performances. I can go completely into one, which is what I want, then out of it tomorrow."

CHAPTER EIGHTEEN

ACROSS A CROWDED ROOM

"Some Enchanted Evening"
RICHARD RODGERS & OSCAR HAMMERSTEIN

THE MCMUNCHUN HOUSE WAS NAMED Ravensview.

It was a mansion, though not nearly the size and extravagant splendor of the Vanderbilt or Rockefeller establishments. Maybe "historic home" would have been the right phrase. But there were historic houses that were much smaller, on much smaller parcels of land, in much less striking locations.

It was clear that I was still underestimating how much money was in play.

A couple of boys—maybe Bard students—were working as valets. They took my car. They weren't impressed with it. They admired Allison. One escorted us the short distance to the house with a large umbrella to protect us from chilly rain.

Madelaine greeted us at the door. I hadn't told her about Allison.

My instinct was that the more surprise there was, all around, the more revelations would follow. Madelaine examined the girl, then me. Her cat's eyes immediately appeared. Before the claws followed, I said, "This is my niece. Her father is a single parent and he had to go to Argentina and he asked me if I could look after her for a bit. I said that of course I would." Allison saw it, too. I presumed it was not the first time that older women, especially wives, had looked at her that way.

She said, "Thank you for having us," very politely and correctly, then, "What a marvelous, amazing house. I'd love to hear about it," which was the perfect thing to say.

Madelaine responded with true property pride. "It originally belonged to one of the Livingstons."

"Who were they?" Allison asked, sounding like she was truly, truly interested.

Our hostess was delighted to explain. Their glory would shine upon her like the reflected light of the moon. She led us into the living room, chatting with Allison beside her, and me trailing behind. There were many guests, standing, sitting, being very civilized indeed. A bartender was serving drinks. Three waitpersons wandered in from the kitchen with trays of tidbits. Exotic little dainties. There was a large fire in the large stone fireplace. That seemed especially right with the nasty weather outside.

Madelaine took Allison to a large chart in a wooden frame hanging on the wall beneath the slope of the stairway to the second floor. It was the perfect spot. Ostentatious—you couldn't miss it—yet humble—after all, it was tucked under the steps. It was illuminated by LED art lights. Like family trees of the British monarchies, each really important person was in their own little rectangle, with vertical lines from their parents and down to their progeny and horizontal lines to whom they married. The Livingstons came to America—New

Netherland—in 1646, with the purchase of 160,000 acres, the south-ern half of today's Columbia County. They married Schuylers, who came from the Netherlands in 1650. One of them, Philip Schuyler, was a general in the American Revolution and Alexander Hamilton's father-in-law. They married into the Rensselaer family—the original patroons of the area around Albany—and into the Vanderbilt, Mills, Bayard, and Fulton families. A Livingston financed Robert Fulton's steamboat.

By then they'd acquired about 1,000,000 acres in upstate New York. They liked large houses and could afford them. Over the next couple of centuries, they built about forty of those mansions along the river. Eleanor Roosevelt was a Livingston. As was George Herbert Walker Bush and, therefore, his son, George W. Bush.

Mick McMunchun spotted Allison Leslie Scott, looking so like a middle school girl, across the crowded room.

I had never met him. But I knew instantly who he was. He was, of course, white. Not much of a distinction, everyone in the room was white, except for one woman who looked to be of Asian Indian heritage and one of the girls wandering through with the trays who was a light-skinned African American. What was it about him? He looked like he owned the place. Which he did. He had a slight smirk. I took it to mean that he'd calculated that he was the richest person in the room.

He headed straight for her.

I didn't want things to happen too quickly. I wanted to string it out. Make him work. Maneuver. I went over to Madelaine, and my niece, Allison, before he could get there. "Allison loves books," I said. "I'd bet she'd like to meet some of the writers."

"Yes, of course," our hostess said. She looked up from the Livingstons to the rest of the room, in search of a writer for the young girl. She saw Mick coming. He moved like a slow but dedicated drone, propellers turning, thwup, thwup, thwup, as he locked on to his target. Madelaine reacted—in her ignorance—as if the situation was completely real. Horndog husband headed for a girl—to make it far worse, one of an inappropriate age—in front of a whole room. She took Allison by the arm and steered her in an arc that took her away from Mick's straight-ahead trajectory. I tagged along, a dutiful uncle, with the odd chore of keeping men from being inappropriate with the teenage girl I was temporarily responsible for.

"There's Beinhart," Maddie said to me. "You already know him, but I'll introduce Allison."

"Call me Allie," my niece said.

"Maddie," Madelaine said to her. They were getting along very well. Beinhart was standing with a couple of people I didn't know, his wife was off in the next room, talking to another small gaggle. They were laughing, lightly and pleasantly. It made me wish I had a life like that. Maddie made the introductions, mentioning *Wag the Dog*. Allison said, "I think I've heard of that," clearly meaning that she hadn't.

"That's fine," Beinhart said, seeming genuinely pleased that she didn't know the film, let alone the book.

Then Mick came over. Speaking to Beinhart, sort of over Allie's shoulder, he said, "Did you ever get that movie off the ground, that script you were trying to sell?" It wasn't a real question. Mick knew—or guessed to a point of certainty—that the writer hadn't gotten the film made or even sold the script. What he was really saying was, "I have the money, I could have financed it, but I didn't, and you don't have the money."

A meet-the-writers fundraiser was not the appropriate venue to play rich-man-taunting-the-artist. Maddie did her best to transform it into something genuinely conversational.

"What project was that?"

"You remember," Mick said, "the one about the cop, the black cop. Named Winston Churchill."

"It was Walker," Beinhart said.

My mind spoke silently to myself. It said, *What the fuck?*

"His name in real life was Winston Walker. I didn't use it in the script."

"Why not?" Allison said, "Doesn't Hollywood love true stories, or based on a true story, or even kind of, sort of like a true story?"

I said, more pointedly, "You knew Winston?"

"Yeah," he said. "I met him, oh, a long time ago. When you were in Europe."

"Back in the late eighties?"

"Eighty-nine. Maybe 1990. I was researching something else. I forget what. Some cop thing. Housing police, maybe. We ran into him, in a bar, I forget the name, which I do a lot lately, but it was on Fifty-Fourth? Fifty-Fifth? Something like that, and Ninth. I was introduced as a writer, then one of the cops said, 'Not a motherfucking scum-sucking lying cocksucker of a journalist . . .'" Beinhart stopped, looked at Allison, and said, "Hey, sorry."

"Oh, not a problem," Allie said, sounding like a kid delighted to hear grown-ups swear, though I suspect that's not a big deal anymore. From time to time I hear kids that age talking to each other. They fucking, sucking swear more than cops did back in the sixties when mother was half a word. "But why wouldn't you use his real name?"

"It's amazing sometimes what people will tell you," Beinhart said. "Sometimes it's strangers-on-a-train syndrome. Where people who think they're strangers and will never see each other again, they say things they want to say, but would never say to anyone who might see them tomorrow. Sometimes it's the moment. Like . . ." He got slightly stuck, then said, "like a short love affair." I realized he'd been looking for a genteel euphemism for a one-night stand out of concern for the ears of the fourteen-year-old junior high school girl who was actually a prostitute.

"At that point, Winston thought a shit-storm was about to break and he'd be standing right under it. He was a character. Did you ever read Chester Himes?"

I said yes. Allison shook her head no. Beinhart took that to be a teaching moment. "You should. Black writer, from a time when that was extremely rare. His biggest success, and what he's known for, is a series of crime novels . . . *Cotton Comes to Harlem*, made into a movie. *Blind Man with a Pistol*, best title, but a mess of a book."

Allison was giving him her gaze of fascination. Good girl. Mick was totally bored. But he couldn't figure a way to interrupt. He wandered off. He'd be back the next moment the girl was detached.

"They all feature two black detectives working in Harlem when it was like a foreign country, Coffin Ed and Gravedigger Jones. Damn, I've searched all my life for character names as great as that. Walker starts talking to me, and it's like one of them has come to life. Some of the things he was telling me . . . which is why I wouldn't use his name . . . were crimes."

"You can say what they were now," I said. "He just died."

"Damn," Beinhart said. "I didn't know. I'm sorry to hear that."

"I went to the funeral," I said.

Maddie pulled me away at that point. She wanted to warn me about how Mick was going to try it on with Allison.

CHAPTER NINETEEN
PRODIGAL

AT ABOUT 10:20 WE NOTICED that my niece Allison seemed to be missing.

By 10:30 it became apparent that Mick had also disappeared.

Madelaine went looking for him. Though she was really looking for *them*. She tried to be discreet about it and to keep her fury capped below socially approved decibel limits. When she'd searched every room, including the bathrooms, she enlisted two of the catering staff, issued them flashlights, and sent them out searching the grounds. She checked to be sure that they both had cell phones. Obviously, they were to call if they found either or both, but also if they were found fucking or sucking, even groping or grasping, unclothed, even significantly disheveled, they were to be photographed and pictures immediately texted to the mothership.

At 1:45 in the morning, Allison came back.

Delivered by a police car.

CHAPTER TWENTY

RIDE OF THE VALKYRIES

THIS IS ALLISON'S STORY OF the missing hours. It's not what she said to the police. She didn't say much of anything in front of Madelaine either. This is what she told to me as I drove her, slowly and carefully, back to the city.

Mick honed in on me. Instantly. You saw that. Everyone saw that. He almost tried to be subtle about it, for someone like that. Wherever I went, he came by. I encouraged it, but didn't bite.

Whenever he got me alone, or nearly so, he kept bringing up different subjects.

He asked me what I was studying. I told him I was trying to learn Chinese and I said the few words I know, badly. He said he did business with the Chinese, a lot of it.

Then he says, an idea that just hit him, "I'm going to Hong Kong and Shanghai in two months. Why don't you come along? Because the best way to learn a language is to be there. It's called 'immersion.'

Don't worry about, I'm not suggesting anything improper. Please. It's just that I like to help out young people. When I see someone as bright and focused as you, I say to myself, that's the future, and Mick, you should do something to contribute."

I politely declined. My father would never permit it. He suggested that I ask him. He offered to talk to my father. He said, "I'm very convincing. People who start out saying no to me, almost always end up saying 'Yes!' " And he went on about why they did.

Madelaine came by, "There's another writer I want you to meet," took me by the arm and led me away.

His next move was to bring me a drink. He said it was a maple-pear mojito, "sweet, delicious, refreshing," he said, "like you." I tasted it, I said it was delicious, but I wasn't used to drinking much. Also, he's the kind of guy who puts things in drinks. When he looked away I dumped most of it in a glass someone else had left on a table.

Then he suggested we go for a walk. We would go down by the river.

I mean, for God's sake, that's like a junior high school move. You'd think a man of his age and experience would have something . . . I don't know . . . more so-phis-ti-cated. I said, "It's kind of cold and rainy."

If I remember correctly, the next suggestion was that we go to his AV room. It's upstairs in what used to be the servants quarters. He said they had to knock out walls to make it right because he has a 98-inch flat-screen Sony, which is like seven feet wide and four feet high, and they'd brought in special luxury furniture to watch it from, plus there's the sound system. Sony has four speakers on the front of the screen so the sounds feel like they're coming right out of the scenes, and then he had their own guy, a specialist, come in and add more sound stuff.

Then he informed me that it had all been soundproofed.

If alarms hadn't gone off before, they would have then.

I wasn't going to get into a room alone with him where he could close the door, let alone one that was soundproofed. Cornered, I would have to swoon, and give in, or he'd force me, or total rejection with me running from the room, which we would have to call a premature conclusion, given that my job was to keep teasing him and drag things out. Right? That's what you wanted.

His next ploy. He starts talking about his car. He said it cost more than $300,000.

Have you read Thorstein Veblen? For about ten minutes I thought I was going to be an economics major. They're not very good at what they do, but some of them make a lot of money at it, so I might reconsider. Conspicuous consumption, that's Veblen. These people, Mr. and Mrs. McMunchun, if you took that away from them, their conspicuous consumption, would they implode?

The car was a McLaren 720S Spider. But you know that by now. It had a turbo-charged V-8 engine and a whole lot of other things and was so super-cool that they didn't measure its power in horsepower but in some other way that I've never heard before.

He said the design was based on the great white shark. I did like that.

He said, "Would you like to see it?"

Getting trapped in a garage with him could be worse than being trapped in the AV room.

I upped it one. I said, "I'd love to go for a ride in it." Which I thought was immensely clever. I knew he would jump on it because it would get me off alone with him. But it was a two-seater—that's what I thought it would be—and I was right—and usually the more expensive and exotic a sports car is, the lower and tighter it is and of all the types of cars, they're the hardest to have sex in. Certainly, the hardest to force it.

He lit up. Right away. We went down to the garage. They have five cars, I think. He tried to corner me a bit, but I kept praising the car and saying "Let's go, I'm dying to see what it does." It really did look totally amazing. One of the most amazing cars ever. It has dihedral doors. There, I remembered the name, you know I love words. It means they don't just swing out, they go *up* and out, and you sort of slither in.

I said, "How amazing." He wanted to hear that.

We got in. The garage door opened electronically. Of course. We had to put on the seat belts.

None of the kids working valet were around so I don't think anyone saw us leave.

We started driving around. It was, what's there to say, it was OK. This is a car that's supposed to go over 200 miles an hour. Zero to sixty in something or other seconds. But around here, this side of the river, there's no place to really go for it, to do anything exciting. The only place we could think of with the kind of straightaway where he could show me what the car can really do was the Thruway. So we went across the river.

People look at you in that car. Even if it's a rainy, kind of miserable night.

Oh, yeah, this is an important part of the important part. He started offering me drugs. Did I want some coke? No, I didn't. He snorted some anyway. How about some weed? No, I didn't like weed, I said. Mostly, I don't. He keeps pushing, "You should get high on something." He turns on his sound system. It's a fabulous, amazing system. "To appreciate it," he says, "you have to get at least a little bit high."

I finally said, "How about some acid?"

That was mine. I picked some up when we made that stop at Bard. It was for myself. Now I was thinking that if any drug was going to open him up, make him reveal himself, acid was it. The coke would just make him pushy and hyper and that's sort of generic when it comes to men, especially men trying to have sex, and what would we learn?

Besides, they were microdoses, and how much of a problem could that be?

Looking back, after the fact, I would say they were not microdoses. Not at all. But at the time, when we dropped, I was sure that's what we were doing.

Wouldn't you know it, just when we're approaching the Thruway entrance, we see two state police cars going in. Then we see another one already cruising the Thruway. We're not even tripping yet but it had that trippy vibe you can get about the nature of a place, that it's good or bad or this or that, and the vibe was that the Thruway was *infested* with police, and we better not go there.

Instead of finding a straightaway—vroom, vroom—we'll go to the mountains where there are twisty, turning roads, there's not a lot of traffic, and if you're not actually in the towns, there aren't that many cops around. It's going to be a total roller-coaster ride. It takes about, I don't really know, about half an hour, until we're sort of away from everyone, from towns, traffic, just these twisty roads.

There was freezing rain. Just like the weather report said there would be. It was freezing on the trees. The higher we got, the more it was doing that. The branches, especially the small ones, were encased in ice. It's dark, they're encased in ice, the beams of the headlights hit them, wow, they glitter and shine.

By then we were tripping.

I know that it was really, really beautiful and it would have been amazingly, astonishingly beautiful without any drugs. But the acid made it . . . magic. Made it something else. It was amazing and getting more so. It was like driving through a magic land draped in gems. Even a movie couldn't show what we were seeing.

One of us said, "Let's open the roof." Or maybe I said, "Can you open the roof without stopping?" I'm not sure exactly how we got to it, but he said he could open the roof while the car was still moving, up to 45 miles an hour I think.

We're cruising along, flying along almost, and he pushes the buttons, and the roof starts to open up, it's a convertible with a hard roof, and the area it goes back into opens up, and we're feeling the coolness and the wind and the rain.

When the roof opens, he changes the music. He puts on Wagner. He starts telling me the story of the Ring Cycle. Which is quite *insane*. A brother and sister fall in love, but they don't know they're brother and sister. After they find out, he goes to kill her husband with a magic sword. Then Wotan's wife shows up to defend marriage. This is all about the Rheingold, which is gold at the bottom of the river, the Rhein, and we're by our Rhein, the Hudson, which is why there's Rhinebeck and Rhinecliff with the train station.

Not much rain gets in, because we're going forward, but when it does, it feels amazing. Just like the trees are covered in that amazing ice that sparkles like diamonds, the rain drops that do touch our faces are almost frozen and they feel like sparks of cool energy . . . zip, zip, zap, zap . . . ahh . . . you know I love words . . . I could say ineffable but all ineffable means is that there are no words for it . . . transcendent? Could that be it? See the crystals, feel the crystals, be the crystals.

I know, I know, it's because we were tripping. I don't know what the doses were, but they were full doses, not microdoses.

A world more beautiful and glittering than diamonds.

The car is part of the magic. We're moving. The lights of the car are moving. Changing dark to light. Shooting out the beams that turn into diffraction and splinter into colors. The sound system is astonishing. Even with the roof open, it sounds perfect. The heat pumps out so that we don't feel cold at all.

Mick still wants sex, of course. That never went away.

I know it. He knows . . . or at least hopes . . . that I know it and that it is going to be part of the trip.

He unzips himself.

His cock is hard.

Under other circumstances I might have laughed—to myself—of course—I try not to be rude—surreal, it was surreal, but so totally typical—and that's how whores—how women—keep our sense of superiority against your sense of superiority—we do that to you and it's like a handle on a suitcase, the kind with wheels, like the one I came with, you grab and it trundles along after you, carrying everything you need.

But then, it was just an erection.

I was outside of so much of the things that I'm normally inside of. It was like I was escaping from myself, as well as the world, in this magic chariot ride.

He reached over and took my hand and—as we all knew he would—he put my hand on it. It was OK. It was more than OK. Outside of us—this world we were hurtling through—that was hard like ice is hard, shining, brittle. This was flesh. It was warm. Gently warm. The skin was very smooth, velvety smooth. Like a commercial for skin conditioner. I let it feel good to me, to my touch, my critical mind, my ego mind—all gone—just floating, flying through this tunnel of magic ice, yet being human animals, pulsing with blood, all sorts of cells—the incredible air coming through the open roof . . . it wasn't sex—not for me—maybe for him—it was something more abstract, maybe more elemental, not inside the limits, the boundaries of the category sex.

He reached over and began to stroke my hair. For a moment, there was a break in the perfection. I knew that was a step toward pushing my head down and trying to get a blow job. I tried to not let that . . . that return to standard, sort of sordid, that cliché of sex actions, take over, because part of me was thinking that maybe it would end up being OK like holding and stroking his erection was.

Then he's sort of thrusting with his hips up against my hand. I say sort of because the seat belt is restraining him, there's not much of a thrust he can do, locked down like that. He releases the belt so he can get more movement and so he can squirm around if he has to, to get my head down there.

I'm trying to be nonjudgmental—pretty much *being* nonjudgmental—not just as a matter of professionalism, as I would normally do—but out of a feeling of that's how we're built, that's what we are. If you want to say it's God that made the trees and encased them temporarily in this magic shining ice, that's what made us, too, with sex and the complications and the transactions . . .

He's pushing up and down more, and more sensually, and more urgently, against my hand.

I feel his hand on my head, the sexual energy coming up through it. OK, a guy getting urgent and pushing harder for me to go down on him, that's totally usual, familiar, boring . . . but now it's not a hand, an arm, a dick . . . I don't feel the hand, I feel the energy, and his arm, the hand, they're just a conduit.

He's going faster and faster. His hips. The music is playing. It's at the part I sort of know the Ride of the Valkyries, totally bombastic. *Dum da da–dum dum, dum de da dadum, dum de da da dummm.*

Then, as we're going over a slight rise, he hits a patch of black ice.

The car gets airborne. We leave the road. We are *really* flying. We're in the air. We hit the trees, I don't know, we're about ten feet in the air. Maybe more. Because we left the road heading off into the downhill side.

That McLaren is truly an amazing car. Mick was telling me, at the beginning somewhere, that it was really a race car modified for commercial use. So it was really safe, with the structure, and the roll bars, and there have been amazing accidents, people going over a cliff, and walking away, completely uninjured. There I am, strapped in, and the car is smashing into branches, particles of ice and pieces of wood flying, and we flip around, and when it finally all stops, I'm OK. Totally unhurt.

Mick had his seat belt off. That made the difference. He flew out of the car. That's why he died.

CHAPTER TWENTY-ONE
WHINE SPRITZER

"Forget talking about our sex lives.
The modern woman is talking about money."

JESSICA BENNETT,
THE NEW YORK TIMES,
January 9, 2020

TWO DAYS AFTER MICK MCMUNCHUN'S death, we stood on the veranda of the mansion—a small one as such things go—looking out on the Hudson, our American Rhine, basking in the gentle warmth of a late afternoon sun as it hovered a half hour above the mountains on the other side, promising that when it slid below those peaks it would produce a sunset worthy of at least a minor Thomas Cole canvas, Elizabeth, Madelaine, and I, each of us with a glass in hand appropriate for the drink it contained, like gentry, or perhaps two members of the gentry and one professional and valued servant of their class, just as if the Gilded Age was not some wisp of genteel nostalgia but lived on in reality and we had the good fortune to have been invited to visit within it as participants in its pleasures and privileges.

The McMunchuns' home bar displayed a trend-filled dedication to an alcoholic version of the farm-to-table and the craft inebriation movements, full of Hudson Valley hard liquors, ciders, and wines, fashionable and high-minded, much to be commended, and so suitable to the moment. My stout, solid glass held a serious splash of Black Dirt Distillery Batch #3 Apple Jack, from 100 percent New York–grown Jonagolds—an excellent and distinctive apple—aged a minimum of five years, and bottled at 100 proof. Elizabeth had gone for the Hudson Single Malt from Tuthilltown Distillery over in Gardiner, just below the Shawangunks. Madelaine was sipping at a white wine spritzer. I had less confidence in our local wines than our beers and whiskeys, but once it's spritzed, how much does it matter?

It was just us in that oversize house. No mourners, no police, no guests, no children, no housekeepers, no cleaners. I did wonder where Madelaine's and Mick's two children might be. You'd expect them to be home, for comfort, to mourn, to be reassured that their lives would somehow remain safe and secure, forty-eight hours after their father had died. But they weren't. Where they might be and why didn't come up in the conversation.

"This feels so good," Madelaine said.

I should have held my tongue, but I said, "Your husband dead feels good?"

Elizabeth said, "You have to understand this."

After a sudden pull from her drink, Madelaine said, "I know it sounds wrong. I'm not heartless. I'm a good person. Not a bad person."

"If you were a woman, you'd understand," Elizabeth said, stepping up to an invisible lectern, to lecture me, her class of one.

"Of course," I said.

"Violence, violence is the essence. Force, force is the issue. We used to be called 'the weaker sex.' And most men are *physically* bigger than most women and *physically* stronger and more willing to be violent. That's the foundation, the bottom line, of everything that keeps women down, that made us second-class citizens, chattel, lower versions of humanity."

"It hurts," Madelaine said plaintively. Having finished her drink, she wandered inside to replenish.

"Yes," Elizabeth said. "It hurts. It creates pain. Women are maimed. Often physically. If not physically, emotionally. In terms of their self-esteem, their self-worth. Men don't see women as people. They're objects."

"Hey," I said. A minor defensive reflex.

"OK, most men," Elizabeth said, dismissing it as a quibble. "Objects. Sometimes decorative. To show off. Trophy wives."

Madelaine came back in time to hear that. She certainly didn't seem offended. If anything, she stood up a little straighter, and her next few steps had a bit of strut in them.

"Sometimes as unpaid servants. Cook, clean, take care of the children, of *his* clothes, *his* schedule, *his* house, *his* lawn. . ."

I looked around. I was reasonably certain that Madelaine didn't mow the lawn. Or clean the house, or cook, unless she chose to, or even do a lot of child care.

"But mostly, of course, as holes to stick their penises in. And the rest of us, our bodies, our minds, our education, our everything, just vehicles to carry around the holes. I'm not talking about sex. Sex would require mutuality. Sex would mean that they understood female sexuality, but that would require them to care about female sexuality, and since they don't, most of them are ignorant and incompetent, and don't care that they are, as long as they get into the holes and squirt. If you're a woman, as you walk down the street, when you go to the office to work, when you're a girl going to school, or at the gym exercising, or doing sports, and men are looking at you, you know that's what they're looking at, oh, here comes a hole, how do I get into it. They whistle, and call, and say stupid things as if we're supposed to be happy that they see us as desirable holes. They reward us for dressing up as desirable holes and dismiss us and punish us when we don't.

"It's wearing, it's stressful, and if you're a woman, you begin to feel it's hopeless. You can't fight it. You can't stop it. It goes on and on.

"Then, an individual woman, like Madelaine, gets trapped in it, by an individual man, and she desperately wants to make it stop, to get out of the trap, and she can't because she can't match his *violence*."

Madelaine was looking out at the river and the mountains, sipping away at her bottomless glass, as if she wasn't there, as if all she heard was the flowing water and the slow whispering wind.

"That's why it feels *good*." Elizabeth said. "Because we finally matched his violence with violence and we stopped him and won."

"But you used a man to do it," I said.

"This time," Elizabeth said.

"Yeah," I said.

"*We* did it," she said. "A gun, a knife, a bomb, a man. Just tools. We used the available tool."

"Are we safe?" Madelaine said suddenly, having turned away from 'the view' and looking at me.

"Yes."

"When they examine the body, if they do a tox screen?" Elizabeth asked, out from behind the lectern, now Miz Bizness, doing straight-up due diligence.

"They'll do a tox screen," I said. Of course, they would.

"What will they find?"

"Whatever they find, he'll have put it in himself. Certainly alcohol. We know that. I'm guessing cocaine. I don't know that," I said, lying somewhat. I looked at Madelaine. "Your guess is better than mine about that."

"That's a good guess," she said.

"Maybe tadalafil," I said.

"Very possibly," Madelaine said, a bitter taste on her tongue. Spritz, quick, to wash it away.

"The police have the car," Elizabeth said. "They're investigating."

"Of course they are," I said.

"Will they find anything?"

I said, "No."

"Are you sure?"

"I guarantee they won't."

"How did you do it?" Elizabeth asked. Maddie looked, too, really wanting to find out.

"Do it? I didn't do anything," I said, trying to sound like it was a double bluff. That I was being disingenuous, devious, and dishonest, trying to cover it up, and failing so badly that they could see through it. "It was an accident."

"Oh, really," Elizabeth said, tones of disbelief.

"Really," I said.

"Then we needn't pay you," she said.

CHAPTER TWENTY-TWO

A SHORT STORY

IT'S A BUTTON. ELECTRIC ZAP. Red as rage, green as the Hulk. Primal as a thirteen-year-old at Sands Jr. High, down by the Brooklyn Navy Yard, some kid who thinks he's tougher says, "Gimme your lunch money." Fight or pay every day. Toxic male violence, motherfucker! But I've had better than six decades to slowly learn some control and how to put on a show, so in spite of the blood going *boomlay, boomlay, boomlay, boom*, inside my skull like the drums of doom, I went all abstract and literary on them. I said, "Beinhart's favorite writer is Dashiell Hammett. Did you know that?"

Madelaine said, "Oh, I think I knew that."

Elizabeth didn't say anything. Her look was a clear *what-the-fuck?*

"There was a collection of short stories." I spoke softly, like we were at the library. "One of them was *The Looting of* . . . a place with a strange name, I forget it . . . an island off the coast of California. There's this massive robbery of the whole island, with fistfights, handguns, machine guns, a murder or two, and they get the bank, the jewelry story, and the wedding gifts at a mansion.

"A detective from the Continental Detective Agency is there. In the middle of all the turmoil, he twists his ankle. He's sees a one-legged newsboy, and, to keep going after the bad guys, he takes the newsie's crutch."

Madelaine had a look of polite interest. It came from long practice. Like a really good toupee, it was impossible to tell if it was real or false. Elizabeth was impatient to know what the point was and said, "Yes, so?"

"At the end of the story," I said, taking my time, "the Op realizes that the beautiful woman he's been with is one of the leaders and probably a murderer. He's got his gun on her. She's not impressed. She says, 'You pretend you'll shoot me, but I don't believe you.'

"Hey, it's 1925, men didn't shoot women, not that they're not in love with, so it's reasonable for her to think he won't. She starts to walk away. He shoots. He hits her in the leg. She's shocked. So is he, for that matter. He'd never shot a woman before.

"He says, 'You ought to have known I'd do it! Didn't I steal a crutch from a cripple?'"

Elizabeth said, "Did you tell that for a reason?"

"The first time we met," I said, "maybe that was instinct or reflex, but each of us established who we were. Very clearly. You're someone who tries to fuck people over for money. I showed you that I would knock you down, take your gun, steal your phone, and walk off with the money. Like stealing a crutch from a cripple.

"Here we are again. I expected you'd try it again. You should have expected that I'd be ready to do something about it. Again."

"You said it was an accident."

"Maybe that's doing you a favor," I said, a little harsh, a little patronizing. "Anybody asks you, you can say that to the very best of your knowledge it was an accident. That you never heard anyone say anything else. You can say it with conviction. Without some little flicker or flutter, inside or out. You can say it with a polygraph and the needle won't twitch. Me saying it was an accident protects you. And you will pay me."

"How's that?" Elizabeth said, with that ace-in-the-hole attitude people learn by binge watching *Billionaire*.

"My tape of you asking and me saying no."

"If you go after us," she said, still sounding like an as-seen-on-TV person, "we definitely won't pay you. Since it's an accident, we're not at risk. Mexican standoff, that's what it's called."

I sighed. "What I'll do is go to each of you. Individually. The first one to pay me gets a pass. Then the other one goes down." I looked back and forth. Like I was trying to calculate who would crack first. Which I was. Madelaine would roll over out of simple fear. Elizabeth was quite crafty enough to know that she was in a race to do it before her client folded.

Maddie placed her drink down on the railing with a drunk's careful attention to making sure it was centered and balanced and wouldn't tumble over and embarrass her. She took a breath. She opened her mouth to speak. Before a single sound emerged, Elizabeth preempted the punchline, "Of course, our intention is to pay you."

"Good," I said.

There was a pause, then, in a more realistic and straightforward way, she said, "I have one last question."

"What?"

"The girl. Will she hold up?"

"Of course," I said, revealing not a single sign of how worried I was about it.

"You're certain?" Madelaine asked.

"*How*," Elizabeth asked, "can you be certain?"

"Because, just like you, the only information she has is that it was an accident. A goddamn accident."

Of course, Allison knew a bit more. That she'd given Mick

McMunchun LSD. She'd been amazingly blithe about it the night it happened. She had also been far more clever than anyone should have been able to be with the police, given her condition and the circumstances. She'd maintained that she was in too much shock to talk. Even better, she maintained that she was just fourteen, so the police couldn't lean on her without the presence of a parent or legal guardian.

It wasn't until the next day that the waves of reality, guilt, remorse, culpability, began bouncing her up, down, and around. I did my best, by telephone, to be reassuring, that McMunchun had no one but himself to blame. He was showing off a car that had no business on real mountain roads, he'd been at the wheel, he'd unfastened his seat belt.

She did, of course, have to go back to the police to be reinterviewed. We'd gone over her story. She now said, right up front, that she'd been there, hired by me, on behalf of Mrs. McMunchun, to determine if the husband was a genuine danger to underage girls. To do so, she'd masqueraded as fourteen, which was completely legal, done by police and by TV shows, to catch a predator. She claimed that she had maintained the masquerade because the accident had put her too deep in shock to stop.

Yes, she had seen McMunchun drink and do cocaine. His own. She'd done neither. They were welcome to do urine and blood tests. Though it was now too late for anything to show. We agreed that she was not to mention LSD. If it showed up in his postmortem tox screen, and if she was asked about it, she was to say she knew nothing about that. She was a smart girl. An exceedingly smart girl. She got that it was the only thing that could harm her. Therefore, her silence shouldn't be limited to police interviews, it better be universal. So long as it was, she was safe, then I was safe, which would keep Elizabeth and Madelaine safe.

"And we're safe?" Madelaine asked, coming close to me, asking for reassurance.

"Yes."

She took each of my hands in her own, held them, looked in my eyes with her own worried eyes.

I said, "Unless one of you, or both of you, have done something that I don't know about, you're safe."

"You're sure?"

"I'm sure. You're safe."

It was as if her tension had been a carapace, a shell that kept her soft and yielding body upright. It dissolved. She came forward, melted forward, as if she needed me to support her.

I was conscious of the press of her breasts. My male response was very much as Elizabeth's anger described it—that they were signals that here's a body with a vagina, the most pleasurable place to put a penis—simple, basic, crude, and often expressed with enthusiastic vulgarity. Even the smell of alcohol coming from her was a message from the signifyin' monkey, here's a woman at work lowering her inhibitions. Take away three, two, maybe just one, of my decades, I'd have let reckless greed rise up, pulled her in tight, even reached for the virago who was standing by, watching us with the lip-locked glower of a Baptist-Opposed-to-Dancing, in an attempt to bring her into a cozy circle of lust.

I gave Madelaine a hug of reassurance, just long enough not to be rude, as I might with a gay male second cousin, then stepped back as I straightened her up to stand on her own. She lifted her head to look at me.

"It's all over," I said. "It's done. It worked. You're safe."

She nodded, with her eyes still looking in mine, and said, "Drink something with me."

Elizabeth spoke up. She was still crisp and businesslike, "Not only are we going to pay you," but also genial and inclusive, and, as my head turned to look at her, she added, "We have great plans for you."

CHAPTER TWENTY-THREE

OUR TOWN, WOODSTOCK

"Boom shaka-laka-laka. Boom shaka-laka-laka."
SYLVESTER "SLY & THE FAMILY STONE" STEWART

I SLEPT THE SLEEP OF the just. Of the innocent. Of the safe.

I woke rested and calm.

I'd pulled it off. I was getting paid for a murder I hadn't committed. It was foolproof. Impenetrable. It could not be unraveled.

Maybe I'd just gotten lucky.

Or the old god who lived in the oak had been so excited by the fact that someone had actually come to him, spoken to him, recognized his divinity, however dated and superannuated, that he had left his root-bound habitat for the night and snuck into modern times to consort with the three Norns, the Fates—Urd, what once was, who finds the threads of our lives, Mick's, Allison's, and mine; Verdandi, what is, who weaves them together; and Skuld, what will come, who picked one thread, Mick's, and cut it short.

————

I kicked the blanket off.

I walked outside, barefoot and bare-assed, while the cats ran in. There was ice. There was frost. It gave me a wake-up shake. I thought I could smell snow, still a long way off, coming from over the mountains. Wishful thinking.

I got dressed, fed the cats, and went into town.

Beinhart was at Bread Alone, as usual, in his regular corner, *The New York Times* open in front of him. He claims to read it for the comedy, and sure enough he broke out cackling.

Jay Samoff, a retired local lawyer, sitting beside him, said, "You know the rules, no snickering unless you share." Jay reads the Kingston paper, the *Daily Freeman*, mostly for the obituaries, and every time he sees that a friend, an acquaintance, or a former client has died, he says, "Did you know" so-and-so. He never seems upset, in mourning, or fearful for his own mortality. It's like he's just keeping track so he can be sure everyone is being filed away where they belong.

Mark Cuddy came in a bit later and joined them. He's the most friendly, social, and jovial of that bunch. He's in the funeral business. I don't know him very well, but I do like him. Passing their table on my way out, I put my hand on his shoulder and said, "Fuck you, Cuddy. It's good to be alive."

"Don't worry," Cuddy said, with his Midwestern smile. "We can be patient."

Our town has no supermarket, but it has two hardware stores. One of them, Houst, is right next to Bread Alone. I needed some bar chain oil, so I ambled over, through the parking area, around the rentals, toward the back door. I noticed a kid who seemed to be looking at me at little quizzically. He didn't say anything. I continued about my business.

Back in 2007, our sheriff formed *U.R.G.E.N.T.*

*U*lster *R*egional *G*ang *E*nforcement *N*arcotics *T*eam. The Team had more than an acronym. They had attitude. They had gear. They were high-tech and well armored. They were undercovers plus SWAT. They were ready if the Crips and Bloods came east from L.A. or the Latin Kings came up the river to rural Ulster County.

There was a long established—one could even say traditional—purveyor of herb right in the center of town.

U.R.G.E.N.T. decided to go total Reefer Madness on him. If you were here at the time, you probably know who I mean. If you weren't, I'll call him Jaz—short for Johnny Apple Zeed—Jones. If you watch TV you might be imagining a high-roller kingpin. Draped in bling. With a pool and a hot tub, both stuffed with buttock models in thongs that dramatized well-rounded cheeks. Nah. Jaz lived in a small third-floor walk-up, in a rickety wood-frame building, over another apartment, which was over a store. He believed in peace and love, in music, and in the spiritual benefits of cannabliss. He was in his seventies and wore tie-dye clothing, not all the time, but sometimes. In sum, if UNESCO had known about him, they'd have named him a living human heritage site.

U.R.G.E.N.T. staked out his domicile. They watched the action. Tailed him. Then they planned their raid.

It was early morn. Barely dawn.

One team charged up the stairs. Another guarded the steps from below. Still another kept watch for a possible escape through the window. They were prepared to break down the door. They'd practiced it. They were eager.

Jaz was lucky. Their clomping feet on the wooden steps roused him from his sleep. He rose up and opened the door before they could knock it down.

Still, they grabbed him. They threw him to the floor. They cuffed his hands behind his back. Tight. They searched the dresser, the closet, the bookshelves, his record collection. They banged on the walls and tapped the floor, testing for the hollow sounds that would reveal hidey holes.

But all that *The Men from U.R.G.E.N.T.* found were seeds and stems.

It was the Youth of Woodstock. They'd watched the watchers watching Jaz. They warned him of what was coming. Jaz cleaned house. Well, as best as an old stoner could. It was good enough to keep him out of felony territory, but, sadly, left enough cannabis detritus for a misdemeanor or two.

That's why I stopped and listened when the kid who watched me enter the hardware store gave me a kind of half wave when I was on my way out.

I knew him slightly. He was about fourteen and probably should have been in school. I recalled that his name was Sly. Not a nickname.

A lot of people in Woodstock have stories. Mini-legends that buffer their arrival and trail along behind him. His reached back to his grandmother, Cindy Lou Citronella, a true God Child of the Sixties, who had been particularly enamored with Sly and the Family Stone. One might even say obsessed. Cindy Lou had three daughters. She gave each of them names related to members of that group, however tenuously. Cynthia Moon Goddess, Verbena, and Cinnamon Girl Rose. She had no sons. When Verbena gave birth to a boy, Grandma Cindy Lou claimed naming rights, and that's how, it was said, Sly got his name.

Sly had curly, light brown hair. His eyes were green. They didn't rove around as most people's do, they seemed to fixate, lock on whatever he was looking at, move abruptly, then fixate again. He said, "Hey," and called me by name. He mentioned my son's name, then said, "You're his dad, right?"

I said, "Yes." Why go into to it that my boy was dead? Sly probably knew that. The kids in town know everything. He said my son and his older sister had been friends and she said I was an OK person.

I thanked him.

Having explained why I qualified to be spoken with, he said, "There's a narc watching you."

"You sure?"

"Yeah."

"How do you know?"

He shrugged and his fixating eyes locked on me with a look that rolled "What are *you*, stupid?" and "Do you think *I'm* stupid?" together as neatly as a Frenchman rolling tobacco and weed in the same joint. How did he know? The same way owls know to hunt after the sun goes down, that trees know to turn their leaves from green to red and gold, and the gods know to trifle with us.

"What's he look like?"

"A narc."

"White? Black?"

Sly thought for a second. "Very white."

"Tall? Short?"

"Like you plus a couple of inches." His eyes got a far-off look. He was processing data. Then he returned with the result. "He's a Fed."

"How do you know?"

"He's got out-of-state plates. He's not fat."

I'd once had to go into exile. It was a matter of not having the right financial records and the existence of the IRS.

I'm not complaining. I went to the Alps. In France and Austria. If you're going into hiding, I recommend it. My daughter was born there. I got married there. I skied in the winters, climbed in the summers. I went into Czechoslovakia and Hungary as the Soviet system fell. It was a time of hope and joy. In which the seeds of gangster capitalism were quickly planted.

If someone was watching, I'd better make sure the money part of what I'd been up to was done right.

I thought I'd been very clever in pushing Madelaine and Elizabeth for more than they'd first offered, but I hadn't thought about taxes. If I declared the money, the bite would be big enough that I probably couldn't pay off the mortgage entirely, something I very much wanted to do. If I didn't declare it and it somehow came to the attention of the IRS, I'd be in a replay of 1984 with my lawyer saying to me, "Leave the country, and while you're at it, change your name," as the great Yogi Berra put it, "déjà vu all over again."

What would be worse, far worse, was if someone came at it from another direction. Looking at me in regard to the death of Mick McMunchun, just because I'd been in the vicinity. Then noticing the money. Discovering that I'd become financially whole almost immediately afterward and then tracking the funds to the widow and her financial backer.

Instead of going home to cut logs and split them for firewood, I headed in the other direction, keeping an eye in my rearview mirror, for a sedan with out-of-state plates, driven by a man who wasn't fat, just as a test. I didn't notice anyone suspicious. When I got into Kingston, I made several sets of extra turns, to see if anyone stayed with me through the meaningless meanders. If they did, they were very good, and I didn't spot them. I parked on Fair Street, by the Department of Motor Vehicles. I strolled around the Old Dutch Church to the Courthouse, went inside, took the elevator up to the

DA's offices, then down the stairs to the side exit, through the parking lot, then around to the Crown, and over to Green Street. I was certainly being paranoid. Better overcautious than caught is a good general rule for life.

I went to see Lucinda Morton, who'd been my accountant back when I was making enough money to need an accountant. It wasn't tax season. She wasn't very busy. I only had wait about fifteen minutes. When we got into her office, I said, "Hypothetically, strictly hypothetically, how would I launder a couple of hundred thousand dollars?" It turned out to be far easier than I'd ever thought it would be. I thanked her, rose to go, and shook her hand.

She said, "If it gets too much more than that, please keep us in mind."

CHAPTER TWENTY-FOUR

THE GOLD DIGGERS OF OUR NEW CENTURY

ELIZABETH HAD ALREADY JUMPED FROM her old company. To start her own. With offices, of course, in DUMBO.

DUMBO is no longer a cute little elephant with ears so large he can fly.

It's the most recent hippest place to be.

For the first half of the twentieth century, Greenwich Village was New York's place—all of America's place—for the arty and avant-garde. By the 1960s, being bohemian was so attractive that it pushed the rents up. There was another neighborhood, right next door, full of rundown factory and warehouse buildings. Back then, it was illegal to live in commercial loft spaces. But these were *artists*. It was their duty to defy conventions. Besides, the space was *cheap*. And big. The artists were often handy, as well as young, lacking in cash, but full of sweat equity. They put in showers, real bathrooms, illegal kitchens, and walls to make separate rooms. Their presence made the neighborhood hip. Real estate dealers and developers moved in. Zoning laws were changed to make the living legal. That area, South of Houston Street, got renamed SOHO, and prices went up, driving the artists out.

They moved a little to the east, which was *north* of *Little Italy*. That became NoLita. Prices went up. They also moved a bit to the south and west, the triangle below Canal Street, which became Tribeca. By then, commercial developers were doing the conversions of loft spaces into apartments. They quickly became so expensive that only people working in finance could afford them.

The next wave of hipsters moved across the East River to Queens and, especially, to Brooklyn. The Brooklyn that I grew up in, blue-collar, segregated into ethnic neighborhoods, with gangs and thugs, became today's Brooklyn, a place so hip that even Parisians reference it as branchée.

One little pocket of that borough, between the Brooklyn-Queens Expressway and the East River, the Brooklyn Navy Yard at one end and the steep hill up to Brooklyn Heights at the other, had gone unnoticed. It was full of buildings constructed for industries that had vanished. Like SOHO had been. It still had cobblestone streets. It had views. All it needed was an intriguing moniker to turn it into real estate riches. It had two bridges going over it. Under the Brooklyn Bridge would just be UBB, but Down Under the Manhattan Bridge Overpass—which it also was—became DUMBO, with all its warm, cuddly, cartoony, Disney connotations.

The transformation was so fast that it hopped and skipped across the standard sequence of artists coming in, redeveloping industrial space to livable quarters, followed by galleries, gourmet grocers, and boutiques to serve them, which would attract visitors, including tourists, and went directly to being the place for trendy businesses.

Elizabeth had half of the fifth floor in a six-story building. It had been built in the 1870s, the boom times after the Civil War, spending most of its life as a coffee warehouse. The ceilings were high. The windows were big. Some of them had views that looked out under the two bridges to the East River, and across it, to Manhattan.

The space was being done over. The door was propped open. I walked in.

An interior design architect was directing construction workers and painters.

A set of huge graphic posters was leaning up against the wall, waiting to be hung. Each one had a banner headline across the top, LITIGATION INVESTMENT for FEMALE EMPOWERMENT. One had a picture of Supreme Court Justice Ruth Bader Ginsburg on the left and the words "The Equality Clause of the 14th Amendment Applies to *Women*" to the right of her. RBG was wearing green earrings and one of her special collars over her judge's robe. The poster was about six feet wide and three feet high.

"Equal Justice Under Law," as it appears carved into the white marble facade of the Supreme Court, was on another poster. The poster then declared "Financial Inequality = Unequal Justice." Followed by, "That's why we're here. Litigation Investment means Female Empowerment."

I could only see part of the poster resting behind it. The top two lines were:

Alta CHRAPLIWY et al., Plaintiffs, v. UNIROYAL, INC. et al., Defendants, $9,318,000 awarded in cash and pension benefits for unlawful sex discrimination.

I guessed the rest would be a list of big financial awards won for women who'd been discriminated against, or harassed, or abused. America's sixteen biggest divorce settlements were listed on two more panels, each six feet tall and three feet wide. Jeff Bezos and MacKenzie Bezos led it off with $35 billion. Rupert Murdoch had both third and fourth place, $1.8 and $1.7 billion. Steven Spielberg was last, with a mere $100 million. It could have been done in one chart, but there were photos of several of the lucky losers and winners, Mel Gibson, Elin Nordegren (formerly married to Tiger Woods), Harrison Ford, Neil Diamond, Maria Shriver, adding much humanity and personality to the financially gargantuan squabbles.

So much money! Such celebrity! It didn't say so, not at all, but the great posters made you *feel* as if they were the accomplishments of Elizabeth's company, LIFE, Inc. No matter that it had just opened and had yet to finance a single case.

Ms. Carter had moved incredibly fast. Leave one business. Start a new one. Find the space, sign a lease. An architect with his plans ready to go. For that specific space. The crews already at work. The graphics would have had to be designed, then argued over, as such things always are, revised, re-argued, finally approved, and then produced. It couldn't have all happened since Mick McMunchun's death. It had to have been planned and organized for some time. A long time. Money committed. A lot of money. A time crunch to get the money. Getting urgent. Needing to make that murder happen.

Elizabeth came up from behind me. I heard her. I turned. She was smiling.

She was a CEO, making it clear that she was breaking away from her busy, busy, very busy, business, to give her full attention to her visitor, to spend some of her very precious time. With me.

She said she was so glad I'd come. She was so looking forward to seeing me. I was a special person who would do special things. She did that very well. If I'd had any desire to feel special, I would have. I would have felt flattered, except that flattery ordinarily makes me suspicious.

She asked if I wanted anything, coffee, tea, water, a drink? I said, nothing, thank you.

She showed me around. The spaces that would be her office, the conference room, then into what would be the secure room. When the IT work was done, it would block out electronics and listening devices with such certainty that you could conference safely with Russian spies—ha ha, that was a joke, but that's the idea—and she closed the door, thick and heavy enough to be a bank vault in a heist movie, making it certain that none of the people working in the rest of the office space could hear us.

"You see what we're about."

"Yes," I said. "Very impressive."

"What happened with Mick McMunchun . . ." she began to ask, presuming I'd engineered it, still wondering how.

"An accident," I said.

Her look said that she couldn't imagine someone just telling the truth, but she'd accept the way I wanted to play it. She said, "Of course. Divine justice. Instant karma. It was a good thing. It removed a bad person. Who was doing bad things with his money. It put that money in the hands of a good person, Madelaine. Who's put it here, where it can do good things, morally good things, great things. Where it can work for the empowerment of women." She was as sincere as a missionary explaining Christ to a heathen who was in need of salvation.

"That being the case," I said, lightly, since I wasn't seeking salvation, "I should probably get a bonus. Not in heaven, here on Earth."

"Yes. Yes, in fact you should," she said, much to my surprise. "And I need to apologize for making things . . . well, difficult . . . challenging you. Obviously, we're in a dangerous high-risk enterprise. Not in the phony way that Wall Street and hedge fund, testosterone-fueled *men*, are always going on about. This is the real thing, risking our freedom, even our lives. You've said as much, warning me, chastising me. You were right. I appreciate it, I appreciated it at the time, but didn't show it. I had to know. Know that you were the right person."

"Thank you," I said, displaying sincerity, to show that I valued her positive words, then switched to what I actually cared about. "We need to talk about *how* you get the money to me. We don't want the money to connect me to you or to Madelaine."

"That makes sense, good sense. Provided . . ."

"Here's what I'm thinking," I said.

"Go on. Sorry to interrupt."

"I presume you have interests, connections, overseas?"

"Yes, of course."

"Where?"

"Oh, all over."

"South America? The Middle East? Where?"

"Brazil. The Caymans. Umm . . . the Philippines."

"Great, all of those are the kinds of places we're looking for. The money is going to be an inheritance . . ."

"Because?"

"We start with the idea of a gift. A gift incurs no tax liability to the recipient. But more important, it's not a *fee*. We don't want a fee, because that means I did something for it."

"I get that," she said, impatient because it was something she already knew.

"Therefore, a gift. The only reporting required, is from the giver. That's there to prevent people from evading inheritance taxes. Our problem is not going to be the tax man. It's if some cop or prosecutor is bothered by Mick's death and he sees that you, me, Madelaine, and Mick were all together the night that he died, then finds out that we all profited, almost immediately thereafter, except Mick, of course, and tries to connect the dots, we are the dots.

"Madelaine inherits. That's what has to be. By itself, that's OK. You were helping Madelaine with her divorce. She was impressed with you, so she invested with you. That stands up. But put me in there and it's possible to connect the dots in a completely different way.

"If the money came to me as a gift, they have to go looking for the gift-giver. Let's say it's from my great aunt—on my mother's side, so there's a different name—died in Brazil—then where does the investigation go? A place like Brazil is good, for us, because who the hell can go through all the deaths in Brazil to prove that no such person as Lucretia Borgia, or whatever her name is going to be, died this year. It's the perfect dead end."

"If that's what you want," she said, "we will do our best to accommodate you."

I didn't like the sound of that. I wanted an outright, absolute, straightforward yes. Not some equivocation that meant that a back door was already open. Then she switched to a pitch. "I'm going to offer you an opportunity," she said, which I liked even less. "A chance to get in on a start-up.

"It's the new American dream. To have a piece of something. That will grow. Exponentially. That once it gets going, it keeps on paying. Whether you work or not. One that could make you *genuinely* rich." She looked at me intently, like good salespeople do, to see how deeply she was drawing me into her world. "The reason that this is going to succeed over others who are doing litigation finance—and will stay ahead when still more discover how lucrative it is—is because of our business model. It has two parts. That fuel each other."

I suddenly got it. I couldn't believe it. Even as I knew I comprehended it correctly. That part of my brain that had left the sane got how perfectly logical it was. And admired the audacity. I did have to check. Not that it couldn't be. Just that it shouldn't be. I gestured toward the larger part of the office space. "You'll have a pool, out there, of unhappy, women. They're talking about divorces. You find the ones where there's a lot of money at stake. You find out who's really, really angry. Full of hate . . ."

"Or fear," she said.

"Or fear." I agreed. "Yeah, that'll do. Then you gently guide them, toward a *special* offer."

"Yes," she said, "a special offer," like she hadn't thought of that phrase for it before.

"Just get rid of the guy. They'll end up with a lot more money. At least double. If there are kids, sole custody. Instead of months or years in court, it'll be quick. And it's really, fully, finally over. No more bickering, no more threats, no more fucking lawyers."

She didn't nod, but I could see from her face that I'd gotten it just about right. I continued and got to the punchline. "You get . . ." I guessed, " . . . half."

"I don't get the money," she claimed.

"No?" That was the point, wasn't it?

"The deal is . . . or will be . . . as with Madelaine . . . they *invest*. With LIFE."

"Oh my." Unable to avoid sounding sarcastic, I said, "That's better then."

"Goddamn it," she said, "It is." She moved her hand, palm up, in a half circle, as if she was conveying funds from where we stood out to the main office thronged with worthy causes.

"It can fund idealistic law suits. Even those with low odds of success. Even those with low payouts when they do succeed. Ones that otherwise no one would finance. Wage theft from domestics and home care workers. Systemic abuse of female farmworkers."

Pardon my skepticism. I said, "You're willing to lose money?"

"Of course we'll keep an eye on the bottom line. A company without profit is like driving a car with no oil in the engine. But this method, as a source of funding, allows us a much greater range of actions."

"Why are you telling me this? What do you want from me?"

She took a moment. Looked hard at me. Finally, she said, "You know what I want."

"Let's not pussyfoot. Or beat around the bush. Let's lay it out. You want me to be your staff assassin?"

"Yes," she said, though she didn't shout it out.

"I don't like killing people."

"It's my understanding . . . well . . . that you have killed people before. . . You shot a couple of gangsters in Miami."

"No," I said.

She looked at me, like she knew better.

"It was in the Bahamas," I said. "And it was to keep them from killing a priest. Who happened to be going out with my mother at the time."

"Episcopal priest?" she asked.

"Catholic."

"Oh, dear."

"Don't worry about it," I said. "It wasn't an exploitive relationship."

She returned to business. "We need someone. To take care of"—her hand moved in a circle over the space between us—"this part."

"You wanted a woman to do it."

"That was the original idea," she admitted.

"Part of equality and empowerment?"

"Yes," she said. "Yes, it would be."

I made a dismissive sound.

She changed tack again. "Don't . . . you wouldn't have to do it yourself."

"It? It? What 'it'?"

"Killings," she said.

"Murders," I said.

She nodded. "If you like. Or executions. Or . . . call it what you like . . . what would be perfect, the perfect answer for all of this, is for you to set things up. Find people. Safe, reliable people. Like yourself. Under your supervision."

"Preferably women?"

"Yes. If you can. That would be good. We'd structure it," she said, "so you'd be our Head of Investigations. Real job, real title. Six-figure salary, plus bonuses . . . all of which you could report, clean, legal, up front . . . perfect . . . plus your piece of the company . . . then once things are up and running, any time after that, at your own choosing, you can walk away. Yet the money keeps flowing to you."

I don't know if she read my face or she read my mind or she simply knew that she had reached the point, gone way past the point, where she had to address the screeching issue, "You think I'm insane."

Yes, I did. I don't doubt it showed.

"You do know what a top lawyer bills? They broke the thousand-dollar-an-hour barrier at least a decade ago.

"Think about it. It's simple math. Two weeks can easily be one hundred hours, billable hours. That's a hundred thousand dollars. For the top guy. He, or she, has associates, paralegals, expenses. How much is that? Figure another hundred and fifty thousand. In two weeks you can run up a bill of a quarter million dollars. Four weeks, you get to half a million. A couple of months, we're at multimillion-dollar legal fees. Think about an ordinary person, let alone an exploited, abused, minimum-wage woman, going up against that."

I didn't look at all convinced.

"You're a *male*," she said. "That's why you don't get it. Let me give you a hyper-*male* example. You know Hulk Hogan."

"Not personally."

"You know *Gawker*?"

"No."

"They were an online gossip magazine. They posted a short video clip of Hulk having sex with a woman named Heather Clem, the wife of a man who was supposed to be one of Hulk's closest friends, Bubba 'the Love Sponge' Clem."

"The Love Sponge?"

"He had a radio show." It was an explanation. She continued, "Hulk sued. He won. The judgment bankrupted *Gawker*. They're gone now.

"Follow along. Follow the money. Hulk's net worth, before he sued, was $8 million. Yet he spent $10 million on legal fees. It turned out that the bills were being paid by Peter Thiel. He's PayPal and an early Facebook investor. He's worth $2.3 *billion*. *Gawker* had outed him. He went looking for revenge by lawsuit. He found Hulk Hogan and used him to destroy *Gawker*.

"A mere multimillionaire can't afford our legal system. Only a billionaire can, and they can use it for their pet peeves. Most of the big money is in the hands of men. We both know it. It's indisputable. 'Equal Justice Under the Law,' is cut into a piece of marble over the entrance to the Supreme Court, but it's just graffiti. We're in a system that's insane. If someone could show me a safe, schoolbook, sane way to battle it, I'd take it. This is a way to redress part of the balance. To find a little bit of justice."

I thought she was quite mad. A black widow who wasn't a widow, corporatizing a rage whose source I didn't know, institutionalizing murder for profit, using a hedge fund to select rich victims and to pay the killers. Perhaps I should have reviled her and marched righteously away. But not until my money had been correctly laundered, transferred to my account, and my mortgage paid off. I said, "I'll think about it."

From her reaction, she seemed to think I actually would.

CHAPTER TWENTY-FIVE

BLACK RAVEN

"There is some ill a-brewing towards my rest,
For I did dream of money-bags to-night."

**SHYLOCK, *THE MERCHANT OF
VENICE*, WILLIAM SHAKESPEARE**

THE ONLY REALLY GOOD ADVICE I ever got from a politician—that I ever heard from a politician—was from Maurice Hinchey, our congressman from 1993 until 2013. I thought he was a good guy and I liked his politics. He told me, "Never use a chainsaw when you're tired."

I have an Austrian stove and two fireplaces. I need a fair amount of wood. I'd neglected that when I was sunk in inertia. Now I knew I was going to keep my home. There was a lot to be done before the snow came. It was a good day, sunny and dry. Cutting, splitting, and stacking are not things to do when the logs are wet, the ground is slippery, and the handles of your tools are slick. I used to be able to do it all day. That was a while ago. After four hours I began to see my body doing careless things so I listened to what Maurice had told me when he had that big bandage on his lower leg.

I stopped. I went inside. I made myself a sandwich. I poured my-self a glass of sweet cider. The sweat began to chill on my body. I took off my shirt, rubbed myself down, put on a sweatshirt. I went outside to eat my lunch sitting in the sun.

It's quiet up on the mountain.

The road is unpaved and rough. I can hear a vehicle coming a long way off. I can recognize UPS, FedEx, and what my neighbors drive by the sounds they make. I heard a car that wasn't one of those. There was no reason for anyone to come to see me. I assumed that it would stop somewhere below. But it kept on coming. Very slowly, inching over the ruts and potholes. Finally, it crept around the last bend and into sight. It was a Cadillac CTS. I guessed it to be about two years old. Black. Cadillac has two blacks. This was the blacker black. Their name for it is black raven.

It stopped. Owen Cohen got out. Bitching and complaining. "Jesus, fuck. You call that a road? Didn't you ever hear of pavement? Look at that . . ." He pointed to the dust and dirt that marred the car's shine. "It won't be enough to wash it. I'm gonna have to have it detailed." He was dressed like a well-off detective would have back in the eighties for a casual day in the country. A hip-length leather jacket. Black. Light-gray shirt with a collar and cuffs. Clean, pressed jeans. Real shoes, black oxfords.

"Hi, Owen," I said, still sitting in the sun. "How are you? Can I get you something?"

"Yeah, sure. I'll take a drink."

"Water, cider, Gatorade . . . "

"A drink, Cassella, a drink. Or are you on some fuckin' twelve-step thing?"

"I have some Scotch . . ."

"That'll do. You got ice? All the way up here?"

I got up. He followed me inside. He looked around while I got the ice and poured some Scotch over it. He said some nice things about the house. I handed him his drink. I said, "What can I do for you?"

He took a sip. He gave a nod that the Scotch was alright. He looked at me, considering. "No chitchat?"

"Owen, you're a surprise guest. I figure there's a reason."

He took another sip. Not like he needed to fortify himself but taking the moment to select his phrasing. "I'll get right to it. I came for my cut of the McMunchun money."

There was only one way to play it. At least for starters. Incredulous as could be. As if all I could say was, "What?"

"Come on," he said, not buying it at all, going on, one smart guy to another. "Make an offer. Then I'll make a counteroffer. Then we'll meet in the middle."

I stuck with incredulous. Added some oblivious. "Owen, what are you talking about?"

"Alright, then I'll start. Two hundred K."

"What are you talking about? I'm repeating myself here. What are you talking about?"

"I was thinking I could make this just about the money and not say those things that should never be spoken aloud."

"Don't worry. Spit it out."

"The McMunchun murder," he said.

"What McMunchun murder?"

"Mick McMunchun, dead on a Saturday night."

"What is that, a Tom Waits song? Dead on a Saturday night?"

"And you did it."

"Owen . . ." I did my best to sound unfazed. I was about to go into a detailed defense, but as I opened my mouth I realized that I didn't need to tell him things, I needed him to tell me things, so I just shrugged and offered a limp, "That's crazy."

"I *know* you did it."

"How do you *know* I did it?"

"Schmuck, what makes you think you were their first stop?"

CHAPTER TWENTY-SIX
TWO LEGAL SCHOLARS

"Your problem is you are too busy holding on to your
unworthiness. You'd rather be a shmuck . . ."

BABA RAM DASS

THE LITTLE PANIC CELLS IN my body came up like gophers from
their holes, their heads swiveling all around, looking for what they
had to run from. I did my best not to let that show. "First stop at
what?" I said.

"They approached Winston."

Those two idiots. My heart was beating faster. Physiology too
deep to immediately control. But I kept my breathing slow and even.
I asked, as if I didn't know the answer, "To do what?"

"Fuck you, Cassella," with a snarl. "Exactly like they did with you."

"How do you know they approached Winston?"

"Because he came to me. Because Winston knew we Hebrews
have alert, scheming minds, flashy trickiness, and artful dodging. He
was right to come to me. Because *I* did my homework." That's what
Owen wanted. Aside from money. To show that he was the smartest
guy around. Maybe he was. I hadn't done the homework. I hadn't
thought. I hadn't planned.

"When the river came to me, I'd just stepped in and let the river decide where we would go. Because . . . good question . . . best answer . . . only answer . . . because when the river came for me the river cared and I did not."

"I found out *McMunchkin*"—he liked the derisive nickname, it was part of the same impulse to display superiority—"was worth a hundred million, give or take. Mrs. McMunchkin had a severe prenup problem, due to drinking, drugging, and the usual fucking of people who weren't Mr. McMunchkin. She was going to end up with maybe five hundred thousand, and just one domicile, which is fine by normal people standards, but pitiful and sad and disappointing for people like her.

"Plus, she had hooked up with *Miz* Bitch Queen, who is am-bitch-ous. I'm figuring she got some game going where if she scores *all* the McMunchkin millions for Mrs. McMunchkin, then Mrs. McMunchkin bankrolls her."

Owen was right. He'd done his homework. While I'd been an idiot.

"With all of that to gain," he spread his hands out wide, "all they wanted to give Winston was fifty K." Just the memory of it made him angry. "Fuckin' rich people." He snapped, forefinger jabbing toward me. "Cheap motherfuckers. You know how it is, Tony. We get crumbs. Tips. Chump change.

"I had to save Winston from himself. It should've been up in the six figures. Way up. Even seven. Who wouldn't spend one million to gain a hundred million? I opened up negotiations with them."

"Them?"

"The wife and her girlfriend, or whatever she is. I explained to them how they were locked in. To Winston. To us. If they had anyone else do it, I could go to the police, and say, hey, these ladies were searching for a contract. That's where we are now, isn't it, Tony? You took him out. Here I am."

I felt sweat prickling down my spine. Not the clean, healthy kind that had been flowing just a little bit earlier, splitting wood. I couldn't see this thing going anywhere good. But I kept my breathing, my face, and my voice under control. "You said you had it locked down. What happened?"

"Winston. Had some other shit in his life. Coochie, coochie, coo. Some young thing with one of those proprietorial husbands. Caught them at it." Owen made a hand gesture, forefinger straight, thumb up. "Pop!" He put his hand down. "After that they didn't want to deal with me, because I knew how much the deal was really worth. They went to you. I hope to hell you didn't do it at some discount dollar-store price. Since I intend to get a substantial payout here."

"Listen to me, Owen. McMunchun's death was an accident."

"Bullshit." He was ready to explode.

The tension inside me rose along with his. I said, "Slow down, Owen. Forget about what I say and what you think, just for a moment, OK? What the cops think is that it was an accident. Officially. Formally."

"Yeah, so?"

"You should very much want it to stay that way. You're a really smart guy, smarter than me. I tell you what I see, and you can tell me if you see a way out of it. First, these two women came to Winston. To solicit a criminal act. Winston came to you. You entered into negotiations over the price." I was doing my best to sound like I was an online voice from *criminal.findlaw.com* or *beenarresstedcallus.net*. Going over the facts. Then hitting the checklist. "Did they give you any money?"

"What? No," he said.

"Did they give Winston any?"

"No."

"Good," I said. I brushed my hair back. Little woodchips fell out, like dandruff.

"Four people. It's a conspiracy. Toward a contract killing. A Class A felony. . . . Give me a second . . . I'm trying to remember . . . 105.15. That's it. *Conspiring* to commit a Class A felony. The crime doesn't have to take place. All it needs is talking about it and *one* overt act.

"That's why prosecutors love conspiracy charges. 105.15 is a felony. With a max of twenty-five years.

"If McMunchun's death was an accident, there's no murder. The only other overt act likely to apply would be if money changed hands. You said it didn't. Good. Then you're down to 105.05 . . . I think that's the right number . . . Conspiracy in the fifth degree. That's only a misdemeanor. Without the overt act, you easily claim that you told them it's stupid, don't do it, figured they wouldn't, and walked away. Nobody's going to prosecute.

"That's where you are now."

I had all this at my fingertips, including the statute numbers because I'd checked it out for myself. I didn't mention that. I wanted to sound like I had Owen's interests at heart and was figuring things out to protect him. I thought I was doing a pretty good job of faking it.

"If you go and say that's a murder . . . doesn't matter who did it . . . you have to say the reason you know is that the four of you talked about it. If the accident gets turned into murder, officially, that's the overt act. Inescapable. It doesn't matter who did it. Because you discussed it, you're part of the felony conspiracy. Inescapable as far as I can figure."

I'd certainly convinced myself that Owen needed this to stay an accident—which it was—nearly as much as the rest of us.

He looked like he was buying it. But he didn't want to let go of his big payday.

"I found you the girl," he said. "I named her price. I named my price. Full retail. Both. You didn't blink. You didn't *hondle*. I knew something was going down. I didn't know what. Until I see the story of McMunchkin flying off the road and she's with him. The things I know are that she's involved, you're involved, that Mrs. McMunchkin was willing to pay for him to be dead, and she's now a widow with a hundred million dollars."

Owen pushed his jacket back, showing me that he was carrying to back up what he said next. "I want my share. I'm going to get it."

The rage came up. Maybe it was the stress of the prolonged confrontation. But I'd go with rage.

In *my house*. He showed me his gun in *my house*.

I masked it. Quickly. Had he seen it? I didn't know.

I said, "Excuse me a second. At my age, my bladder . . ." turning, ". . . at our age . . ." walking toward the bedroom, ". . . how's yours?" as I disappeared behind the door.

CHAPTER TWENTY-SEVEN
SHOTGUN BOOGIE

"Shotgun Boogie," written and sung by
Tennessee Ernie Ford, was #1 on
the country charts for fourteen weeks.

WHEN I WALKED BACK INTO the living room, I was holding a
Benelli M4.

I'm not much of a gun guy. This one had belonged to Seymour
Herschkowitz, the killer dry cleaner, when he feared people might come
to do him harm. It had been included with the home furnishings. There's
no sportsman bullshit that it's for hunting. It was designed from scratch
for professional killers. Ostensibly the legal ones, soldiers and armed-
response police. It's a semiautomatic. It holds six rounds in the magazine
and one in the chamber. It has a collapsible stock, which is exactly what
it sounds like, so you can hold it like a giant pistol instead of a rifle.

Cohen stood still. Staring at me. Trying to breathe steady.

I didn't say anything.

He didn't say anything.

Cohen slowly raised his hands up. Not high overhead like in a
Western movie. Or like kids marching out of a middle school after a
mass shooting. Just to about shoulder height, palms forward.

I still didn't say anything.

Finally, he spoke. "I don't know what I did to upset you."

I pointed at the handgun he'd revealed by pushing back his jacket.

He said, "It's hot in here. I was just getting comfortable."

I shook my head, no.

"Come on, Tony, I'm not going to pull on you."

I still didn't say anything.

"You want me to just take it out, put it on the ground or something?"

"No."

"No?"

"No. You don't have to do that. Do what you want. Go for it. If you win, you have big problems. What do you do with the body? What were you doing here? They trace cars and phones. If I win, I don't have any problems. You came in with a gun. Even in blue state New York, this is *my* house."

"You're misreading an innocent gesture."

"No. I'm not. What we have here, Owen, is . . . a breach of etiquette. Yeah, a breach of etiquette. Bad manners. A misperception of who each of us is in this situation." I gestured with the Benelli. It's Italian. It has style, style that communicates. As Ferrari says speed and Gucci says conspicuous consumption, a Benelli shotgun says kill. I said, "Sit down."

Owen backed up slowly, until he felt the couch behind him, then lowered himself. It's big, cushiony and soft. He sank low. If he pulled his gun, he'd shoot himself in the knee before he shot me.

"We go back a long way," I said. "We've done business together. Always worked out. If you want to talk to me, you could call and I'd chat with you any time. Hey, if you think it's better to visit with no invitation . . . and surprise me just 'cause you're in the neighborhood . . . I can accept that. If you have something to say, I'm willing to listen. Like I said, why not? But don't think you can come up here and threaten me. Not with words. Not by showing you own a gun. Don't come up here . . . for that matter, don't talk to me anywhere, any time . . . like you think you're a cop and I'm a civilian."

"Wrong impression," he said. "It's just that there was a big payday that I was a part of making happen." He did his best to make it sound thoughtful, rather than like blackmail. "Just knowing about it and having some early participation, I figure it's best for everyone, if I get included in."

"Owen, here's the problem. It wasn't a murder. It really was an accident. The police ruled it an accident. Because it was. Also, I never discussed murder with Mrs. McMunchun or Miz Carter. You might have. That puts *you* in the frame, but not me."

"OK, sure. Can I go now?"

"You can go any time."

He pushed himself up. He was sunk deep in soft cushions on a low couch, and what the hell, he was old, just like I was, so he had to struggle to get back on his feet.

My adrenals had stopped pumping. I felt very calm, a little tired, very spacey, and probably sounded that way. "It's been weird. I've been thinking about death a lot lately. My own, other people's. You and me, our age, what's ahead is nowhere near what's behind. If we get more time, what would it be, drooling, pissing ourselves, in some facility?" He was moving slowly toward the door. He watched me carefully, like he thought I might be insane. I said, "Who wants that?"

He'd opened the door. He stood there a moment. "Bullshit," he said. It was very dramatic. All back light coming in from behind him, leaving his face and body in silhouette, nearly black, his voice coming from that darkness, with rays of light all around it. "You might be able to keep your act up, but I can make somebody crack, the two of them, or the girl. One of you will crack. I'll get paid."

CHAPTER TWENTY-EIGHT
DETAILS

IF I HAD TO MAKE a list of three things that were rare to see in Woodstock, they would be a new Chevy or Ford sedan, a guy between thirty and forty who was neither a Brooklyn hipster nor a musician moonlighting as a carpenter, with the third being that guy, driving that car, wearing pressed chinos and a pressed shirt.

It was a Chevy Malibu. Nice and clean, this year's or last, no bumper stickers, nothing hanging from the rearview mirror. Virginia plates. He looked like he'd do thirty-five sit-ups in one minute, twenty-four push-ups without stopping, 300 meters in a single minute, a mile and a half in under thirteen minutes. The FBI standards for his age group. He had a fresh shave and a Quantico haircut. Even the pressed chinos and a pressed shirt.

No wonder Sly had pegged him as a Fed.

There were two things to wonder about. Why was he watching me, and why did he want me to know it? If he hadn't been aware how obvious he was to start with, he should have been after two minutes in town. He could have gone to Kingston, rented a Subaru, and come back disguised as a lesbian. That's a Subaru joke, not a lesbian joke. The car of choice in Woodstock, as long as I've been here, has always been the least expensive, truly reliable, four-wheel or all-wheel drive vehicle. For obvious reasons. It used to be the Isuzu Trooper. Now it's a Subaru. Which also happens to be the car of choice for lesbians. The reasons for that are not at all obvious.

I'd spotted him following me at least once. He didn't seem to be working too hard at it. I thought he might have put some kind of tracking device on my car.

When I got home, I jacked it up and crawled underneath with a flashlight.

In recent years, I've grown used to silence. Now, the minute I'm on my back in the dirt with 3,500 pounds looming over me, my cell phone rings. Allison. She got right to the point. I liked that about her. She said, "I think someone's watching me."

"Are you sure?"

"No. If I was sure that's what I would have said. I could even be . . . you know . . . paranoid . . . but I think so."

"Just be careful," I said. "Very careful."

"Yeah," she said, like maybe she wouldn't.

"Come on."

Silence.

I said, "For a couple of days. Then I'll come down. Hang out and watch your back. If that will make you feel better."

"It would. Saturday would be good."

I told her, "Be more cautious than usual until then."

"Alright. Yes."

———

Fifteen minutes later, still poking around under the car, my phone rang again. Elizabeth. She wanted to see me. She said she had exciting news. Amazing progress. We needed to meet. It had to be tomorrow. I tried to make it Saturday so it would be just one trip. No. Had to be tomorrow. OK. I ended the call and returned to poking about. Then I heard a car coming up the road.

I was accustomed to solitude as well as silence. I don't count the company of cats. I don't think my company means much to them, except for the food. I'd already had four visitors this month. Three who'd made it all the way up to my house. Any more, and I'd have to be on the Woodstock tourist maps and put up a sign, *The concert wasn't here and neither was Bob Dylan*. I got out and brushed myself off. I thought that maybe I should have a gun to greet a prospective guest, then decided it was probably me that was getting out of hand.

It was a blue Ford Explorer. Not particularly new.

A black woman was at the wheel. I recognized her. Edwina Walker, Winston's widow, his second wife. She was about fifteen years younger than he'd been. She'd been here before. Long ago, with Winston. She'd always made me think of some of the black women I'd known as a child, like Mrs. Ferrer, my teacher from fourth to sixth grade. They were determined to be four times more proper and twice as bourgeois as any of their white peers. And they were, but still didn't get as much credit as they deserved or the opportunities they'd earned. A generation later they would be Michelle Obama, Venus and Serena Williams, Oprah Winfrey, and Condoleezza Rice. That's who she reminded me of, Mrs. Ferrer, who taught us never to put anything smaller than our elbow in our ear and not to try to put our pants on standing up, because her husband got a heart attack that way.

I walked up to her car, greeted her, held the door open to help her out.

This thing was getting terribly complicated for a murder that I didn't commit. That nobody committed.

CHAPTER TWENTY-NINE
WHAT A WIFE KNOWS

"When a man's partner is killed
he's supposed to do something about it."

DASHIELL HAMMETT, *THE MALTESE FALCON*
Hammett had been a detective, the real thing,
a Pinkerton, before he became a writer. He said,
"All my characters were based on people I've known
personally or known about." So that ethos,
you could figure there was actually something to it.

"I'M NOT INTERRUPTING? IS THIS a bad time? Should I have
called first?"

"No problem. You're always welcome." After they got married,
knowing that names almost always get shortened, she insisted on being called Eddie out of sheer dread that Winston and Edwina Walker
would become Winnie and Winnie and the only Winnie she knew
was Winnie the Pooh.

"It's still such a beautiful spot," she said.

"I guess we should have had you up here more often. Sorry we
didn't. And . . . well . . . I'm sorry for your loss."

She took both my hands in hers. "Thank you. And I am for yours."

"Thanks," I said, feeling the pain. Hers. And my own. Maybe it
showed, so before she could say anything more, I said, "Do you want
to come inside?" and offered refreshment.

"It's a little chilly," she said, "But the air is good and the view is beautiful. Maybe we could sit outside for a while."

"I could get you a blanket," I said, "Put it over your shoulders, and if we sit facing the sun, it should be OK."

"Yes, I think I'd like that."

We walked up toward the house, to the bench out front, under the eaves. I rushed forward and brushed some fallen leaves off it. "I'm sorry, if I'd known I'd have a guest . . ."

She laughed a little, then sat herself down.

I came back out with a Pendleton blanket. It had been a gift from Beinhart and his wife when we first moved up here. It was wool, indigo with some yellow, red, white, and some other blue tints, in a Native American pattern. It was one of those objects that seemed to be imbued with meaning. My wife had loved it. She used to sit out here, on chilly days, with it wrapped around her the way Eddie was wearing it now. The way they smiled was sort of the same, too, in an odd sort of way, and I wanted to break down—something was breaking down inside of me—break down and cry. But I didn't because one doesn't in front of guests. Does one?

Turning my back to her, heading away, I said, "Let me lower the car down. It'll only take a minute." I did that because I wanted the time to get myself back together, then returned and sat beside her. I knew it wasn't a social visit. "Eddie, what's happening? What do you need?"

"I don't know where to turn. I need to understand some things."

"Go on."

"It's about money."

"OK."

"We never had a problem with money. Between my job"—she was, in fact, a grade-school teacher—"and his, we were quite well enough off."

I wasn't keeping much of a poker face.

She read it. Then nodded. It was going to be one of those it-will-all-go-better-to-be-really-honest conversations. "And when he was on the force there was . . . extra. I never knew the details, nor should I have, but neither did I pretend to myself that I was blind. Then, when he left the force, and he and Cohen bought your business, we were still doing well. But the last few years the money seemed to dry up. After he died I expected there would be more than what was covered by the partners' insurance to buy me out."

"Could he have been . . ."—euphemism time, and a shrug—". . . spending it other places?"

She laughed, it somehow mixed an earthy sort of R&B attitude with a drier cackle. "I learned long ago what to check for. A woman who can't smell it on her man, who can't tell it from his conduct and timing, and for that matter, when he's taking care of business, is no woman at all. He was good and we were good, especially these last several years."

"You're sure?"

"Very sure."

"Because . . ."

"Because when I wasn't sure, I checked up on him."

I laughed.

She asked, "How come you sound so unsure?"

"Something someone said."

"You mean Owen?"

"Yes."

"I don't trust that man. You shouldn't trust that man."

"They were partners," I said. "In the great myths . . ."

"What great myths?"

"All of them," I sighed. "In reality and fiction. Partners are supposed to back each other up, protect each other, lie for each other, and do something about it if one of them gets killed."

"They didn't like each other," she said.

"It's not supposed to matter," I said.

We were side by side. She looked out at the mountains, not at me. She said, "The race thing. Blacks and whites. The race thing. Always. You can bend around it, paper over it, pretend it's died and gone to heaven, but there's always the race thing."

"Come on," I said. "I'm not saying it's not true, but they were together a long time."

"They knew how to use it," she said, looking at me. Professionals talking. "They played it like good cop, bad cop, on people's expectations. If it was down and dirty it was 'send the big nigga.' If it was financial stuff, embezzlement and such, Owen would do his tricky Hebe shtick. It worked when they were police and clients ate it up when they went private.

"Then the things that are underneath started coming out, like the old grudges in a marriage that's not quite right. Owen started acting like a white motherfucker who thinks people of color shouldn't get too uppity. My Winston was a hard man in the ways he had to be and wild in his time, I knew that, you know that, but he wasn't stupid, I promise you that."

I said, "Yes, I know."

"That wild stuff . . . Winston was getting old . . . you know how the parts that been hurt, they turn into slow aches and they're heavy. I'd see him getting out of bed in the morning and it was like he was wearing shackles and chains. At least until he got moving." She gave me a once-over. She said, "You're looking good, like you're hardly getting old, but what's it like in the morning for you? Do all the parts that been hurt, are they right there keeping you company when you head for the bathroom, when you try to put your pants on, when you bend down to tie your shoes?"

"The ones in my heart," I said.

"Yes. I see the sadness in you."

"Yes."

"You got religion?"

"No. No, I'd say I don't."

"It could help."

I thought about what religion I did have. Talking trees, screeching ravens, trickster gods, pagan doomsayers, and death-lovers. Even though I'd met them, been with them, spoke to them, and heard them speak to me, I'd place odds that they were hallucinations. If pressed, I'd say the same about her religion. About anyone's. "Well," I said, "Well . . . tell me what you want. Tell me what you're here for."

"I want to know . . . I want to know if, if there was money, and if Owen was stealing it."

I was sure she had more to say. I prompted her, "And?"

"Who killed him?"

"I have a question for *you* . . . Did Winston, shortly before he died, talk to you about a job, a special job, for a lot of money?"

"Yes. We were talking about our bills. I was being worrisome. He said he was going to fix things. That business was about to get a lot better."

"Did he say what it was? Did he say anything specific?"

"No."

"That it might be extreme or dangerous?"

"No, nothing like that. What? What do you know?"

I found myself not wanting to tell her that her husband might have been cutting a deal to be a contract killer. The only thing I knew for a fact was that he hadn't done it. Instead, I said, "Owen thinks it was a jealous husband."

"He's a lying, scandalizing man. I told you, I'm no fool. I know what men do. And I know that in his time, Winston did his share and maybe more. But I know that he wasn't stealing around . . . oh . . . for quite a while."

I stood up, took a few steps, making a half circle, until I was facing her. "Come on, Eddie, how can you be sure?"

She paused and pursed her lips, then let it pop out, "Because I put one of those apps on his phone."

"What kind of app?"

"Spyware. I could see almost everything. Facebook, Messenger, his phone calls, Instagram, email, where he went. All of it."

"Did you tell the police?"

She didn't say anything, but eventually shook her head no.

With a gesture, not words, I asked, why not?

"I didn't want them to see me as a woman who needed to track her man."

"Was it still working? When he died?"

"Yes."

"Would it show where he was and where he went the night he died?"

"Yes."

CHAPTER THIRTY

SPACE TO BE

Who Do You Want on Your Divorce Team?
Team Member No. 1: The Wealth Advisor.

"YOU SAID WE WERE SAFE," Maddie said. She sounded exactly like a woman at the customer service window at Bloomingdale's who'd been told her warranty no longer applies.

I replied as if I was on the other side of the counter, patiently, courteously, telling her that she had voided the warranty. "Yes, we were safe. Provided that you hadn't done things you hadn't told me about."

Her protest came out with a whine, "You *promised* me."

"I need to know everything."

"You put your arms around me and told me we were safe."

Getting irritated, I said, "Where the fuck is your girlfriend." Meaning Liz. We were there on Elizabeth's schedule, in her offices— LIFE, Inc., *Litigation Investment for Female Empowerment*—a world under construction—half the pre-fab interior walls up, some waiting, much of the wiring done, but she wasn't there.

For whatever reason, none of the work crews were there. Just us.

The full space was a large rectangle, deeper than it was wide. The plan for the offices was now quite visible. Double doors, for entry, were in the middle of the short side facing the interior of the building. Once you came through them—sometime in the near future—you'd meet the receptionist, at a nicely curved reception desk.

Looking ahead and to the right there were cubicles for fund managers and lawyers. Bathrooms were about halfway down that line. The women's much larger than the men's. As it ought to be. To the left, there was a conference room, the secure room, and Liz's personal CEO corner office.

There were two places to wait. An unappealing, bare one, in front of the receptionist. Monied people would be escorted to an area behind her, hidden by a half wall, akin to one of the better airport lounges or an upscale coffee bar, with comfortable upholstered chairs, nice little tables, plants, reading material, snacks, and fancy coffee from a live barista.

The far end was to be the Investigators' Section, alongside the CEO's office. The plan was for that department to have two lawyers, since the job was ostensibly to evaluate lawsuits, two PIs, two assistants, two secretaries, even a couple of interns. Plus, one person in charge. I was the current nominee. I'd have my own space. I would even have a window. A big one. Wowzer. So far it had walls and a door, one office chair, one plain chair, a cast-off from somewhere unknown, and a piece of plywood across sawhorses where a desk might go. That's where the two of us were.

Madelaine was in the rickety chair. I was standing.

The only light was natural light. It was afternoon. We were facing west. It was coming in strong and bright. I had Madelaine facing the window. The light was in her eyes. If I stood in front of her, I was a dark presence. When I circled around behind her, she had to twist to see me, while her eyes worked to adjust. It was excellent as an impromptu interrogation room.

"Tell me about your deal with Winston Walker." Before she could deny it, I said, "I know you had a deal with him." I could tell from the way she moved her mouth, she was still going to waffle and weasel. I had to narrow it down, make it specific. "Who found him?"

"I did. I did."

"How?"

"I told you."

"No."

"I told you."

"Now tell me again."

"Beinhart," she said.

"You asked Beinhart how to find a contract killer?" That was ridiculous. But maybe he'd surprise me.

"No. His screenplay. I told you about it. He said it was all true. Only the names were changed to protect the guilty. In it, the Winston character—person—had killed people for money."

Oh, Winston. I knew he'd been, well, a cop in the crack-crazy eighties, in Spanish Harlem. I knew he'd killed people but thought he'd restricted himself to the standard kill-or-be-killed situations. Well, well, Winston. "Who? Who did he kill?"

"I don't know. Some drug dealer types. They weren't real names anyway and I don't remember. Except Winston's."

"Beinhart used Winston's real name?"

"Not in the screenplay. But he told us, because that was part of the pitch. 'Based on a true story' was supposed to be the hook. Hollywood likes that."

"Who approached Winston?"

"I did. I mean to start."

"About killing your husband?"

She twisted away, squirming from the light. "Don't say that."

"Who? You? Liz? Or someone else?"

"Liz," she said, eager to lay it off on someone else. "*She* did it."

"Alone?"

"No. I . . . I was there."

"Then what happened?"

"I don't know. It came apart."

"How? Why?"

"I don't know. Ask *Liz*."

"I will. How did Owen Cohen get involved?"

"Owen Cohen?" Like she'd never heard the name.

"Come on," I barked at her.

"How do you know . . ."

"Because the bastard came to see me. He wants money. He thinks I murdered Mick, and he wants a piece of the action."

"What did you say?"

"I put a shotgun in his face and told him there was no murder."

"That's good," she said, eager for any reassurance at all.

"That it was an accident."

"That's good." Oh, she felt that was better yet.

"Did you give him money?"

"No."

"Or Winston?"

She shook her head. I said, "Anything at all?"

"No."

"Are you sure?"

"Yes, I'm sure." Then very plaintively, "Why? Why are you asking that?"

CHAPTER THIRTY-ONE

JUST THE THREE OF US

THE DOOR SWUNG OPEN. LIZ stepped in. She looked at Madelaine. She turned her head and glared at me. "Why are you making her cry?"

Sure enough, there were actual tears on Maddie's face. At least coming from one eye, with the other working up to it. As for her expression, imagine an actress, somewhere in her third and fourth decades, playing an abused child.

"I was just about to explain criminal conspiracy to her."

"Oh, yes," Elizabeth said. "When two or more people agree to commit an illegal act and take some step toward its completion."

"When it was just the three of us," I said, "I was reasonably certain—*unreasonably* certain—that this could be contained. Now I know that there are at least five of us. Three who have benefited. One who hasn't—Owen Cohen—who is very upset. And one who's dead."

"Owen doesn't know anything."

"Oh, Liz," Madelaine said, not knowing enough to keep her mouth shut.

"Bullshit," I said. "I need you to tell me what happened with Winston and Owen. Every bit of it." I knew they'd wanted a female killer. Or several. I was sure they'd tried. "I need to know if you approached anyone else."

Both of them claimed that they'd never spoken to any women about it *in a direct way*. But, well, when they encountered women who seemed particularly disgruntled, they did try to spin conversations in that direction. Just as a sort of gossipy possibility. Sort of like the way men say, "Women. You can't live with them, you can't live without them," trying out lines like, "Husbands, don't you sometimes wish you could just eliminate the current one?" and "What if there were a service to get rid of husbands for you?" They got lots of positives, but never anything even slightly serious.

"We just don't know people like that," Madelaine said.

"We travel in very limited circles," Liz said, dry and sarcastic.

After they'd heard about Winston from Beinhart and his screenplay, Madelaine made the approach. Liz came in to make the deal. As Cohen told me, they'd agreed on $50,000. Then, out of the blue, Cohen showed up claiming to be Winston's negotiator. "Just a mere one percent of a hundred million, one million," is what he said. Liz told him, very crisply, "Never mind. Goodbye."

Owen's response was like it had been with me. Since he knew, if something happened to Mick without him and his partner getting paid, he'd put in a call to One Police Plaza.

"I don't do business with people who renege on their deals," Liz said, with full sanctimony, not even a whiff of irony. "Besides, if I showed myself the sort of person who would roll over the first time, he'd be the sort of person who would never stop."

Liz broke off all communication with Owen and with Winston. As did Madelaine, following Elizabeth's orders. Owen called both of

them. Multiple times. Neither took his calls. Owen tried to approach
Liz on the street. There'd been a uniformed cop nearby. Liz had rushed
over to say she was being harassed, "by that man there!," pointing
at Owen. It was in the East 60s, a region where the word of a well-
dressed businesswoman carried unassailable clout. Owen slunk away.

Winston tried next. Somehow, Liz found his approach more
amenable. "I rather liked him," Liz said. "Certainly much more than
Owen. I thought he was more honest and . . . I guess it's very odd to
say so . . . less dangerous. That's not a deduction from facts, I admit
it. It was a feeling, which is foolish, but there you are, and I let him
approach me. He started by apologizing for Owen. Then he asked if
he could speak to me for five minutes." My interpretation was that she
figured they were about to jump off the $1,000,000 demand right back
down to an affordable number. They went to the Astro, a Greek diner
on the corner of Fifty-Fifth Street and Sixth Avenue, busy enough
that Liz felt safe, slow enough to find a table out of earshot, cheap
enough that she wouldn't be seen by anyone who knew her.

Winston apologized again. Liz said, "I don't want anything to
do with you now."

"Because of him?"

"Yes."

"I'll take care of him," Winston said. "Don't worry."

"No. Absolutely not."

"I can do this for you. For the original price."

"Winston, I think it's best that we both pretend . . . that we both
believe . . . none of this happened. Pffft. Gone."

"I'll do it for thirty."

"The money's not the problem. The problem is . . ."

". . . Owen," Winston said.

Liz nodded.

"I'll take care of it."

Liz looked skeptical.

"I guarantee it."

"In my business, I know a lot of people driven by greed. You can see it. Owen's one of them. He won't stop."

Winston was very emphatic and definite about it, "I will take care of him."

Liz paused in telling the story. I stepped into the silence. "Who said it, Liz? You or Winston?"

"Neither, really. Not like that."

"Somebody said the only way to stop someone *like* Owen, to stop Owen, is to kill him."

Liz didn't answer. She did sigh.

"That's the logic of it," I said. As I tried to figure what went on, I spoke the thoughts out loud. "No. I don't see Winston saying, 'The only way is to kill him, so don't worry, I'll kill him.' No, it didn't go like that . . . You said it. Didn't you?" I was certain that was the truth. With that, the masquerade—the educated speech and advanced degrees, the expensive, precise but conservative hair and makeup—and the facade— the slick, sophisticated, architect-designed office, the advertising agency pitches and graphics—all started dissolving—not a metaphor—I was seeing this—there she was and the truth of it spoke the words that I heard—we three heard—coming through my mouth. "You are . . . or you've become . . . a sociopath. Kill this one, kill that one, and another one . . ."

She reacted. Not instantly. She knew straight-up denial would not work. She had to reweave the illusions that she kept around her. "It was not like that," she said. "Yes. I did express what I thought Cohen's character was. Something to the effect of the only way to stop him or get him out of the equation or, you know, something like that, would be if he weren't around."

"Uh-huh."

"Don't take it out of context. That was only half the statement. I immediately, *immediately* added, because I saw that he might misinterpret, 'We don't want to go there. I don't want that, and I'm sure you don't want that.' That's what I said. Then I was done. I got up to go. He stood up, too. He didn't block me, but we both paused, almost had to pause, to get around the tables. He said, 'I'll take care of the problem. I will demonstrate to you that it's taken care of. Then the deal's back on."

"Did you say yes?" I asked.

"Nothing as definite as a word," Liz said. "I did nod." As if that was really less damning. "Then he said, 'At the original price. Since the problem's not money, it's Owen.' Then I did say, 'Yes, that's OK.' He said, 'I'll get back to you in a week, maybe less.'"

"Then?"

"Then we both left."

"Then?"

"Then I never heard from him."

"Come on, Liz. Then? Then what?"

"Then he was dead."

"Dropped dead? Natural causes? Heart attack? Old fucking age?"

"He was shot."

"Right. Murdered is usually the term."

"We had nothing to do with that," Madelaine said, near tears, maybe with tears.

"Absolutely nothing," Liz said, cool and secure about it. "Are we done with this now? Can we get to real business?"

"Not yet," I said. "I have another question. Where were you the night of the fourteenth? Both of you. Between about eleven p.m. and two a.m.?"

Madelaine blurted out, "What?" sounding bewildered and childlike.

"You two have the best motives that I'm aware of. He could put you in the frame, conspiracy to commit murder. Do you have alibis?" There was no immediate answer. Which didn't mean much. Most people don't know, offhand, where they were by date and time. Still, I pushed. "You need alibis. For the cops, if it comes to that. What I need is the truth, so I know what I have to deal with."

Elizabeth looked at her watch.

She actually had a watch. She wasn't just digitized into time through her cell phone. It was slender and silver with a face in the shape of a teardrop. The strap was like a snake's skin, presuming there's a viper with scales made of a shining, polished metal. Elizabeth was clearly feeling pressured by the movements of the hands. Tick-tock, tick-tock. She said, "The way to deal with all of this, all of this, is to move forward. That's what we're going to do. Move forward.

"I'm going to make that happen now. Right now. In a big way. Maybe the biggest ever. I need the two of you to buck up and be on your game. Your A game. We can do it. And we will."

CHAPTER THIRTY-TWO

IS IT POSSIBLE TO HAVE A SATIRICAL HALLUCINATION?

WITH THE QUESTIONS UNANSWERED, THE goal unknown, Elizabeth led us from the unfinished space we were in through the unfinished space that was going to be her large corner office and out of that via her special side entrance—a door that actually existed in a wall that was already in place—to what was to be the secure room.

Elizabeth had another woman for us to see. To meet. To kill for?

Sanity. Is. A funny thing.

I. Felt. Mine slipping. Away.

Age? Some strange disease? Chemical imbalance? Something slipped into a drink? But I hadn't had one.

Cognitive dissonance? That. Yes! Probably. Certainly? Certainty slip-sliding. Away.

That was it. Hold on. The cognitively correct thing to do was to have walked away. Early. At the start. Having failed that, immediately. In the now. Maybe I was just tired. At a breaking point.

This new one sat like a drawing of a princess in a fairy tale. Like a drawing of a Norse goddess, who are always depicted, for reasons unknown, like comic book heroines, two steps even more idealized than women on the covers of bodice-rippers. Freya, conveniently the goddess of love *and* death.

Two rooms back, I had placed Maddie so that the light abused her. Intimidated. Revealed. Interrogated. This one, whomever she was, had placed herself so that the light gifted her with illuminations, gold that shimmered. I suspected that she always did that, always found the key light, like the old-time movie stars, Garbo, Bergman, Bacall, knew how to do. The other alternative was impossible, that she was such that the light sought her out.

Elizabeth began to tell the woman's story. Young, beautiful, American, from the Midwest, junior year trip abroad. In Firenze, or Mykonos, or Lake Como, one of those places, maybe Paris, it didn't matter, it was gilt, gelt, gold, glamour. A man who was immensely, impossibly, wealthy, though significantly older, spotted her. It was enticing. But she wouldn't be rented or even purchased. Elizabeth didn't say it that way, but it's how it sounded when it reached my ears. He proposed. Swept up by it all, she succumbed.

I found Elizabeth's voice to be harsh. Her tale to be tedious. Hackneyed. Vexatious. Irksome. Nagging. So, apparently, I replaced it. With a song. Unfortunately, the voice singing it in my head was from 1904 or thereabouts and had its own trilling irritations. These are the words it sang, both plaintive and self-righteous:

She's only a bird in a gilded cage,
A beautiful sight to see.
You might think she's happy and free from care,
She's not, though she seems to be.
Her beauty was sold for an old man's gold,
She's a bird in a gilded cage.

Her maiden name was Kaylee Biggs Posey.

The man was Russian. A billionaire. An actual billionaire, that's one thousand millions. Of dollars. Not rubles. The voice in my head sang on.

Her gems were the purest, her gown divine,
And what could a woman want more?
But happiness cannot be bought with gold,
Although she's a rich man's bride.

His name was Grigor God Voloshin. God? Yes. That was his middle name. Really. OK.

They had a son. Leo. He was three years old. Pictures of him were passed around. He was cuter than a button. Blond hair, bright blue eyes. A lively, intelligent expression. Playful and boyish. In the photos with his mother, the two appeared to utterly adore each other. But what mother shows pictures of her children looking upon her with anger, hatred, or even plain indifference. Therefore, adoration mandatory.

God could not come to America. Because of the Magnitsky Act.

The Magnitsky Act was the invention of Bill Browder. He started a hedge fund in Russia that made a fortune. He bought shares in corrupt

THE DEAL GOES DOWN

companies. As a shareholder he could expose them. That forced them to reform. That made the share price rocket up.

The Russians came after him. He got out with most of his money. However, the Russian police seized corporate documents and used them to commit massive frauds. Browder's lawyer, Sergei Magnitsky, who had stayed in Russia, discovered the scams. But the perps were the police. They counter-accused. Sergei was arrested. The application of bail in Russia is arbitrary and rare. Magnitsky was held in pretrial detention. During that year, he was tormented, tortured, and finally murdered.

Browder knew Russia in depth and detail. He crafted a plan that targeted the individuals responsible and got it passed as American law. It froze the assets they held in the United States, banned them from bringing more money in, and stopped them from getting U.S. visas. The act could be expanded, and it was, to cover more people. Uniquely, it targeted the rich, powerful, and criminal, Putin's inner circle.

A syllogism is deductive reasoning based on two or more propositions assumed to be true. Oligarchs who are not friends of Putin are no longer oligarchs, or are in exile, or they're dead. Therefore, a live oligarch, domiciled in Russia, or even passing through regularly, is a friend of Putin. If Voloshin was a Russian billionaire, he was a friend of Putin. If he was listed under the Magnitsky Act, the U.S. State Department considered him some sort of criminal.

> *There's riches at her command.*
> *She married for wealth, not for love.*
> *'Though she lives in a mansion grand,*
> *She's only a bird in a gilded cage.*

Kaylee wanted to come to America. Her parents, her family, were here. Even to move back. God only allowed her the shortest trips.

One, two, three days, at the most. When she came to America, where he couldn't follow, he kept Leo. Whenever she traveled alone, anywhere, he kept Leo.

She wanted a divorce. He'd said no.

"Aren't divorces easy in Russia? Very common, too," I said.

"Judges are easy to bribe in Russia," Kaylee stated. Silver chains and diamond-studded shackles.

She had multiple homes, servants, gowns, shoes, jewelry, and she had all those *nevers*, never having to earn a dime, do a budget, pay a bill, pass up a sparkly for a necessity, and never go without. But she was but a possession to Grigor God Voloshin. A bauble, a bangle, at best a Fabergé egg. Prized. Displayed. But unable to live by her feelings. It was *degradation*. Sad, tragic, piteous, wretched. The old vinyl recording playing the song in my head had a scratch and the needle started to jump making repetitions, "a bird in a gilded cage"—*screech*—"bird in a gilded cage"—*screech*—"bird in a gilded cage"—*screech*.

God was a tyrant. Cruel. Unjust. Given to rages. A drunk. With thugs. Enforcers. He called them "security personnel." Kaylee was constantly on the verge of terror, but knew stress ruins beauty, both short-term and long, creating wrinkles as surely as smoking. She needed to have Leo, her beautiful, wonderful son. She needed Leo *to be an American*. She needed to *leave God*. She dared not. *He would kill her.*

"We can fix this," Elizabeth said. Sounding as certain of her own notion of justice as Sergeant Joe Friday in *Dragnet*, from when television screens had rounded corners and everything was made right, in black-and-white, in twenty-six minutes.

"Can you?" Kaylee asked, the tiniest light of hope in her eyes.

"Yes," Elizabeth said, then cued Madelaine, "Tell her."

Maddie came forward, reciting, "I had a life much like yours. I, too, was a prisoner, wedded to the warden. My children were his hostages, as your Leo is for you. I know that sadness, that fear, that hopeless feeling when you think there's no way out. But there is one. With their help"—she pointed to Elizabeth and me—"we found the way."

"And that is . . ." Kaylee asked, though I expected she'd already been told.

"That is . . ." Elizabeth spoke, quite rightly not trusting Madelaine to do so, "to eliminate the problem."

"Eliminate?" Kaylee asked.

"Yes. *Eliminate*. Remove," Elizabeth said. "Then you will be free. To be with your son. To be the mother you wish to be. To return to your own country. And, of course, to inherit that fortune."

"Can you really?"

"Yes," Elizabeth said. "This is the man who can make it happen." It was time for me to recite my lines. Elizabeth looked and suddenly knew that I'd say the wrong thing or not speak at all, so quick as a wink, she said, "Isn't he, Maddie?"

"He did it for me," Maddie said. "My husband is . . . he passed on. The police ruled that it was an accident. There is no question that it was . . . an accident. He can do it for you. I know he can."

I looked at the three women. One so desperate. One so grateful. One so greedy and determined. Nonetheless, the answer had to be no. Anything else was . . . that simple, on syllable, two letter word began to form on my lips.

Such a short word, yet before I could get it out, Kaylee said, "The time. What's the time?" She looked at her phone.

Elizabeth looked at her watch.

Kaylee said, "Oh dear, I have to go," a little frantic, "I should have left already."

Liz turned to me and said, "Kaylee could only escape for a very short time. God sends security people with her. Keepers. KGB types. Right now, she's supposedly with her mother. Her mother helped her sneak away. But she has to get back before something terrible happens."

Kaylee was already standing, trying to figure out how to leave. Elizabeth said, "Come on, I'll walk you out." Off they went.

As they tapped, tapped away, I went into Elizabeth's space, where the corner window was. Looking down, I could see Elizabeth and Kaylee. There was a car waiting. Elizabeth signaled. It pulled up. Kaylee got in.

There was a guy leaning into a shadow on the other side of the street. He seemed to be watching. He looked a lot like the guy I'd seen up in Woodstock, the one Sly said was a narc.

CHAPTER THIRTY-THREE
WHAT? WHERE?
HOW? WHEN?

"In a Russian tragedy, everybody dies. In a
Russian comedy, everybody dies, too. But they die happy."

BARRY FARBER, *WMCA*

WHEN LIZ CAME BACK UPSTAIRS, I finally said it, "No." I repeated it, "No."

"That's a billion dollars," she said.

"Plus a damsel in distress," I said. "No."

"Think . . ."

"Where do they live?"

"In Moscow, mostly."

"Moscow. You want to try . . . you want me to try . . . you want *any-one* to try . . . to kill someone in fucking Moscow? Russia, Russian police, his personal security people, and then get out of Russia?" I was building up into a pretty good rant. "As bad as American prisons are, what do you think Russian prisons are like? As bad as American gangs might be, what do you think Russian mobsters are like? In prison and out?"

"They're going on vacation," Elizabeth said.

"So what."

"Don't you want to know where?"

"No. I don't. Because wherever they go, he'll have security with him. Because he's listed under the Magnitsky Act, which means that he's connected to Putin, who uses the FSB as his personal toy, and to the Russian mob."

"Calm down."

"No."

"Let me tell you where they're going. They're going to St. Anton."

St. Anton is both a town and the generic reference to one of those sprawling ski areas that includes several villages. There're almost ninety lifts, roughly two hundred miles of marked runs, and since there are no rules restricting you to the official routes, endless amounts of off-piste skiing. I lived there once upon a time.

"She's going tomorrow. He'll meet her there. They'll stay for two weeks." Elizabeth had her gotcha face on. "That's your second home."

It was where I lived when my daughter was born. Where I got married.

"Rick's Laundromat Americaine," Liz said. "That's right, isn't it?"

That was my business. It did well, too. And *Rick* had been my name then. Elizabeth knew a lot about me. New dots, worthy of connecting, had appeared. I looked at Maddie, "You didn't meet me by chance, did you?"

Liz started to say something. I snapped at her, "Shut up." Back to Maddie. I had her conditioned to answer my questions, "Tell me."

"No," she said.

"How did you pick me?"

"Beinhart," Maddie said.

"Tell me."

Maddie looked to Liz. "Go ahead, tell him," Liz said.

"After Winston died, I . . . we . . . we didn't know what to do . . . then I saw him . . ."

"Beinhart?"

"Yes. At a restaurant in Rhinebeck. Cinnamon. It's Indian, but very good. Right?"

We all agreed, Elizabeth, Madelaine, and I, that Cinnamon was very good. "We were at a table next to them . . ."

"Who?"

"Him, his wife, and another couple, she's Indian, sort of exotically beautiful, he's African American, umm, a musician . . ."

"David Sancious," I said. I knew who he was. I'd seen him play and watched genius come out of his fingertips onto the keys of a piano.

"Yes," she said. "Then I brought up that I'd heard or read that the guy he'd written the screenplay about . . . I pretended not to remember the name . . . then he said it, Winston . . . then I said I just heard that he died . . . Beinhart knew that . . . then I asked him, did he know many people who had actually killed anyone. He said, 'not counting war?' . . . I said, 'Right, that's what I meant.' He said, 'maybe a couple.' 'Like who,' I asked. That's when he mentioned you. 'Wow,' I said, then we started talking about . . . I don't know . . . music and *The Marvelous Mrs. Maisel.*"

"That's all?"

"I think so."

"Come on, there's more. There has to be more."

"I guess. Umm . . . somewhere in there he said you and Winston knew each other, did business together. You were both part of that time and place, New York in the seventies and eighties, and you'd probably go the funeral. He would go, he said, but there was some other thing he was committed to."

"So, you knew I'd be going?"

"Yes."

"How did you work out meeting me on the train?"

"That was a guess," Elizabeth said. "That you'd take the train. I asked Madelaine to look for you."

"I had to let three trains go by," Madelaine said. "Before you showed up."

"What if I'd driven or taken the bus?"

"I went down to the funeral," Elizabeth said. "As a backup. I was sure that a woman on the train would be much, much better." That was done as far as she was concerned. Time to switch to the exciting subject. "Now, this." The absent Kaylee Voloshin. "She will put in half—as an investment—of however much she inherits. That will be huge. Then we're really funded. We can't fail. We can handle anything."

I said, "You haven't even paid me what you already owe me. Where is it?"

"I have a contract here for you," she said, enthusiastic and ready to close her deal. "It puts you in charge of our investigatory unit. There's a $200,000 signing bonus. A guaranteed $300,000 a year. An expense account. It would cover, for example, all your travel expenses going to St. Anton. Though it might actually be Lech? That's sort of a suburb . . ."

"A separate village. Nearby." I said. "But part of the same ski circuit."

"Right, that's fine then. We'll get you an Amex Black Card. Bills to the company. Sign the contract. I call a bank in the Caymans; the signing bonus goes to your bank on Monday."

"When you were downstairs," I said, "putting Kaylee in the car, I was looking out your window. There was someone watching you. He looked a lot like a guy I think was watching me in Woodstock. I think of him as the Mormon because he has that look. The FBI has a lot of them that look like that. They clone them out in Utah. Using multiple wives.

"Money first. With some kindly letter of bereavement. About my dead aunt. You can make up a name or I'll give you one. In my bank on Monday. First thing." I had no intention of killing anyone, of investigating another trophy marriage, of going to St. Anton. No matter how good the skiing was there. But I wanted my money.

"Money first," I repeated. "We only talk after that."

CHAPTER THIRTY-FOUR

RULES & RHYME

"I was working on the proof of one of my
poems all the morning, and took out a comma.
In the afternoon I put it back again."

OSCAR WILDE

THE BROOKLYN POETRY SLAM HAD good rules. Rule #4 was:
Competitors are prohibited from using animal acts, props, or musical
accompaniment.

It was at BRIC—Brooklyn Information & Culture—on Fulton
Street, two short blocks southeast of Flatbush Avenue. That puts it in
Fort Greene, though right next to Downtown Brooklyn. Allison was
performing.

Was someone actually watching her? Maybe.

She invited me. I said no.

If she thought I was there, her behavior would change. She'd look
for me, look at me, and the unknown mysterious maybe-person would
pick up on it. I made some reassuring sounds that I would find a way
to check things out.

Was someone watching me? It seemed likely.

Elizabeth said that Kaylee Biggs Posey had slipped her leash and come to the office unobserved. Maybe. Maybe not. If her minders had tracked her, they might have picked up on me. All things considered, it seemed sensible to be armed. If things did go off the rails, better a gun that traced back to someone else. I went to my hiding place, lifted the rock, opened the box, and took out Elizabeth's little hot pink and black Glock 43.

It was a wet, windy, ugly night. Traffic was slow. I was late. It was hard to find a parking spot. I ended up farther away than I wanted to be.

The wind came in gusts, abrupt and hard, blowing the rain sideways. I don't like umbrellas. If a hard rain is going to fall, I wear a Western hat and a duster. Imagine a ten-year-old dressing up for a Sergio Leone Western. It keeps me drier than most other things.

The slam was in a small theater with a stage and raked seating called, for no apparent reason, The Ballroom. It was well attended. The very few empty seats were in the back, near the corners. That suited me.

Within the first few moments, I was glad that I was late. A young black man was yelling at me about how badly oppressed he and all his people were. For a really long time. It was all true. Or close enough. I couldn't complain about that. I agreed that black lives matter and I even believe in reparations so long as the Baptist Church and Princeton University are paying them. But I'd heard every word he was saying by 1962.

Rule #2 was: Poets are given three minutes to read their own original work.

Another excellent rule. Yet time stretched. As it did for Einstein on that trolley in Bern, making him envision relativity and change the very meaning of time.

At last it was over. There was applause. He left.

There was an introduction. A four-woman crew was next.

They had not simply memorized their material; they had created an act, individual bits, echoed responses, and moments when they all recited together. They were angry. As well they should have been. For the abuse, exploitation, and body shaming they had suffered. They were loud. Strident. Over and over, I thought of the question, "How many feminists does it take to change a light bulb?" and the answer, "That's not funny." I knew that it was only my status as a privileged white male that permitted—nay, that demanded—that I respond that way and I sincerely tried to feel guilt.

Three minutes used to be the standard length of a pop song, but I'd never heard one that seemed this long.

Another team was next. Three young gay men of Asian ancestry, a Vietnamese, a Chinese, and a Malaysian who was also Muslim. They had it tough. They declaimed, shrieked, squawked, and ululated.

The MC announced the next poet as Phryne Impiety. Her hair was darker and shinier than Cadillac's raven black. It was thick and straight. Her lips were also black, but less so. Her makeup was intense. Her midriff was bare. A glittery dangle hung down from her navel. I braced myself for another three minutes of stress and tried to remember breathing exercises.

There were microphones on stage. They were working. This girl, Phryne, seemed to be the first to realize that electronics amplified even a whisper. She didn't have to yell. She began her recitation at a normal, even playful, conversational level. What a relief it was.

A floozy, a doxie, a harlot, a tart.
Such exciting words, they'll do for a start.

Only her voice made me recognize Allison.

A bawd, a hussy, streetwalker, a jade
when men with money want to get laid.

A fresh sugar baby, a kept woman, a mistress.
Whatever you want, a website will list us.

What had she done, I wondered, swallowed a thesaurus? Then it was as if she'd answered my thought.

I've swallowed the thesaurus a lot more than semen.
It's synonyms and antonyms that set me to dreaming.

I'm an actor, a therapist, wearing masks, playing roles,
not just along for the ride and collecting the tolls.

I'm the girlfriend experience, I'm a sweet jezebel
there's five stars on Yelp for the coochie I sell.

I was fascinated by her. Probably more than I should have been. She was young, wickedly smart, sharp and funny, impulsive, dangerous, willing to sell herself. I was old, dragged down with ennui, and, I recently discovered, still impulsive and willing to sell myself. Where does that go?

We do Greek and Roman, Swedish and Brit,
Latex and anal, and would you like to be hit.

I'll wear the catsuit, I'll break out the lash,
you want what you want, and I want the cash.

Your fille de joie, votre belle chatelaine,
We'll be priest and penitent, or Tarzan and Jane.

Prostitute is a verb. It's not just a noun.
Which of you stays pure, with money around?

The audience was confused. Sex workers had huge cred as an oppressed class. But her verses were not about misery, abuse, and terrible suffering. She didn't yell, rant, or harangue.

There's more prostituting than there are prostitutes,
watched over by lawyers all dressed up in suits.

Ladies of low virtue, creatures of pleasure
to relish, to savor, to enjoy at your leisure.

In the life, on the street, girl in the game,
the trick is to do tricks without any shame.

Want an escort, a call girl, an old-fashioned hooker?
Open your laptop, your browser, and book her.

I spotted a man of about my age. I couldn't see his face, just the back of his head and his clothing from his collar to his mid-back. Men in their sixties and seventies who come to an event like this should look like Bernie Sanders. Or volunteers who've canvassed for Bernie. He didn't. I thought it could be Owen.

While I'm voguing and posing and dancing on poles,
has your great career sucked away all your soul?

Are you better than me because I'm paid to play?
Who here has a talent that they won't sell for pay?

In your days at the office are you a knight brave and bold?
Always guided by conscience, or do you do what you're told?

Here's my story for what it's worth.
I offer it to you in rhyme and verse.
When you think about yours, is it better, is it worse?

She got some applause, but it was clear that she wouldn't win. What did I care? I know little about poetry. I wasn't her mother. As she left the stage, the man I'd noted got up from his seat. As he went up the aisle I saw his profile. It was Owen.

CHAPTER THIRTY-FIVE
"I'M SINGIN' . . .

. . . and dancin' in the rain."

OWEN HELD AN OVERSIZE BLACK umbrella over his head. Huge and round, like it had been made from the wings of a giant bat, its metal struts like skinny bones. I hate umbrellas. When Allison came out, he walked up to her. He held the thing so that they were both beneath it. He spoke. She nodded and smiled. Knowing who was who and what was what, I took it to be a professional conversation on her part, probably something different on his.

If they went somewhere in a car, I needed to be in a vehicle, right then, right there, to follow. If I went to get my own car, they'd be long gone before I got back. Cabs were going to be rare, but I saw one. I dashed through the rain, cut off a couple who thought it would be theirs, wrenched the door open and hopped in.

The driver said, "Where to?"

I said, "Hold on," as I twisted around to keep watching. Owen asked something. Allison agreed. I told the cabbie, "Those two. We're going to follow them."

"Oh shit. One of those," he said in a thick Arabic accent.

"Yeah, well. It'll pay well."

"It better. Fuck Uber. And the cost of medallions."

A car service town car pulled up. Owen opened the door. Allison passed beneath his umbrella and got in.

The rain kept coming.

The asphalt showed off its grit, trash rising and floating. The water showed off its glitter. Water shimmered and shuddered in puddles. Water flowed toward sewer gratings. Water splashed as tires drove through puddles. Imagine if blood was drained of its color and ran clear and took its character from all the things that it touched as it flowed through the night.

We went up Flatbush.

Junior's on the left. LIU on the right, in the building that used to be the Brooklyn Paramount, where Alan Freed staged his rock 'n' roll shows: Chuck Berry, Frankie Avalon, Jackie Wilson, Bobby Rydell, Santo & Johnny, The Elegants, The Royal Teens, Duane Eddy, The Cleftones, King Curtis, The Del Vikings.

An easy uphill slope, past the corner of Myrtle Avenue, where there used to be an el, then onto the upper level of the Manhattan Bridge. There was nothing to block the wind. It came harder, battering the windows with rain, the wipers, *whop, whop, whop*, one of them with a little whine as it dragged on the glass. It was hard to see the cars in front of us. No matter. We were on the bridge, nowhere to go but straight. Once we were off it, in a landscape ruled by traffic lights and the rules randomly and constantly disrupted by vehicles double parking, trying to make turns, and maneuvering around each other, following was going to become difficult. It was time to think. Lift the game out of mere physical reality, up into the realm of thought. Go from the movement of a machine into a construct of the mind that dictated it. An obscenely fancy way to say guess where they're going. Yet that's how the figuring felt, as if I were lifting that small part of the pattern they had already created, extending it into the pattern they were going to create, and seeing it as if it already existed, as if the car would be driven by predestination, going where it must and where I must follow.

They took that first early exit, on to Chrystie Street. They went straight and made the light where Chrystie ended, at East Houston. We did not. The cabbie turned to me. I said, "Left when we get the light. Try to catch them. If you can't, I have a bet with myself where they're going."

"I was hoping for a fare to JFK," he said.

"Bullshit, you would have been lucky to get a couple of hipsters going fifteen blocks to Bed-Stuy."

"Or even LaGuardia," he said. "Everybody wants to fly somewhere." I passed a twenty up to the front. He said, "OK."

We got the light. He pushed it as hard as a sensible man would on a rainy night in Manhattan. We spotted a big black Lincoln sedan. He did his best to catch it. We didn't quite make it.

"We'll go north on Sixth," I said.

This time we made the same light. I shoved another twenty to the front. He sped, braked, swerved, and slid between trucks, cabs, and cars. We caught up. Got parallel. I looked over, from our window into theirs. Someone completely different was inside.

"Fuck," I said.

"Not them?" the cabbie said.

"Keep going, then . . . turn on Fourteenth. Left on Fourteenth."

"Whatever you say."

I was far more certain than I should have been. I felt like I knew.

He made the left. "We're going to head uptown. Which is going to be faster, Tenth or Twelfth?"

"How far?"

"Forty-Sixth Street."

"I don't know," he said, "this time of night, this weather, either one could be a mess."

"Tenth," I said.

He said, "OK," then turned his radio to Arabic music and kept on trying to make good time.

Just after we crossed Forty-Second Street I saw another town car that could have been them. We were close. It signaled a turn on Forty-Sixth and made it. We didn't. No matter. It was either them or it wasn't and I was willing to take the bet. "Good job," I told the cabbie. The meter said $48. I gave him three more twenties.

"OK," he said with genuine enthusiasm. I grabbed my hat off the seat, pulled it down low, and pushed myself out the door.

The weather hit me in the face and pulled at my clothes. I looked down the block and saw Owen and his too big umbrella opening the back door of the Lincoln—such a gentleman—for Allison—still in her black wig—getting out. Going to his office. Which used to be mine.

I scrambled down the opposite side of the street until I got to where I could see into the building. Owen still had the round black shroud open, even indoors, partially hiding Allison.

I leaned against the bricks behind me, getting as much shelter from the storm as I could.

The security guy knew Owen. He and Allison got past him with a simple wave. Water dripped as they went toward the elevators. That annoyed the security guy. Owen didn't close the umbrella until an elevator arrived.

I pulled out my wallet. I had two nearly real law enforcement IDs in there, one federal, one state. I chose the federal and put it in the plastic window so it would show if I did a G-man ID flip. I pulled my hat down low over my eyes, dodged the traffic, and went across the street. I walked in, water dripping from the brim of my hat and falling from my coat, my shoes squeaking. The security guy said the usual and shoved the sign-in book toward me. I flashed the fake ID. I signed a fake name, put JTF next to it, and NYB for my destination.

He said, "JTF? NYB?"

I said, "Joint Task Force," as I turned toward the elevators, and, "Not Your Business," as I began to walk away. That was a clearly satisfactory answer since he said nothing further.

CHAPTER THIRTY-SIX

WALK ON GILDED SPLINTERS

"Few men get killed. Most of those who meet sudden ends, get themselves killed."

DASHIEL HAMMETT, *THE WHOSIS KID*

THE DOOR TO TOTAL CONFIDENTIALITY Investigations, Ltd. was locked.

I needed to find a way to break in. A pry bar or some such. Back in my time, the janitor often left his closet unlocked, and there were all sorts of things in there. It was down the hall, by the stair landing. I started in that direction.

Why not knock?

Was I getting caught up in some overdramatized, crazy fantasy scenario? Real people, in real circumstances, knock. Even cops should go with a simple knock on the door before they go all SWAT. I turned around. Walked back. Took the little Glock from the pocket of my sport jacket and put it my coat pocket. Just in case I wasn't overdramatizing. Then I knocked on the door.

I heard voices on the other side. His and hers. Though I couldn't make out any words.

The door opened. When Owen saw me he said, "My house," and lifted the gun that he had in his hand until it was pointing at me. "Come in."

It was a 9mm. I didn't know the brand. I knew it could kill me. The name of the manufacturer didn't make much difference. They were all sufficiently reliable that I wouldn't bet my life on a malfunction. Whichever one of them this was, it would kill me as dead as any of the others. For that matter, the fact that it was an automatic rather than a revolver and that it was a 9mm rather than a .38, a .44, or a .45 was irrelevant in the immediate context.

I accepted the invitation. He shoved the door closed behind me.

We were in the reception area. Allison appeared in the doorway between there and Owen's private office. She called my name. I said, "Hi. Good to see you. I think we should go now."

"No," Owen said. "We're going to settle things now. I'm going to get my share."

"Of what?" Allison asked.

"Has he threatened you?" I asked her.

"No," she said.

"Good," I said, "Come on."

"You're staying," Owen snapped at her.

"Let it go," I said to him. "Game's over."

"Not at all," he said.

"It is," I said. "Let's not get crazy. Yeah, you got a gun on me, but you're not going to shoot me. Or her. What would you do with the body? Or bodies? The last place we were seen alive was here. Everybody's phone says so. Mine. Hers. Yours. *And* we're signed in down below, at the desk."

"I'm not signed in," Owen said with a smirk, and Allison shook her head, no she hadn't signed in.

"Yeah, you are. The security guy signed you in. He's got to protect his job. I saw it when I signed in. *Owen Cohen and guest*, destination *TCI, Inc.* It means he recognized you, it wasn't someone pretending to be you or some shit like that," I said, making it up as I went along. As long as I was lying, I kept at it, "Then I signed in. Also going to TCI, Inc."

"You don't walk out of here until I've got my share."

"Whatever you imagine it is, do you think I have it on me?"

"You have the information on you. And so does she, and I'm going to get it out of one of you. Or both of you. I'm going to get what's mine."

"What's he talking about?" Allison said.

"Let's just get out of here," I said to her.

"I want to know," she said.

"You don't know?" Owen said. "Your murder was a multimillion-dollar enterprise. A hundred-million-dollar enterprise. This mother-fucker got a nice piece of change, what was it, Cassella? A hundred grand? Two hundred? You could've gotten more. I'm guessing . . ."

"What murder?" Allison said, her voice, for once, without confidence or bravado, guessing—knowing—what it was.

"There was no murder," I said, adamantly. "It was an accident."

"Mr. McMunchun?" Allison said, her innocent act back, nearly intact, "It was an accident." Good girl, sticking to her story. With good reason. If there was anyone to blame—besides stoned, horny McMunchun himself—it was her.

Owen sneered, "Sure it was."

"It was," she said.

"You don't know, do you?"

"Know what?"

"Miziz McMunchkin was looking for a contract on her husband."

"What?"

"This one," Owen pointed his gun at me, "took that contract. Then he used *you* to make it happen. Didn't you, Tony?"

"No. I agreed to investigate. Go ahead, Allie, tell him what I asked you to do. To just find out how he'd react to a fourteen-year-old girl. Right?"

"That's leading the witness. Excessively. Putting words in her mouth instead of a dick."

"Hey. You heard me," Allison said, sassy, talking back. "*I've swallowed the thesaurus, a lot more than semen.* I don't need anyone to put words in my mouth. That's exactly what he asked me to do. Just find out how the sleazy husband acted with underage girls. Which he did. He showed off a hot car like he was a stupid teenager and I would be impressed by it, and drove too fucking fast, and not using his seat belt so he could wave his *dick* around. It was icy rain, and he drove off the road."

"That's what the police report says," I said. "An accident. The insurance company examined the car. It was in perfect condition. They may argue that he was a DUI, but he did that to himself, and there are witnesses to it, well most of it, the drinking, and I'm sure if someone really, really cared they could show the coke was his coke, too."

Owen said, "I don't believe it." But he was starting to.

"We've known each other a long time. I'm not going to claim we're best friends, but we've done business. Was I ever anything but square with you? Did I ever cheat you? Lie to you? If there was ever something I didn't want to tell you, I just said none of your business. Owen, we're two old men, we're too old for this shit."

I'd talked him down. He had to throw in one last threat, "I'm gonna keep watching," he said. "If I ever find out . . ." but he was starting to put his gun back in his belt holster and we were going to walk out.

My phone made one of its many irritating sound effects. Owen's Full Alert Switch snapped back to the On position. His gun swung back up, pointing at me. "Gimme! Gimme!" he said. I took my phone out of my pocket and handed it to him. Slowly. It was a text.

He looked at who it was from. Something bad was happening.

He tapped it. To read what it said. Something even worse.

CHAPTER THIRTY-SEVEN

DANSE MACABRE

Ziggety, zig, zig, zig, Death got a beat
tapping the tomb with both his feet;
Death plays his tunes of ruin and sin

Ziggety, zig, on his violin.
The night is dark, winter winds freeze,
groaning and moaning, through barren trees.
White bones run through the shadowy gloom
dressed in nothing but the shrouds of doom.

Ziggety, zig, zig, zig, struts and shakes
bones banging like the rattles on snakes.
Lecherous skeletons try to do again,
what they did when they had a skin.

HENRI CAZALIS, *DANSE MACABRE*
(TRANS. BEINHART)

OWEN SAID, "I'M IN TOO deep," and herded us into his inner office.

Allison had her handbag. She held it like a nervous grandmother riding in the passenger seat, clutching it to her bosom with both hands.

Keeping his eyes and his gun on me, Owen tried to knock her down. She just backed away from his shove. All that happened was she staggered a little. Angry, he grabbed her by the hair, forgetting, or not knowing, that it was a wig. It came off in his hand and she was a blonde again. I thought he was going to shoot out of pure frustration. His eyes went back and forth, back and forth, like Christmas lights going on and off, on and off. "Too deep," he mumbled, half a sob. He backhanded her. She managed to lessen the force of the blow by backing away again. Even so, twenty, thirty years ago, he would have knocked her into the wall. We were getting old.

She still clutched her bag.

Frustrated by the girl, and even more by his own weakness, Owen pulled the trigger.

A shot in an enclosed space is loud. Go to the range. Take one shot without ear protection. It'll be a quarter hour before you carry on a conversation normally. It wasn't at anybody. Just at the wall.

We all froze.

"You," he barked at Allie, "down on the ground."

She moved slowly to her knees.

Owen went to his desk. Pulled open a drawer. Took out a glass bottle. He unscrewed the top. Awkwardly because his right hand still held the gun. When the lid was off, he just dropped it. He held the bottle up for all to see. "Acid," he said. He looked around the room. He spotted the wig that had tricked and embarrassed him. Keeping the gun moving between the two of us, but mostly at me, he walked over to the limp wad of fake hair and splashed some of the liquid on it. It sizzled and stank as the acid ate through it. It scared the hell out of me and I assume Allie felt the same.

"You. Bitch. Lie down."

She didn't move.

"Owen, come on, come on," I said. "You don't want to . . . this isn't you."

"I'm in too deep. Too deep. One of you, or the two of you, are going to say it and I'm going to record it, how you killed the motherfucker, and how much money you made from it. Either she'll talk because she doesn't want to be a scarred lab specimen for the rest of her life, or you'll talk to protect her, or she'll talk after I start shooting you. You," he said at Allison again, "you little whore," pronouncing it *who-er* like they did in the neighborhoods when we were young. "Do it! Lie down. You'll be much happier if I start at your feet instead of your face."

Whimpering, fearful, she lay on her back, looking up. Still clutching her handbag.

Owen walked around her. I started to say something, to talk him down. "Shut up," he yelled. He stopped. Standing over her. By her feet. He poured. Not a lot. Just enough. On to her shoes. It began to eat through the leather or whatever they were made of. Allison shrieked and started to kick her shoes off.

I yelled, "Stop it, motherfucker!"

Owen turned to look at me. A thin-lipped smirk. Uneven, a diagonal line cutting across the lower part of his face. Intense eyes. Two steps over the sanity line. As his focus moved toward me, his whole head turned. Allison's hand went into her bag. It came out with a revolver. A small one. A tiny thing. She shot. It hit Owen.

Surprised, like he'd been punched by a ghost, he turned back to her, acid in one hand, 9mm in the other.

It gave me time to pull Liz's hot pink and black Glock from my pocket and shoot. It hit him on the side somewhere. There was more surprise. But he was still alive. Still standing. Still holding a weapon in his hand. I shot again. Then two more. *Womp, womp,* into his body. He fell backward against his desk, then slid, his back against it, alive or dead or nearly dead, I couldn't say, but without enough strength left to lift his hands. The bottle of acid fell from his fingers, spilling on the carpet, cooking it and stinking. He kept hold of the gun, but the hand that clutched it went down to the floor. It twitched, but it couldn't rise.

Allison rose to her feet. She let go of the handbag. She held her little revolver in her right hand, steadied it with her left. It was a .22. She stepped forward, until she was standing right over Owen, one foot between his sprawled legs, the other outside his left leg. Then she fired. The bullet went in his left eye, through his brain, and bounced around the back of his skull.

CHAPTER THIRTY-EIGHT
NOW AND ZEN

"One day, death will come. Before
it knocks you down, have a good laugh . . ."

OSHO: Never born, never died.
Only visited this Planet Earth
between December 11, 1931 and
January 19, 1990

ALLISON SAID, "WE SHOULD CALL the police." But her tone made
it a question.

"Seven minutes," I said.

"What?"

I sat down. I was tired. "I told him," I said, meaning Owen, "right
at the start, that I was too old for this shit."

"What's seven minutes? What does that mean?"

I took off my hat. Kept my coat on. Put the hat in my lap. I closed
my eyes.

"Are you going to sleep?"

"No," I said. "But if I start to snore you can wake me."

"I'm going to call them. It was self-defense. He shot first. He was
going to burn me. Look at my shoe and my wig. That proves it."

"Wait. Be quiet. Four minutes, is that OK? Quiet for four minutes. Sit if you want. Don't touch anything new." I made it as close to
an order as I could. "Do it!"

Quiet. Like a dream. Was four minutes enough? That was not the question. Nor the need. The need was to erase as much static as possible. Reduce things to their key elements. Then see how those items might march into the future along their diverging paths, drawing the multiplying paths as a child draws a tree, this branch takes us there, that branch the other way, each splits, and splits again. Where would actual futures actually go? Like a dream. A meditation. No path was absolutely perfect or foolproof. All had hazards. Nor was anything entirely up to us. The future had its own life. We would move. It would move. In concord or in conflict. In both.

"Well," she said.

"Was I snoring?"

"No," she said.

I didn't respond.

She squirmed and complained, "Just sitting here is crazy."

"Mind is like a mad monkey. Moving fast is crazier."

"Are we having a Zen moment?"

"I live in Woodstock," I said. "We have a lot of them. Most of our Buddhists started as Jews. We call them Jew-Boos. I prefer to call them Zen Cohens," I said, looking down at Owen Cohen. We both started to laugh.

Back when I was in junior high in Brooklyn, I used to go to Junior's, the restaurant, with my two best friends, and the three of us would order a banana split. This was way back when there were only four flavors of ice cream, ice cream sundaes were the ultimate extravagance, and the biggest and most excessive manifestation of that form was the banana split. Each of us would try to make the others laugh. Two of us would always dissolve into that hysterical laughter that makes it impossible to do anything but giggle, chortle, and cackle, while he who did not laugh, would sit there calmly devouring the remaining ice cream, whipped cream, fruit, nuts, and chocolate syrup.

It was that kind of laughter. Uncontrollable. Beyond reason. A release unrelated to the joke that launched it. It went on for a long time. It stopped several times as each of us tried to get our breath back, then started again, several times.

When the laughter ceased enough that we could speak, I said, "It's at least seven minutes. The answer is, we don't call the police."

"Because?"

"If someone had heard the shooting and called the police, they'd be here now. At the very least, we'd hear the sirens, and even with the blinds down like they are, we'd see the lights flashing."

"You're sure? So soon?"

"Yeah. Cops are excitement junkies in a job that's mostly boring and tedious. A report of shots fired in Midtown Manhattan, half the cars in the borough would be roaring here. If they were, it would be a good idea to have called them ourselves. It's what innocent people would be presumed to do. We could claim self-defense like you said and having called them would help. The problem is explaining why we're here . . ."

"I have an explanation . . ." she said, sounding sure that the obvious explanation, given her profession, would cover the matter.

"Why am I here? Am I your pimp? Protector? Your father? Come on. The two of us here and then, maybe, probably, someone puts together that we two, both of us, were also there when McMunchun died. You were in the car with him. This time, your hand was on the gun. The fact that the cops aren't here yet, makes me think that the building is empty or mostly empty, nobody heard . . ."

"What about the security, downstairs . . ."

"You had a black wig on. You were half hidden by Cohen's umbrella. I had my hat down over my eyes . . ."

"The signing in?"

"The guard didn't sign you guys in. I didn't use my real name."

"What do we do?"

"My guess is that maintenance, the cleaning crew, comes in around three, that's how it used to be. We have at least an hour, hour and a half. What we do, is sort of empty your mind, go to the front door, then slowly go through each step you took. Take the bag out of the garbage bin there, anything you see that might connect to you, put it in there. Any place you touched with your hands, muss it up. I'll do the same. We take his phone, too. I'm guessing that Owen has other clothes around. We change our clothes as much as we can. Whatever works to make us look different than the way we came in. He'll have a gym bag, maybe even a suitcase for rush travel, we put our stuff in that. We also take a bunch of his files, his laptop, any backup device or extra hard drives. Make a mess. Like someone was after him about one of his cases. Now the cops have to track down all those different things."

"Alright. That all makes sense."

"Then we walk out the side entrance, the one they use for trash and such."

"But what about my shoes?" she said, looking at the one that the acid had burned through.

"Duct tape," I said. "I bet we can find some duct tape."

CHAPTER THIRTY-NINE

THE ABYSS

"WHEN YOU FIGHT WITH MONSTERS, beware that you do not become the monster. When you stare into the Abyss, the Abyss is staring back at you."

What the hell was I doing, listening to Nietzsche? Not to the man himself or to books on tape. From my own mind. I had been told by a god, personally told by a *god*, that "Nietzsche was a humbug asshole." OK, it was an archaic, minor deity disguised as a large oak tree in the forest near my own house, and common sense suggests it was me talking to myself, but what spoken message from a divine source, minor or Most Major, isn't? The "monster," in this case, for a fair definition, would be a contract killer. Murderer for hire. Assassin. Hit man. Clipper. Ice Man. *Sicario. Gatillero.*

I was so far in, there seemed to be no way back. I could find no sound advice to give myself. I could not come up with some sound plan of my own. I therefore took Elizabeth's, even though I disliked her, distrusted her, and was certain she was a sociopath.

———

On Monday, I made some handwritten changes to Elizabeth's contract, initialed them, then signed and dated it where indicated, then went to her offices. They were humming. Workers busy as bees. Walls going up, doors being hung. Painters painting. Furniture coming in. Oh, joy.

I gave her the contract. She looked. She noticed the changes, read them, and looked perturbed.

The first kicked the signing bonus up to $400,000.

The second was to indemnify myself and my associates (to be named later) for all legal expenses incurred on behalf of LIFE, Inc., its principals, its primary investors (defined as over $1 million), its clients, by The Company (as named in the contract), and, should The Company be dissolved or cease to exist, that liability would be incurred by its successors, should there be any, and if not, by its principals.

"I can't do this," she said.

"Which part?"

"Both."

"You had a problem. A big problem."

"Which? What?"

"Cohen."

"Well . . ."

"Your problem. Your screw up. Your disaster, waiting and eager to happen."

"Are you going to fix it?"

"It's fixed," I said.

She looked blank.

"You read the *Times*. And *The Wall Street Journal*. You don't read the *Post*. I bet you watch MSNBC . . ." Oh, the sneer that prompted. ". . . or Fox? You're a Fox News person. I should have known. Anyway, you don't watch New York 1." She still looked blank. "Mr. Cohen died late Saturday night, early Sunday morning."

It seemed as if she was about to say, "Thank God," or at least, "Oh, good," but she didn't. She left that alone. For the moment. Instead she switched to a mental calculation as to whether $200,000 was the right price for what was, ostensibly, the second hit. Since that had been roughly the price of the first, it damn well should be. She accepted that. She went to the next item.

"This other thing is ridiculous."

"No. It's not. We both know, top lawyers are over a thousand an hour. Experts, research, all the horseshit, ain't no justice anymore, money is how we mostly keep score. Something goes off the rails, or even looks like it might cause stress, we both want the kind of lawyer that can drop in on the DA and not have to mention how much he contributed to the DA's campaign fund, since they both know the amount down to the dime—and oh, the power of words unspoken—and the DA can decide it's not enough to go to trial on, and he pushes it away like he did for the Trump kids and Weinstein and Epstein. We know of those, only because other factors pulled them out of obscurity and made them famous, but I'd guess there are plenty more. Read your own giant posters."

"To make a commitment . . ."

I leaned in close and whispered, "Do we need to do it this way? Do you want to know how fucked you are before you sign it?"

She didn't say anything but she did need it laid out. Because that's who she was. Short term, it was a game. Long term, would one of us have to destroy the other?

I explained it, starting nice and reasonable, casual and conversational. "I'm pretty sure that there's no evidence at the scene that definitely connects to anyone. Nothing that can't be explained away or accounted for." Then to the point: "Except for one thing. There are bullets. A couple in his body and one or two that probably passed through. Which the police now have as evidence. They need a gun to match them to. It could turn out to be yours. The pink and black one. If they had the cartridges, the cartridges would have your prints on them. They don't have them, but they could have them."

"I want the gun back," she said. Who wouldn't?

"Forget it."

"I insist."

"Not negotiable. Don't even try."

She let that stand. For now. She switched, "Who are these associates? It can't be unlimited."

Not a bad question. Allison might be on. Or maybe that was terribly wrong. The way things were going, there might be another. Not more than that. I hoped. "Two," I said. "You can make it no more than two."

"Is one of them that girl?"

"I'll let you know names when appropriate."

"If it is, she could well be what we're looking for."

I had to admit, Elizabeth was, in her own sociopathic way, truly amazing. No matter the danger or difficulties, her only urge was to lunge forward to devour more and more of what was ahead of her. Shark is the popular image.

"Well, wouldn't she be?"

She was possibly correct. Would Allison want to be among the mad?

Maybe it was just the names, Alice and Allison, that prompted my own voice from impossibly long ago, reading to my children—oh my, how I'd loved them—in that way of speaking you use with kids, with bits of character acting thrown in—reading *Alice in Wonderland*.

Allison had gone down the rabbit hole. No, no, no. It was Alice who had. When she'd met the Cheshire Cat, she told him, "I don't want to be among mad people."

"Oh, you can't help that," said the Cat, "we're all mad here. I'm mad. You're mad."

"How do you know I'm mad?" said Alice.

"You must be," said the Cat, "or you wouldn't have come here."

I had to agree with the diagnosis. This Allison was mad—I don't know if that was clinically accurate—but close enough. Her road ahead had a three-way fork. One would take her to incarceration. One would require serious change, therapy, and medication to become someone she was not. The third was to plunge down the rabbit hole with the hope that she'd land in a world quite as mad as she was. It was clear that the last was her choice. Did I want to be the one to take her there? Had I already done so? With nothing left to do but sit up in a tree, looking down to see what I'd done, as I slowly disappeared, leaving nothing but a grin.

I wasn't going to deal with who was mad and who was responsible. Not at that moment. I needed to deal with something tangible. With that which is fungible.

Pull my mind out of my mind, put it in the present. Reality? Of sorts. Snapped it back, aimed at Elizabeth, "The money. Now. You have an hour."

"All four hundred?"

"Fuck yes. Plus there'll be a bill for expenses."

"How much?"

"Under . . ." I was going to say ten, but then I said, ". . . twenty. We'll do it later, I'm just letting you know."

"Alright."

"Good."

"And you'll go to Austria?"

I went to the window. Like I was thinking about it. I looked out. There was the fucking Mormon.

Yesterday, I'd had the opportunity to ask him if he was one but failed to do so. That had been Sunday—shouldn't Mormons have a thing about not working on Sunday?—he'd come up to my house. Wanting to talk to me. Allison had stayed inside. It felt like he knew she was there. He asked if I'd been to the city. I said, "You know why I live up here? End of a dirt road. You can barely make it up here in that sedan, I heard you skidding and slipping for the last fifteen minutes, and that's after Marcel came and plowed."

"Well, it is pretty country," he said. "Though a little bleak."

"It's winter. It should be bleak." I wanted him gone, before he learned any tidbits of use. I made it clear. "I'm here because I like to be alone. Because nobody comes up that road. I don't particularly like to talk to people. Especially about things that're nobody's business but my own."

"Sorry. I didn't mean to intrude."

"Goodbye, then. Be careful heading down the hill."

Here we were. One day later. Monday. There he was, down there, in trendy Brooklyn. With an ugly puffy parka and a wool hat that looked like he'd purchased it within the hour from a Nigerian side-walk peddler. Also, strolling along, and being reasonably subtle about it, with her face mostly covered by a funny furry hat, a wooly scarf, and wearing a peacoat, was Allison, keeping an eye on him. He didn't seem to take notice of her. Maybe she was good at these things. More important, I was sure that there was no way the Mormon could have tailed me. I'd ducked and dodged enough to be sure of it. But there he was, looking very certain. How?

It had been my intention, at least my first-choice inclination, to take Elizabeth's money and say, "so long, it's been good to know you." There was certainly enough of it. But it might be a good idea to disappear for a while. Weeks. Not years, like the last time. Just out of range of casual inquiries. Give things time to settle and reveal themselves.

I wanted that to be a workable resolution. But that was desire.

I turned back from the window.

"If I do," I said to her—hedging the bet, altering, at least blurring, the game—"I will go and look. I will endeavor to find a way to get your client safely away from her husband with her son. In such a way that they will be safe and you will be able to secure her an excellent settlement. That's what I can commit to, as your chief investigator."

"Of course," she said. "I would never ask for anything more."

"I'll let you know once I've received the money. And you should give me my Black Amex Card."

"It will probably take a couple of days for that. But if you leave before it arrives, just give me an address. They're wonderful about delivering such things."

"As they should be," I said.

She returned to the contract. She scrawled a note on my note that limited the additional indemnified associates to two. She initialed my changes and her own. She passed it back to me to initial her changes, which I did. She took out her copy. We made the changes there as well. Now we each had originals.

"The young woman," she asked, "is she going with you?"

"If I go," I said, "I'll need two of those Amex cards. In two different names. The other one is Victor Vasquez."

CHAPTER FORTY

TRIBUTE, OF SORTS

TRAVEL / Spring skiing: Bloodied but unbowed
on a knife-edge in the sky.

DOUG SAGER, *THE INDEPENDENT,*
March 21, 1993

I OFFER AN OBSCURE METAPHOR. It's from Doug Sager.

Doug taught me to ski off-piste and in the backcountry. Once, using his own word, he'd been a "real" journalist, in Egypt for CBS, when Sadat signed the peace deal with Begin. Then, somehow, he never said why, he'd wandered off to Verbier, Switzerland, and became a ski journalist. He skied all the most dramatic and dangerous locations in Europe. In his late sixties he returned to the U.S. In April 2019, on a bicycle ride in Lancaster, Pennsylvania, he got hit from behind by a car. He died there, age seventy.

The only meaning in that is meaninglessness. A morsel tainted with asphalt to toss to the nihilists coming up behind us.

Doug taught me, "Never take off your skis in the mountains."

Off-piste you get to places that scare you. Slopes that look far too steep for your skills, windblown slabs that look like they'll break, rotten snow that feels like it will slide, and if the weather comes in when you're above the tree line you can't even tell if you're moving or standing still. Your every instinct, your whole life's experience, begins to cry and tell you you'd be better off to kick off those boards and get back to your feet. But you'd be wrong. Your skis are the only thing that would get you out of there alive.

It seemed to me—I knew for a fact—it was obvious beyond dispute—that I'd left the marked routes—trails, pistes, whatever you'd like to call them—and wandered off into the wilds of the mountain range called murder—lo, I walk—slide—through the valley of the shadow of death—and I do fear evil.

If there was logic to it, it went like this.

Like the weather, like the winter, like the snows, what was happening would not stop. Elizabeth would not stop. If I walked off, trudging thigh deep to I know not where, she'd find someone else. Odds on, someone less able, or less lucky, or less careful, than I had been. Even if they were good, the best of the worst as it were, cunning and sharp, as well trained as a mythical ninja, Elizabeth and Madelaine were amateurs, impulsive, greedy, prone to—guaranteed to—make mistakes. They were not organized crime with some code of omertà. Once they were in a cell with cops questioning them, they'd fold. They'd compete to be the quickest to blame others, and the odds were that my name would appear in that short chain of laying it off on someone else.

True or false, right or wrong, the thing inside me said that it would go better to stay with it—or rather, if I did the sensible thing, walk away and leave it to others, it would go worse, far worse.

There I was, where I'd taken myself, back of the beyond—stuck in a fucking metaphor that included crevasses and avalanches—and the only advice that seemed pertinent was from an old friend killed on a bicycle ride, "Never take off your skis in the mountains."

CHAPTER FORTY-ONE
GOD IN THE NIGHT—LECH

"Buyers would struggle to find a more exclusive resort
than Lech in the Vorarlberg province
of Austria . . . reliable snow, vast network of pistes,
stunning scenery and impeccable style."

FINANCIAL TIMES

WE ARE SITTING OUTSIDE IN the night. Just the two of us, God and I.

When you think about it, being one-on-one with this God, Grigor God Voloshin, was infinitely more unique than being with the traditional God, the one called Jehovah, Yahweh, King of Kings, Lord of Hosts, Elohim, the Supreme Being. Everyone does that, praying to Him—"Please cancel the test I didn't study for"—"Don't let the Customs Man search my bags"—"Let me meet that special her"—"Tell me I didn't catch an STD from the angel you helped me meet"—"Find me a parking space"—and bargaining with Him—"I'll pray a lot," "go to church," "tithe," "never do it again," "be really, really good," and "never ask for another thing, ever." A fair number of people will even hear Him—or an important representative, Jesus, Mary, one of the saints—talking back.

There are only ninety-six Russian billionaires. According to Wikipedia, which, like the U.S. government, got their list from *Forbes*. They travel to exclusive places, stay in special residences, have entourages around them, intermediaries and security to block access, they're much harder to get to.

We are in God's hot tub. Behind God's chalet. A chalet sitting splendidly alone on a hill above Lech.

Lech was once a tiny, rural huddle in the high mountains in the western tip of Austria, inaccessible in winter, barely accessible even in the mild seasons, and a family with seven cows were the rich folks. A river runs through it. The church was built in 1390, as a best guess. It is now a luxury ski resort. It's still small. Population, about 1,700. It has retained its "character" as these things go. All the buildings are wood and stone. They all have pitched roofs. There are no high-rises. The tallest is five and a half stories high, the half being the space under the inverted V of the roof. It's in a region called the Vorarlberg, which means in front of the Arlberg. There is no border, no distinction, absolutely no way to discern a difference between the two regions unless you're a native and your ancestry goes back several centuries. It's part of a giant ski region that crosses back and forth over that indecipherable border and connects to seven other towns, Oberlech, Zürs, Warth, Schröcken, Stuben, and St. Christoph, with populations between forty and a few hundred, and St. Anton, the biggest and best known of the lot, with a population of 2,700.

It is an unusual night.

Even in the coldest months, January and February, the temperature in the region stays between a very comfortable 35° and 26° Fahrenheit. In this age of excitable weather, a strange freezing finger had come down from the Arctic. It was about 5° below zero. Minus 20.5 Celsius.

Snow is falling. The colder it is, the lighter and finer the flakes. This is fine stuff indeed. Baccarat crystal. Comparable to the best of high Rocky Mountains powder. The flakes are invisible in the dark, but when they're touched by light, it's a slow falling glitter of white incandescence.

It is a promise that tomorrow's skiing will be as good as it can get.

Of course, from time to time, not very often, but it does happen, depending on how much new snow there is, how it binds with what's beneath it, how steep the slope is, even on whether a skier or snow-boarder enters into a section and how they do so, it breaks and slides and if the people caught in it are unlucky, the snow kills. From time to time. Not very often.

It is as perfect a night, as perfect a moment, as anyone could wish for.

Snow is piled loose and ankle-deep all around us. God has a bot-tle of vodka and two glasses plunked down in it to chill. He has cigars, too. In a box to keep them dry. He has a lighter of precious metal that he said had been gifted to him by Putin himself. There are assorted recreational drugs in the box as well, pills and powder. Billionaires are often great hosts. God is drinking. He is urging me to drink. I know he could drink me under any given table, drink me underneath the warm bubbling water for that matter, leaving me to sleepily drown. I mime it as best I can, spilling when I have the chance, holding shots in my mouth without swallowing and spitting it out when his head is turned, to be stirred away by the bubbling water.

Elizabeth wants me to kill God.

If I do, will Nietzsche suddenly appear like an old-fashioned Russian icon, a flat halo of gold leaf around the outside of his head and spirochetes of syphilis filling up the inside of it?

What I want is to merely slip his wife, Kaylee, along with their son, Leo, out from under his ponderous embrace and away from his watchful eye and scurry them safely off to the States. From whence she could sue for some hundreds of millions, more than enough to keep her and her son in style, and satiate even Elizabeth's greed. Temporarily.

God, of course, has his own aims and goals.

No matter. It is as perfect a moment as I, or even you, could wish for. Unless you knew what happened immediately before and immediately after.

CHAPTER FORTY-TWO

TRANSATLANTIC FLIGHT OR FIGHT

ON THE WAY TO AUSTRIA.

We sat beside each other. Allison and me. In relative luxury. Not maximum luxury. That would have been a private jet. Not even great luxury, which would have been First Class. Relative luxury. Business class. New York to Zurich. Nonstop.

Why did I bring her with me?

I didn't have a plan that required a young woman. I was going to improvise. I could say that another person expanded the options. Or that I was worried about leaving her alone back in New York, to do something foolish, or get caught in some random twists of the thread of her fate, tangled with mine. That since she'd helped me solve a problem, she deserved a reward, the sort of thing the salesperson of the year might receive, a holiday at a posh resort.

A more—accurate?—honest?—best?—explanation was that it was a relationship.

We'd saved each other. We'd killed together. That should make people close.

Before that. In New York.

After we killed Owen Cohen, cleaned up the scene, and went out the freight entrance, we walked two blocks before we tried for a cab. She wanted to use her Uber app. I said, "No, that's an e-track—is that a word yet?—with your name on it.

"Cabs and cash are anonymous. It's all analog. Human, vague, confusing, and time consuming." It was still raining. Making it a typical bitch of a New York night to catch a cab, even as late as it was, and it took another fifteen or twenty minutes, trudging to Forty-Second Street and Eighth Avenue, water squishing in our shoes, especially hers with the duct tape wrappings—we'd done both to make them look more uniform—and I wish we'd kept them as art pieces since that banana duct-taped to a wall went for $120,000. Even though I hate umbrellas, I'd taken Owen's batwing version to mask our faces and create the type of image that misdirects memories. I could imagine a witness, "Uh, it was, uh, like a walking black dome with four legs, I didn't see no faces, that's what I remember, a moving black dome, four legs."

We didn't catch a cab until the lineup in front of Port Authority. More misdirection. If the driver remembered us at all, it would be as people who'd come in on a bus from New Jersey or upstate or some other distant realm. The cab was a Toyota sedan, neither too old, nor too new. The driver was a Haitian, Johnny-Wolf Juste.

As we headed downtown, Allie asked, "What happened? It seemed like it was all under control, then, what?"

Johnny-Wolf Juste had some Haitian music on. A Caribbean sound, the lyrics more incomprehensible than reggae and its heirs, since it was in an actual other language. I encouraged him to turn it up. He was pleased to do so.

"A ghost," I explained to Allie. "A text from a dead man. Winston Walker, who'd been Owen's partner.

"It was actually Winston's wife using Winston's phone. Owen would have figured it out quick enough. Wouldn't have made a difference. Maybe he did. He probably did. Then the text. It was a map of Winston's last half hour or so. He was at the office. Where we just were. It shows that he walks to his car. Stops on the street. Briefly. Walks faster. Into the garage. Where he was killed.

"They're the lines in a coloring book. It tells you what you should fill in.

"If you're the cops, you go to Owen's phone, if it tracked him and the track matches Winston's, you have them both moving to the place where Winston died and arriving at the same moment. If Owen's phone didn't track him, Winston's still gives you exact times and places. That narrows the window and it makes it far more likely you'll find witnesses.

"After you color it in, you visualize Owen and Winston together in the office. They argue. Winston leaves. Owen stays, then goes after him. That's a guess. Catches up with him. Winston stands still. I expect they were continuing the argument. Standing in the street. Then Winston tells him to fuck off and heads for his car. He's walking faster, like angry people do. Owen watches him. Fuming. Coming to a boil. Goes after him again. He would've known Winston was going to the parking garage, because that was the normal thing. Finds him there. There's whatever, whatever, back and forth, it ends up Owen shoots him.

"Owen knew that once I saw it, I'd figure it out. So would the cops."

Allison said, "I want to do what you do."

"What do you think I do?"

"Rescue girls and kill bad guys."

"That makes it sound like a bad TV show. An old one. In the new ones, girls kill bad guys and rescue boys. And they do a lot of karate. In spike heels, too."

"I can do that."

"The spike heels?"

"I can walk in them," she said.

"Kicks and stuff?"

"No."

"Karate? Kung fu? Tae kwon do?"

"None of them," she said. "Can you?"

"No."

"Can you even walk in spike heels?"

"I don't think so."

"There you go. I'm one up on you already. But there's one thing I need to know."

"What's that?"

"Does it make good money?"

"You called me and said you were worried because someone was maybe following you. I came all the way to Brooklyn."

"That's the place to be now."

"And it was late. I knew it would keep me up past my bedtime. Am I charging you?"

She gave me a quick look, sharp and wary, was I? If I was, how much, did she have it, could she negotiate it down?

"Don't worry," I said.

She relaxed.

"There's your answer," I said. "About making good money."

"It should," she said.

"You're right."

"But not by charging me. Though you really should get yourself organized so it makes good money."

"Like poetry," I replied.

"Verse, verse."

"What's the difference?"

"Poetry is so deadly serious it arrives in a hearse. What could be sadder, what could be worse? If I were judgmental, I'd call it perverse. I want rhythm and rhyme, pointed and terse, and so, my friend, I end up with verse."

I didn't laugh. Neither did she. But I smiled. She did, too, softly, sadly, perhaps.

"Can I stay with you?" she asked. When I didn't answer right away, she said, "Tonight . . . just . . . I don't want to be alone . . . just for a bit."

I said, "Of course."

She leaned into me. Like a girl. A child. Maybe like a woman. I put my arm around her. Reflex. Because that's where it fits when someone—a child or a woman—leans against you. I had a beautiful, young woman pressing her body against my side, molded there as bodies do in important moments. She aches just like a woman, but this one doesn't break like a little girl. I knew I had feelings. I let them exist. Not so much in me as suspended in space around me, as if I were a cartoon character and I put my feelings into thought bubbles. So there they were, contained and restrained inside their lines, one up against the ceiling of the cab—*she constantly surprises me, the surprises delight me*—one bumping up against my window—*this is very like having feelings*—another over in that space that she'd left empty—*I like her here beside me*—when she leans into me.

We got to Brooklyn. We found my car.

"Do you have a license?" I asked her.

"Yes," she said.

I was tired. "You drive," I said, and handed her the keys.

I watched for a little bit. She drove well enough. I told her not to listen to the talking map in her phone. Just go straight up Flatbush to the Manhattan Bridge. That would take her right onto Canal Street. Go straight to the West Side Drive, up to the George Washington Bridge, then Palisades Parkway to Exit 9W, not *Route* 9W, to the thruway, to Exit 19.

It being after three in the morning, the traffic was light going over the Manhattan Bridge, allowing mental space for rumination. "I don't want to be a whore anymore," she said. "I don't have a problem with it. About how I think of myself. But so many other people do and you can't wear a condom against aspersion. Do people disapprove of what you do?"

"Sure," I said.

"But not like that," she said.

I made a noncommittal noise.

"Then there's the age thing. It's one thing to be a young courtesan, it's another to be an old whore. That's a reality that I recognize. In what you do, is there ageism? I don't think so, and if there is, it's not like that. You see what I mean, don't you? I think I should make a change. I think I would like to do what you do."

It seemed nice that someone thought well of what I did.

"I want to do what you do," she said again, then added, quite thoughtfully, "if it makes good money."

Kids today. I was very tired. "Drive carefully," I said, and fell asleep.

On the way to Austria.

On the flight, I had a stack of reading. Russian oligarchs, *Vory*, the Russian Mafiya, the FSB, successor to the KGB, all reputed to be in orbit around Putin, a soft-core, non-Commie Stalin, autocrat for a country that was never without one.

My name, at this point, was Victor Vasquez.

When I returned to the States in 1990, there was a strong possibility that things might turn out for the worse. I thought it wise, like the playwright Bertolt Brecht, to have an alternate passport. He lived in East Berlin, as the showcase artist of Communism, but kept Austrian papers. Also a Swiss bank account. For my purposes, I thought a different name would suffice. We were staying on West 123rd Street, just off of Broadway. I got friendly with owner of the bodega down the block. Our conversation turned to travel. He had no interest whatsoever in leaving America. Did he have a passport? No need, he declared. He looked a bit like me. Enough that in a small, black-and-white, slightly smudged photo we might pass for each other. Who looks that closely anyway? I did the paperwork. He got the passport. He handed it to me. I handed him $1,250, which was a lot at the time.

It was good for ten years. Every nine, I renewed it, the old one serving as proof of identity, slipping in photos of myself. This trip seemed the right time to bring it out. If, afterward, the *Vory* or the FSB or someone came looking, let them search for Victor Vasquez, a name so common that Wikipedia will take you to a singer, a comedian, at least two professional soccer players, a rapper, to the DEA agent who took down El Chapo, to characters in the TV series *The Walking Dead*, and to the superhero movie *Shazam*, but not to my guy who retired many years ago to Vieques. To prevent cognitive dissonance when I needed to present ID at a point of purchase and to avoid leaving financial footprints with my real name, I had Elizabeth get Victor his own company credit card.

She had given me a packet of information on Russian divorces and told me it was must-read material.

Elena Rybolovleva won four billion dollars. From Dmitry Rybolovlev. It was the biggest divorce award in history in the whole world. Although they were Russian, the suit had been in Switzerland. Then another Swiss court knocked it down to a mere $400 million.

The message was that you can't trust the courts when it comes to divorce. It was ultimately settled in private for an undisclosed amount. The process took seven years. A painfully long time if you were investing in the litigation.

Tatiana Akhmedova got her divorce from Farkhan Akhmedov in the U.K. The court said she should have £453 million, about $600 million. But Farkhan didn't give it to her. She managed to have his yacht, said to be worth $500 million, seized in Dubai. But the Dubaites changed their mind. They let the yacht go, even though Tatiana had yet to extract a dirham, a pound, or a dollar, from Farkhan.

The Panama Papers revealed that a firm called Mossack Fonseca had moved assets through shell companies and offshore banks, hither, yon, and elsewhere, mostly to avoid taxes, but also to hide money from spouses and their attorneys. They were said to have been the fourth-largest purveyor of offshore financial services. Meaning there were three bigger ones and an unknown number of smaller ones, all busier than burrowing rodents, making millions, tens of millions, hundreds of millions, even billions, disappear beneath the ground. It was not enough to win a settlement. The money still had to be found. Then seized. You could see where it could drive someone in the divorce industry to murderous frustration and come to believe that inheritance was a much more efficient solution.

Allison, meanwhile, was reading Nadya Tolokonnikova, *Read & Riot: A Pussy Riot Guide to Activism*. It was much more fun. It was downright inspiring. From time to time, she insisted on reading bits to me.

"I had become lifeless and apathetic. My spirit was broken." That was when Nadya was in prison. "I was obedient because of the endless abuse, trauma, and psychological pressure. I thought, What can I do against this totalitarian machine . . ." But someone gave her *The Power of the Powerless* by Václav Havel, who had been sentenced to five years in prison for political acts, and then, after the fall of the Soviet system, emerged to became president of Czechoslovakia. "I read it, hiding it from the prison officers. Then, tears of joy. And the tears brought my confidence back. We're not broken until we allow ourselves to be broken. Tears brought my courage back."

"I was there," I told Allison. "Not with Nadya. In the time of Václav Havel. Prague. January 1990.

"The Berlin Wall had come down. All the countries in Eastern Europe were declaring themselves free. A crowd had gathered in Wenceslas Square. It isn't a square. It's more like a boulevard, like Park Avenue, but shorter, about half a mile long, and the center portion is much wider, about two hundred feet. There was a demonstration in memory of a student who had burned himself to death, there, in the square, back in 1968, to protest the Russians coming in with tanks to crush the Prague Spring. It was also because Václav Havel had become the new president. He'd just been in Washington to address the U.S. Congress . . . back when that was still a good thing . . . he was in Prague . . . on his way to Moscow, to tell the Russians to pull their troops out. There were TV sets in the shop windows and they were playing videos of the old Communist leaders. I say old, but they'd been running the place just three or four months earlier and they were feared because they had their secret police and political prisons. But now people were standing outside those store windows, watching reruns of those guys giving speeches, and laughing.

"Wenceslas Square was full. A hundred thousand people, maybe two hundred thousand. They were singing. It was in Czech, but I kept thinking, I know this song, I know this song. Then I realized, it was 'We Shall Overcome.'

"It was a time of hope," I said, trying to convey some of what I'd felt. "Such as I'd never seen before. That I've never seen since.

"I hope that once in your lifetime, you get to see such a time."

CHAPTER FORTY-THREE

HEAVEN

"Heaven goes by favor. If it went by merit, you would
stay out and your dog would go in."

MARK TWAIN

THE WEATHER WAS GOOD. THE snow was good. The sun shone and
reflected back from the mountains, roofs, and byways, all covered in
white. The lift system was extensive, well-maintained, and very reliable. The skiing was good. The hotel was excellent. Four stars. All necessary amenities and many unnecessary ones. When I was last in the
region, way back in 1990, the food was very *mitteleuropäische*, sausages,
stews, and schnitzels, dumplings, strudels, and tortes. It still mostly
was, but with international, nouvelle, foodie influences. That was good,
too. If you liked wine, the more expensive hotels and restaurants had
world-competitive wine lists. Doing it on an expense account with no
apparent top end or any real accountability made it all infinitely better.
It struck me that if I put that all together, it was what people imagined
heaven would be: clean, luxurious, orderly, your beds made for you and
your tables bussed, with never a bill to pay.

The only thing wrong was the job.

The Voloshin family was there for two weeks, fourteen days.

We got there four days after them. We had ten days to make it happen.

We started by just watching. Looking for a moment in which we could strike up a casual conversation. On a lift, in a restaurant, strolling through town. Grigor's motto could have been, *Russian bodyguards, never leave home without them.* He had his own security team. Four people, three men and one woman. They all had that ex–special forces look. Fit, trained, alert, tough, protective.

I gave them the names Boris One, usually with Grigor; Boris Two, with Leo; Boris Three worked the night shift, and the Borisova who escorted Kaylee.

Each morning, three ski instructors would show up at God's chalet, and each of the principals would go off with one of them, plus their individual Boris. It certainly made sense for Leo to be taught on his own. Any ski instructor will tell you, never let the parents come along. Don't even let the kid catch sight of them. Particularly the mother. It turns them whiny, weak, inattentive, disobedient, prone to tears and tantrums.

I watched each of them ski.

Grigor and Kaylee going off separately could be explained generically or personally and it would be about the same. Grigor saw himself as strong, manly, and adventurous. The function of his *skiführer* was to be an adventure guide, go off-piste, find stashes of untouched snow. Kaylee, by contrast, expected her instructor to teach her. She was actually the better skier of the two or was at least becoming so. Grigor was sure he was God and not to be improved upon. He constantly assumed he was much better than his actual skills. Or that skills didn't really enter into it. Gusto, bluster, and daring would get him through anything and everything. Those were the qualities that had served him well through the peaks and cliffs, crevasses and rifts, of those rich and treacherous ranges where Russian capitalism mixed with Russian politics and Russian organized crime. Charge ahead like you're the best there is and if you're still standing at the end, then yes, you were.

Kaylee was quite different. By nature. She was to measure up in all things to the high standard set by her own physical beauty, a very cool, plastic, Nicole Kidman sort of thing. She took ski instruction like one of the good girls in ballet class. She followed orders. She practiced the exercises. She never ventured beyond the range of her established competence. Something might happen out there that would make her appear less than perfect.

I made sure that my path crossed Grigor's on the slopes, at a restaurant in the mountains, and walking through town, each time with a nod and a casual American "hiya." I got no response. Except from Boris One. He was about 6 foot 3, with shoulders wide enough for 1.7 normal people and quite capable of making up for his lack of refined skiing skills with muscle and athleticism. The area over his left eye was thick from scarring and his nose had a lumpy look to it. Boxing or some other kind of battering. His eyeballs ran up and down me like they had a built-in scanning device for evaluating threat levels. I calculated that a pushier approach would be counterproductive.

Boris Two had a more pleasant and less pugilistic demeanor. He was Leo's keeper. He either liked kids or felt it was his duty to act as if he did. Leo usually only skied half a day. If he did more, he would sometimes fall asleep on the chairlift or even standing on skis, not when he was in motion, just if he had to be still for some reason. If I'd been close with the family, I would have recommended he go into a group with other kids. Kittens like to play with kittens, puppies with puppies, and kids with kids. But I was not close and it was none of my business.

Virtue has its limits. Its borders are best marked by opportunity. Grigor was not assigning a younger, fitter, handsomer man to keep his radiantly beautiful wife company. He'd assigned the Borisova to be her watchdog. She had a pleasant smile. I noticed the ski instructor that went with them treated Kaylee with a certain formality. I could see it in his posture and in those few moments, like waiting for a lift, that I got close enough to overhear them. It was odd and slightly comic. I guessed it was because when Borisova dropped her smile she looked like she carried a Makarov in her pocket and a razor in her shoe.

So it went for three days.

Late on the third day, after the lifts were closed but before dinnertime, we spotted Kaylee in town with Leo. Escorted by both Boris Two and the Borisova. Allison made the approach. Without me. As she walked by, she looked at Leo, and exclaimed to his mother, "What a cute boy." It's a ploy you can market with a money-back guarantee. It also works with people walking their dogs. Kaylee's initial response was positive, "Oh, thank you," with warmth and a gratified smiled. The Borisova said, "Who are you?" strict and suspicious as a U.S. border patrol officer staring at a guy named José, speaking right over Allison's cheery, "Hey, you're an American," and over Kaylee's reply, "Yes," which was equally friendly, two natives of the same place meeting in a foreign land. Then the Borisova cut them off, verbally, with "Excuse us, please," in a thick Russian accent, and physically, by stepping between them.

Allison came back to me and we strolled on, window shopping. She said, "That's one scary bitch," about Kaylee's keeper. "If I were a guy,

I'd be scared she had vagina dentata." Continuing her report, she added, without transition, "Kaylee's husband's hitting her."

"You're sure?"

"Someone is," a verbal shrug. The social logic was that he'd be the only one allowed to.

"Her makeup. And she's using her hair and her hat to cover bruising."

Thursday. Friday. Saturday. Three days gone. Nothing accomplished. Seven left.

CHAPTER FORTY-FOUR
HOME AGAIN

"You can't go back home to your family, back home to your
childhood, back home to romantic love, back home to
a young man's dreams of glory and of fame, back home to
exile, to escape to Europe and some foreign
land, back home to lyricism, to singing just for singing's
sake . . . back home to someone who can help you,
save you, ease the burden for you . . . back home to the
escapes of Time and Memory."

THOMAS WOLFE, *YOU CAN'T GO HOME AGAIN*

ON THE MORNING OF THE fourth day, Sunday, God's day, Grigor
took the Rüfikopf cable car.

We followed along. He, his Boris, and his skiführer skied down
to the Schuttboden drag lift. They rode up, then skied down to Zürs.
They got on another lift, Trittkopf 1. Grigor used his phone while they
rode. They got off before it became Trittkopf 2, which would have
taken them up to the top of the peak called Trittkopf, and switched to
the Flexen lift, to Alpe Ruiz. Grigor kept making calls. They got on
another lift, the Valfagehrbahn. Grigor was growing visibly impatient.
At last they got off and they took off.

It's easy to go psychotically fast on modern skis. They rushed
down the long, winding blue run into St. Anton. It was Sunday. It was
crowded and the lower down they got, the more people there were. It
didn't slow Grigor and his crew at all. We followed at an easier pace,

got to town, kicked off our skis, and strolled in the direction that Grigor had gone, into the pedestrian zone.

We hadn't been in St. Anton more than five minutes when I felt someone staring at me. I looked around. It was a cop. A large one. At first, his expression was quizzical. Then a mixture of searching and puzzlement. His mouth hung open and he said, quite loudly, calling across the street, "Rick?"

Allison looked at me. She'd known me as Tony, now as Victor, was I Rick as well?

The cop had a dog with him. A large Alsatian. They were coming toward me.

"Rick, is that you?" It was phrased as a question, but said as a certainty.

"Franz?" I asked. He looked like Franz, but that was thirty years ago. A big man, over six feet, more than two hundred pounds, solid as the ceramic of an Austrian stove, with big hands, gray eyes, thin lips, and weathered lines in an otherwise genial face.

Allison looked bewildered. "Go with it," I mumbled to her.

The big cop laughed, "Son of Franz."

Then I laughed, too. "Lukas. Of course." By then he was right in front of me. We embraced and slapped each other on the back. "Good God," I said, "you look just like him."

"Ja, ja, I know."

"How is he?" Then I wondered if I should have asked. "Is he . . ."

"Yes. He's still alive. Eighty-seven. Still got it all up here," he tapped his head. "And you, you look the same."

"Bullshit," I said. "It's thirty years."

"Who's this?" he asked about Allison. "Your daughter."

"No," I said. "My niece," and I introduced them.

He gave a policeman's man of the world look but didn't challenge it. He said, "We still have the Laundromat."

"Is it still making money?"

"Yes. The business has changed. Fewer tourists come in to use it, but the guest houses and smaller hotels and such, they use it and we fold and make everything nice. Good business. Cash business," he chuckled. Then, with a laugh and a big forefinger poking my shoulder, "You're not going to make any trouble, are you?"

"No, of course not."

"No dead bodies?"

"No. Of course not. That wasn't my doing. Not really. You know that."

He laughed. "I know that. My father still talks about it. The biggest case he ever had. The biggest mess he ever had to cover up. You have to come for dinner."

"Yeah, sure," I said.

"Tonight," Lukas said. "I will call him now. Quiet, I'm just going to say we have two guests. It will be a surprise." He punched a number into his cellphone. He spoke quickly in German. There was agreement. We were invited to dine at eight.

"Where?" I asked.

"The same place," he said. "It's bigger now. But the same place."

I looked at his jacket. "Police now, not gendarmes anymore?"

"Ja, ja. A few years back. We're all federal, all polizie."

"Is that better or worse?"

"The same, pretty much."

I took that to mean in the small towns they still ran things their own way. "I have one more question." I pointed to the dog. "That can't be Rudi?"

"No, that Rudi passed on. This is great-grandson of Rudi."

I knelt down. Looked up to Lukas, to make sure it was acceptable. Lukas nodded yes. I ruffled the big dog's fur, scratched him behind the ears, looked into his warm brown eyes. "Your great-grandfather saved my life," I told him. "Thanks."

"What was that?" Allison said, when they were gone. "Who's Rick? If I may ask. Or when were you Rick? Or something like that."

"Come on, I'll show you."

It was near the end of town, half behind the Shell station. The same sign, repainted, *Rick's Laundromat Americaine.* "That was my business when I lived here. It was before the EU. It was hard for a foreigner to own a business. I bet it still is. These towns, these villages, they're centuries old and they're tight-knit. Anyway, I needed a local partner. Franz, he was the gendarme then, *the* cop in town. He actually put it in Lukas's name. I barely knew Lukas. He was a kid then, away doing his national service."

"You sold it to him when you left?"

I laughed. "It was more like it was the price of my ticket out of town."

As Lukas said, the house had grown, longer, and higher. It had been a modest two stories. Now it was four. Where it had been three rooms deep, now it was six. Franz had the ground floor, Lukas and his wife and their two children a full apartment over him, and the top two stories were rented out, mostly weekly, and were a good source of income.

Franz greeted me with appropriate enthusiasm and astonishment.

His wife had passed on. I'd met her had but barely known her. Back then, thirty years ago, which might have been a long time and might not have been, when I penetrated the host-tourist barrier, to the degree that I did, I slowly began to understand that I was dealing with mountain people whose families had lived in these villages for a thousand years, give or take a few centuries. That is not to say they were backward, just that time was more viscous here, thick and slow moving. He was the gendarme. She was the frau. I expressed my sympathies. There was now a Polish woman who cleaned and cooked and had a room at the back.

Franz had a big, broad, wooden table. Sausages, cheese, and bread were already laid out. The Polish woman brought out more as we ate. There was *bier* and schnapps and whatever other alcohol anyone wanted.

Franz asked after my wife. I told him that she too had passed on.

"I'm sorry," he said, "she was a lovely woman."

"The best," I said. "Or better than that." It was sort of comic and got some smiles, but inside it was sadder than sad.

"How?" he asked.

"Cancer," I said.

He nodded sympathetically. "That can be . . ."

"Long and painful," I admitted.

"Ja."

"The daughter? I remember you pulling her on the wooden sled."

"Yeah, and it always tipped over. It got so she cried the minute she saw it. An indictment of Austrian design."

He laughed. Then asked if I saw her much. I said she was well, living in France, but we were not close. Any other children, he asked. A son, I said.

"Ah," he said, with male chauvinist pleasure. But then looked at me. I could hardly speak, but sometimes things need to be said. "He . . . he was a great kid . . . smart . . . idealistic . . . after college . . . he was going to go to med school . . . but first he went off to volunteer for Medecins Sans Frontiers . . . in Africa . . . one of those . . . things got violent."

Franz sighed. "I shouldn't have asked."

"It's OK."

He pushed a big glass of beer toward me. A flagon. To wash down the sorrow.

The Polish woman served a goulash, which was rich and hearty. Franz said, "After we took over the Laundromat, we found out how much money you were making, cash money."

I said, "You like cash money, don't you?"

"But you didn't tell me how much."

"I never cheated you. Not a groschen. I paid a fixed amount, minus documented costs, as agreed. If I had reported all that cash, there would have been taxes, then the costs would have been higher, and you would have had less."

Franz laughed, "You see, you see what kind of guy this guy is. It is true. You didn't cheat. And I would have made less. But it feels like you tricked me. But it was a good trick. I missed you, Rick."

A few drinks later, he said, "The winter of '89, '90, that was a crazy time. Their whole world collapsed . . ." he waved, vaguely, to the north and the east. "It was going to be paradise. Well, maybe it is. Look around, how well we are doing."

Lukas said, "We are doing well. Old men always think the old days were better."

"No," Franz said. "We don't. We know plenty of old days . . . that were bad. Very bad. So, yes, this is better. But that year . . . And the things you did," he meant me. He looked at Allison, "There was this girl, American, nice enough, too many boyfriends maybe. She died. In an avalanche. Her mother shows up . . ."

"You know that I tried to stay out of it, you know that Franz."

"You would not believe the things that happened. *His* mother showed up." He gestured with his bier glass toward me. My mother. "And a priest. She was dating a priest, the serious kind, Catholic. And his girlfriend's mother, she wasn't his wife yet. There was the Japanese guy and the other Japanese guy and two Bulgarians . . . Rick, here, shot two Bulgarians, and there was the CIA guy . . ."

"We were never sure about that," I said. "And I only shot one Bulgarian. The other one was stabbed by the mother." "Your mother?" Allison asked.

"No, no," Franz and I said together, "the girl's mother."

"It was crazy. It was not my fault," I said.

"Back then," Franz said, "Austria was perfect. We had the lowest murder rate in world." It wasn't true. But it was close. "Except for those little places that aren't even countries, and some others that lied about it." OK, that fudged the numbers enough. "They were all dead, I couldn't hide the bodies, but I blamed it all on foreigners."

"But wasn't . . ." Allison hesitated over the name. ". . . Rick a foreigner?"

"Of course," Franz said. "But it was different. We were in business." Directly to me, he said, "And I was the witness at your wedding. Under your real name." Back to Allison, "Do you know what his passport said, not the real one, the fake one he was living here under? It said he was a Catholic priest, another one, from Ireland." Franz and Lukas thought that was hysterically funny and laughed so hard that even the Polish woman joined in.

When I was at last alone in my hotel room, I sank to the floor on my knees, then pressed my forehead to the rug, the way Muslims pray, and I let myself know my emptiness and then let the sorrow of my losses fill that emptiness, and I began to weep. There was a knock at the door. I ignored it. It came several times more, then I heard Allison say, "If you don't let me in, I'll tell the concierge there's something wrong and make him open the door."

I rose and let her in. She looked at me, and I said, "It's an ugly thing to watch old men cry."

"Why don't you see your daughter?"

"You mean why won't she see me?"

"I guess."

"She blamed me . . . blames me . . . for it all. She's the sort of person who believes in psychosomatic illness. That a husband's sins create a wife's cancer."

"What were your sins?"

"The ones she knows about? That are involved in this . . . alienation. They're that I did things that were too dangerous. Risky. That caused stress. The thing is that she encouraged it, my wife did. Like the events that Franz and Lukas were talking about. I tried to walk away . . . I was a new father . . . It changed me . . . it did . . . I wanted to be careful. Stay out of things that were none of my business. But Marie-Laure she said she wanted me to be the man she'd met and fallen in love with and wanted to be with . . . every time I said this is getting crazy . . . she said I had to go on."

"But can't you explain?"

"Then our son . . . he wanted . . . this is my daughter's vision of it . . . he wanted to be like me. Daring. But also, moral and doing good things. Better than me. Which is how it should be. I wanted that. Approved of it. That's what drove him. To his death. Add that, and that was the pain that became physical, you see, in his mother, the pain of that, and so, for my daughter, it's me that killed both her brother and her mother."

"That doesn't sound right or fair."

"You're hearing it from me. I'm sure I'm soft-peddling it. Taking the worst of the ugliness out of it. Maybe if you heard it from her, it would be different."

Allison looked at me. Maybe it was with pity. Maybe with sadness. She started to move closer to me, not just physical distance, searching for a role through which she might offer comfort and solace.

Sexual healing? No, I was certain that wouldn't do and guessed that she sensed that too. That in that half moment, we both caught glimpses of the insidious twists and turns in the erotic poisons and putrefaction waiting if we entered such swamps. Could we play at substitute daughter and pseudo-papa? A different bearing, simple and caring. No, that wouldn't do either. Blood is blood, though that, too, is beyond reason. I appreciated the impulse. I nodded, as close to thanks as I could go. And a shrug—it is what it is. As death is what it is.

I felt I had to say something, some explanation of the distance that remained. That we—that I—retained. "Young men run on passion. Old men are filled with broken shards of memories. As if we've been looking at our lives in mirrors, all along, through all those years, lots of them forgotten, some lost, most of them broken, nothing really true or completely whole is left, just all those bits and pieces, sharp edges, and silver peeling off the backs. That's all there is."

CHAPTER FORTY-FIVE
FROM THE SKY

"They call it stormy Monday . . ."

AARON "T-BONE" WALKER

THE NEXT MORNING, I WANTED to be alone. I caught the first lift. I went off-piste. It may sound snobbish, but the truth is that skiing on the trails in the Alps, at least in the high stations, is a waste. They get crowded, chopped up, and scraped off. It's all better off-piste.

Whomp, whomp, whomp . . . that chopper sound . . . *Thicka, thicka, thicka* . . .

Chopper coming in. I was just on my second run.

There's a helipad in Lech. Actually, there are two. The Flexenpass Helipad is the general commercial one. A helipad doesn't need to be much more than a reasonably flat area and that's what this one was, paved, with a circle painted on it, like a target, which would be visible when it wasn't covered by snow. That's enough to get it listed in the international airport guide. Technically, it's in Zürs, not Lech, but not by much.

Flexenpass is an actual pass, a way through the mountains, and, more recently, a road. It's one of those twisty and narrow tracks, with whole sections tunneling beneath avalanche shields, that makes you glad you've obeyed Austrian traffic laws and carried tire chains with you.

Whomp, whomp, whomp . . . of course there were helicopters. There are always helicopters. They do search and rescue. I knew that. One had come to find me when I was deep in a crevasse, the sun going down, and I was likely to die. They come in when someone's injuries are so severe they have to be coptered to a big hospital with the facilities and the skills for major surgeries.

There's heli-skiing. That's a big mountain thing for rich people. It's fairly common in Italy and Switzerland. It's banned in France and Germany. Only one place in Austria permits it. Lech. Most of the heli-skiing departs from the other helipad, at Balmalp, which is officially part of Lech.

Whomp, whomp, whomp . . .

I looked to the sound. The choppers that fly into Flexenpass are two-seaters to eight-seaters. This was one of the big ones, an AgustaWestland, which, in spite of its name, is an Italian machine. Like my Benelli shotgun, it's got style. It's sleek and dark, with a shark's look.

Whomp, whomp, whomp . . . looking up, I felt dizzy . . . Oh, Francis Ford Coppola . . . with your fleet of choppers coming in over the jungle and the sea . . . *Apocalypse Now* . . . speakers hung upon them blasting "Flight of the Valkyries" . . . Wagner's stirring salute to dying by violence . . . the Valkyries come from out of the sky to pick through the corpses, selecting the ones they want to carry off as heroes to Valhalla . . . *Dum da da-dum dum, dum de da dadum, dum de da da dummm* . . . *Whomp, whomp, whomp* . . . farewell Mick McMunchun . . . you flew a $325,000 McLaren 720S Spider off the road and into the trees with your seat belt off and your penis pointing forth . . . are you in Valhalla now, drinking and whoring and boasting . . . I was audio-hallucinating, multiplying the rotor blades of a single machine into a Coppola-sized fleet . . . I was laying in a music track to increase the drama . . . it was a different kind of dizziness . . . not falling down . . . a weightless rising . . . detached from the Earth . . . buffeted by the winds from the rotors . . . though in actual physical truth they were too far away for me to feel them at all.

Was the madness returning? Was that ancient deity—the one intent on deconstructing Nietzsche—about to reappear disguised as a snowman?

I willed myself down. Down until I felt my feet in my boots and my boots on my skis, my skis on the mountain, as the music faded to silence.

I saw a shadow pass over the snow. Not as a bird might fly. I looked for what caused it. It seemed to be a tiny helicopter. A toy. A drone. A hallucination within a hallucination? It seemed real. The resort taking promotional pictures? Ski patrol examining the snowpack? A rich person, child or adult, playing with the modern version of a model airplane?

Helicopter.

That could be it. If I could get mother and child to a helicopter, it could whisk them away faster than a pursuit could be organized to stop them. But with the three Borises and the one Borisova always on watch, on behalf of their God, Grigor Voloshin, how could that be done? What the hell, if I could actually get the two of them away from their keepers, speed probably wouldn't be the issue, and we could make our escape in a horse-drawn sleigh.

Still, since I'd had the thought, I wanted to see more. I began to ski toward the helipad.

The AW109 settled neatly down to the ground and shut its engines off. Four men got out. I was much too far away to make out faces or real details. But certain things were clear. They weren't skiers. They wore winter clothes, but for warmth, not for sport. They didn't have skis. No luggage at all. Two of them were . . . businessmen? Officials? There for business, not fun. The other two—if I were to guess—were their security. Younger, leaner. Alert guard dogs, ears and noses twitching, scan 360 degrees, then their heads swivel, swivel, swivel, as they proceeded toward two Mercedes SUVs. The drivers popped out. Each held open a rear door for their clients, chauffeur style. The two business types got into one back seat, and one of the security guys got into the front, beside the driver. The other security guy got in the car that was in front, which then led the way, as if it were scouting for IEDs.

Did this have anything to do with me? I didn't know. I didn't think so. I was on a mission with no solution that I was a fool for doing, except, of course, that it was an all-expenses paid luxury ski vacation. Good gosh, I was lucky. I returned to riding up and sliding down and called it meditation.

Whomp, whomp, whomp . . . two hours later. The same chopper flying away.

That evening, walking through town, we saw Kaylee and Leo with Boris Two and the Borisova. This time, Kaylee looked to Allison and gave her a slight smile.

CHAPTER FORTY-SIX

YOU CALL THAT A PLAN?

" . . . but Tuesday's just as bad."

AARON "T-BONE" WALKER

KAYLEE HAD INVITED ALLISON TO ski with her. Two American girls in a foreign land. Every time they got on a chairlift, they were chattering away, especially if it was a two-seater and it was just them. By the time the day was done, Allison was Kaylee's new best friend. Possibly, so it seemed, her only friend.

"This is a big deal, isn't it?" Allison said to me.

"By big, you mean?"

"A lot of money. This is worth a lot of money, if we pull this off."

"It probably is. Sure," I said.

"I want to talk money. I am helping you," she said.

"I brought you to keep you safe, you know," I said. "And you're getting a four-star vacation. Free and clear."

"True," she said. "With no sugar baby or hooking stuff. You're being very good to me, Uncle Tony. Uncle Victor. Uncle Rick. But it's different now. I'm part of it. And I'm your way in."

"Part way, anyway. It's a start." And it was.

We now knew, through Allison's chats with Kaylee, that the name of Boris One, Grigor's guardian, was Pavel. Boris Two, who watched over little Leo, was Lev. Boris Three, Tomas, did the night shift and was the swing man when it was necessary to cover for one of the others. The Borisova was Yvetta. She was the boss of the crew, outranking them here, just as she had in the Russian military.

There was also a nanny. A Frenchwoman with a White Russian background. Political White, not racial white. From one of those families who'd fled the Bolsheviks, the Reds, back in 1917, and ended up as impoverished exiles in Paris. Something that's sadly no longer possible. You'd best be wealthy if you're going to be an expat in Paris today. She had a growing obsession with the Romanovs and was convinced that after Putin, Russia would go back to the tsars. The aristocracy would be revived, and she was awaiting the day when she would be called back to the life she'd been born for. Nonetheless, she was good with Leo, and Grigor wanted his son to be fluent in French as well as English and Russian.

The rest of the staff was local. A chef with an assistant who doubled as a bartender. A maid to fetch and to pick up after everyone. A pair of cleaners who came in every morning, just as they would in a hotel, to do the beds and the laundry, to vacuum, scrub, and scour.

Something was going on with Grigor. Kaylee didn't know what. It had become much more intense. He was skiing less and on the phone a lot more. He was also drinking more. Sometimes alcohol made him loquacious and grandiose and he was likely to give away a diamond or a sports car. Sometimes drinking made him silent and brooding. Sometimes horny and he'd insist on sex with whomever was nearest, Kaylee or the left-hand wife or one of the fortune-hunting whores that thronged around him and his rich friends.

The rich Russians notoriously favored Courchevel. They all went there on the same dates. They went out to the clubs every night for what Kaylee called whore-parties with gaggles of skimpy-clothed wannabe models flown in like it was school holidays for Russky rich dicks. Coming to St. Anton instead had been a favor to Kaylee. To make it a "family" holiday. But she suspected he'd brought the left-hand wife. Since Kaylee hadn't actually spotted her, she thought he was keeping her in one of the nearby villages, Zürs, Oberlech, or St. Anton. That might have explained the impatience and the urgency with which Grigor had raced into St. Anton when we'd followed him.

Other times, the drinking made him raging and violent.

He always insisted it barely affected him and that he never got drunk.

"Do you have a plan?" Allison asked.

"Helicopter," I said. "If we could get them alone, Kaylee and Leo, and get them to the helipad, with a chopper standing by, and if the weather was good enough to fly. Fly them to Zurich. Timing it so they could get right on a flight, before Grigor or his crew or his lawyers could intercept them at the boarding gate, and it should be nonstop to the states, so they can't be intercepted changing planes in Paris or Munich or someplace."

"Can we make that work?" she said.

"No," I said.

We were in my hotel room. I went to the minibar. I took out four bottles, three candy bars, and a bag of nuts. "Here's the helipad," the bag of nuts. "Now we have three pairs," each of them a bottle and a candy bar, "and one single security guy," just a bottle. "Let's say that we get lucky, and Grigor and Pavel are fairly far away, off-piste," I pushed that pair, a vodka and a package of Manner Wafers, way over to the left. "Here's Kaylee and Yvetta," another vodka and a Mozart Ball, near the middle of the table. "Here's Leo," I said, ecstatic that I had a Milka candy actually called a Leo, the biggest achievement of my planning so far. I paired it with a half bottle of a rather ordinary red wine, "and Lev." I put them over on my right. "And here," a bier, right in front of me, home base, "is Tomas. It's daytime. Maybe he's at the chalet, sleeping, or eating, or whatever.

But he's on call. There's a car at the chalet and the helipad is right on the road. Tomas gets there . . . I don't know, five minutes, seven at the most."

"Really what we have to worry about," Allison said, "is two people. Lev and Yvetta."

"If we're lucky. We only have a few days to pull it off. Bad weather, meaning no-fly weather, or Grigor decides to ski with his son, or hang nearby to watch, and the plan doesn't work. Also . . ." I took out another candy bar. I tore the wrapper off, broke it into thirds, and put a piece with each pair. "The skif`ührers. What do they do, when Kaylee and Leo head for the helicopter? Say OK? Or call someone? Or call Grigor? Or help the keepers stop them?"

Allison said, "If a mother wants to go somewhere with her son, won't they accept that?"

"Maybe. Probably. Unless Grigor's already had a word in their ear, 'My wife is a little unstable, please be careful, don't let her run off, especially with our boy, we have a restraining order,' and his money in their pocket."

"But if we make it happen, there's a lot of money, isn't there?"

"Yes."

"How much are we talking about? For me."

I should have given it some thought. But I hadn't. Back when I was in the PI business I paid people by the hour. Usually about $30, billed them out at $50. An eight-hour day was $240, a forty-hour week was $1,200. A lot of it was just watching and waiting so there were lots of ten-hour days and longer. Most of the guys were ex-cops or moonlighting cops. For them it was money on top of their base money. That had been a long time ago. Normal thinking would be that it should be much more now, but American life wasn't running that way. The rising tide had only been lifting the yachts, the rest had been left in the mudflats of the Great Stagnation, and as best as I could tell, people were as likely to be making less as they were to be making more. On that scale, $2,000, maybe $2,500.

On the other hand, we'd started with $7,000 for a single night. This was a ten-day job. Seventy thousand dollars sounded insanely high. However, assuming that I could name her as my associate, or as part of LIFE, Inc.'s investigation section, or just put her on my expense account, and presuming Elizabeth came through, it wasn't my money. I offered what I considered to be an extremely good number. "Fifteen thousand dollars."

"That's not a lot," Allison said.

I said, "I thought it was."

"Tuition at Bard is $51,000, and with books and all the extras, like a place to live and eating, it's a lot more."

"I thought you were a scholarship student."

"I am. But I also have student loans. What if I want to go to grad school? Or law school. Or med school."

"You're not going to pay for your whole life with ten days' work, most of which is a luxury holiday."

"Let me ask you something first. Are we going to kill this guy?"

"What?"

"I've been thinking. A lot. We killed Owen Cohen."

"That was self-defense."

"At dinner, with your Austrian friends, Franz and Lukas, I found out you killed several people here. Three, four, five, something like that."

"There was a girl. About your age . . ."

"I know. I understand," she said, meaning acceptance of what was. "But it started me thinking. About what I did. I killed Mick McMunchun."

"It was an accident."

"Sure. It was. But it wasn't. You trying to shield me from thinking I killed him, I appreciate that. I think you are really doing that to be protective, because that's sort of who you are. But here's what I think, I think it was what everyone wanted."

"No. That's not . . ."

She cut me off, "Don't say it. Let's not lie. If it wasn't what everyone wanted, you would have been mad at me. *'You stupid little bitch,'* " she said in a voice that mimicked an angry parent or teacher or probation officer, " *'What are you crazy, giving him LSD? And taking it with him so there was no one straight enough to say don't drive so fast, you lunatic!'* " Then returned to her normal voice. "The widow and her friend, they should have been all upset. At least crying. But no, their eyes were drier than a dry martini. They were almost smiling. I bet after we left they were high-fiving. I think it was what everyone wanted." I started to say something, but she waved me off. "That was what the whole thing with Owen was about. He wanted to be paid for Mick's death. He was sure you killed him."

"But I didn't. And I wasn't going to."

She shook her head. "I've killed two people. Put any wrapper you want on it, it's still what it is. That's changed everything."

I called Elizabeth.

I told her that if we were going to get mother and child away from father and thugs, we would do it by helicopter, hopefully connecting to a direct flight out of Zurich.

Elizabeth said, "No, no, no."

"No?"

"We're not going to fly her commercial. We have to show Kaylee that we care. We'll get a private jet."

"That would make things more flexible." Simpler and easier. Life is grand when money doesn't matter. I had to keep reminding myself.

"She has to know how valued she is. That we love her. That we will treat her better than he does, so she wants to be in our hands. We'll make sure it's a good one. A big one."

"Can you arrange it to have both on standby? The helicopter and the jet."

"Zurich?"

"A private jet making a direct flight . . . then Innsbruck is probably better. It's closer. No border to cross. You might want to have lawyers standing by."

"Criminal?"

"No. Divorce. Custody. Guys in really good suits and arrogant, establishment attitudes, like they're representing established money, deeper than the deep state."

She said, "Make sure you have a list of Kaylee's favorite foods. And the boy's, too."

"What?"

"So they'll be on the jet. Oh, and find out the boy's favorite toys and videos and such."

"Yeah, sure."

"How are you going to do it?"

"Get the lists?"

"No. The whole thing. The . . . what are you going to do with the husband?"

"He'll be fine. He'll be able to fly back to Moscow. Buy some new toys. Grown-up toys."

"Oh," Elizabeth said. She sounded disappointed, her voice tinged with regret at missing out on an event that she was anticipating with salacious delight. She quickly recovered and resumed being business-like. "If that's the case, make sure you collect some list of his assets and where to track them."

"Make sure?"

As if I hadn't said a word, she continued on into a lecture, "That's more than half the battle, the way these husbands hide their money. I'd say it should be against the law, but it already is, and it doesn't seem to matter. It's an invidious and insidious corruption. That's what we're fighting."

"The girl," I said, referring to Allison. "I brought her."

"I thought you might."

"It was for our protection and hers. Keep her away from anyone who might ask questions. Or for her getting bored and reckless, for that matter. It turns out she's helping. I want money for her."

"How much?"

"Minimum seven, even if we can't make it work. Maximum," I impulsively put a cushion on it, "say fifty." I think it was the private jet that prompted me. We all have to find ways to say how much we care.

"Are you going to get them out?"

"As things stand now, no."

"Damn it. Why not?"

"Because he has four security people. Two of them, at least, I'm sure are Spetsnaz, Russian special forces. I'm no match for them. Neither is Allison. Even if we were, this is Austria. They don't have murders and they have lots of police."

"I see," she said, sounding as if she thought it was something she definitely shouldn't have to see, like Queen Victoria stumbling across Prince Albert fornicating with a page in a water closet.

After that I called Caroline Sunshine, the woman I'd hired to come in twice a day for the cats. "They are fine," she said. "But Huba is scary. He sits and stares at me. I tried to be nice to him, but if I get close he disappears. Then he finds a new place and stares. I managed to pet him once when he was eating. Scotty is much nicer. Not as friendly as a regular cat, but not as spooky as Huba. Oh, yes, they killed two mice today. Outside, not inside. They left them at the front door, which I thought was good."

CHAPTER FORTY-SEVEN

PLAN—PART II

Wednesday [is] . . . The Mouseketeers Anything
Can Happen Day.

THE MICKEY MOUSE CLUB,
WORDS AND MUSIC BY JIMMY DODD

PLANS MEET REALITIES. PLANS FAIL. Plans are reinvented.
Resurrected. It's not all up to us.

Kaylee and Allison, Yvetta and Stephan, their skiführer, stopped
for lunch at Der Wolfe, a mountain restaurant. It's a new place, all
wood, but so spare and clean it's almost a satire on Scandinavian design. The views are magnificent. The food is good and costly.

There was a moment after the waiter had taken their order. Yvetta
had gone to the toilet and Stephan had seen friends on the other side
of the room and had excused himself for a quick visit. Allison put her
hand on Kaylee's arm, leaned in close and said, very softly, "We're here
to help you."

Instead of the thrilling excitement and relief that Allison had
been looking forward to, Kaylee became an instant frostcicle.

Allison tried, "Elizabeth sent us."

The moment turned worse, not better. Kaylee's expression was
immobile but her eyes radiated panic.

Soft, warm, and caring, Allison said, "We're going to get you . . . *and Leo* . . . away."

"You can't," Kaylee said.

"Isn't that you want?"

No answer.

"What you need?"

Nothing.

"What Leo needs?"

A slight nod, almost a yes.

"Good."

"That man, that you're with," Kaylee asked, "is he the one I saw in New York?"

"Yes."

"I wasn't sure. I only saw him for a few moments. And I didn't have my contacts in."

Allison was relieved. The goddess had a flaw. Yvetta returned. Then Stephan. Yvetta had a burger which she devoured with both gusto and deliberation. Stephan had a regional dish that involved potatoes and cheese. Kaylee and Allison had salads. Kaylee just picked at hers, too frightened to eat.

After lunch, it got worse. Instead of maneuvering to sit with Allison when they rode the lifts, Kaylee placed herself with Yvetta or Stephan.

While that was happening, I was trying to keep an eye on Grigor. He seemed distracted. He stopped to answer his phone. I had to ski on by. I was fairly sure Pavel, his oversized security guy, noticed me and made a check mark on his mental slate. I had to stay farther away.

About an hour later, *Whomp, whomp, whomp* . . . that chopper sound . . . *Thicka, thicka, thicka* . . .

Since I was keeping my distance from God and his guard dog anyway, I decided to ski down toward the helipad. Look around, scout it out, in case the impossible opportunity arrived and we did make a dash for it. A blue run named Madlochalm ran along above the landing place. It had cliffs on one side, the one I was on, steep hills on the other, and if we were going out that way, we'd sure as hell want good weather. The chopper was an AW109 again. Maybe the same one, maybe not. It looked like the same four men coming out. This time, only one car came to meet them. Two men got out of it. They were too far for me to make out their faces, but by their ski jackets and general look, posture and coloring and such, I was sure of who they were, Grigor and Pavel.

Pavel and the two security guys who'd arrived in the helicopter stood off at a discreet distance, while Grigor and the two principals took off their gloves to greet each other with firm handshakes, walked a few steps farther from their guardians to talk. My impression, from too far off, with too little information, was that the three of them were deliberately maintaining an appearance of calm while engaged in an exchange of great intensity.

This is what Allison told me, later that evening, about what happened with Kaylee.

I admit it, I sort of, not sort of, *totally*, felt like we were doing something heroic. And dashing, too. Rescuing the beautiful princess from the dragon. Or the villain. Like every story and fairy tale and Disney movie we all grew up on, except this time, it was a girl hero rescuing the princess. In my mind, I wasn't your sidekick or assistant or an accident, I was the daring, dashing, sneaky, heroic rescuer.

And this dumb twit wasn't having any of it.

Do you encounter that much? Rescuing people and they say, "Uh, duh, I'd rather lay here like a drunk in the mud?" Do they? Or wives saying, "Oh, he beats me, he beats me . . . I think I'll just go home for another black eye." What is that about? Inertia should be a concept for psychology not physics.

Well, I wasn't going to take it. When we got to a two-person chairlift, I elbowed my way past Stephan and got on the lift with Kaylee. Once we were up in the air, I said, "Come on. What's going on?"

She said, "I can't."

I said, "Why not?"

She said, "I just can't."

I would have yelled at her, but I couldn't let anyone hear us, I kind of whisper yelled—snarled?—that might be it, I snarled. "You said this was what you wanted. We flew four thousand miles. For you. Just for you. We've been here days, maneuvering, watching, trying to get close, and now you're telling me that what, we're a pair of shoes that you didn't mean to order?"

Kaylee didn't say anything. Just sort of drew herself straighter, like I was supposed to notice how beautiful and perfect she was. She is amazingly beautiful, but she's not perfect, I knew that now that I knew that she needed contacts. And she's not that bright. At first, I figured she dumbed herself down for all the girly chitchat we'd been having, but now, no. She's really not that bright. I kept at her. I said, "You better do it!"

Something happened. She nodded. Then she spoke, very politely and meekly. I don't know how often I've ever seen anyone do "meekly." Who does "meekly" anymore? She said, "Tell me what to do." I think that's the key to her. She takes orders.

Once I got that, I started pushing her to where we need her to go. It's not enough for her to be ready to rush to the helicopter with Leo. If Grigor is off with Pavel and Tomas is at the chalet, that leaves Yvetta and Lev. I told her she had to seduce Lev. She looked at me like it was the sort of thing she simply doesn't do. You know what, I suspect that she doesn't. It's the curse of great beauty, homage without effort. I said, "You do realize he's head over heels in love with you." She looks at me again like I'm telephoning in from Andromeda. "You don't see how he glances at you, how he tries to almost touch you." Again, she looks blank because men look at her that way so often she can't even see it. I explained it to her. And that the way Lev dotes on Leo is part of it. Then she slowly starts to get it. She says, "He's always saying things like, 'If I had a son, I'd want him to be just like Leo.' 'I hope, someday, to have a boy like Leo.'"

I said, "Yes."

Then she said, "You want me to have sex with him?"

"I want you to look at him, very occasionally, the way he looks at you."

"How many times would that be, very occasionally?"

Phew. Wow. OK, we only have a couple of days to make this happen. I told her four times today and eight times tomorrow. She nods and I can see she's making little notes in her head. She will, exactly that many times. She will do it well, too. It probably won't be with feeling, but it will be sort of perfect. Also, I told her, "You have to touch him. Very slightly, like the edge of your hand to the edge of his. For him, it will be electric. Adjust his shirt, like it's askew, even if it's not. And once, just once, something with his hair. It's really short, so it doesn't get mussed, but do it anyway."

I told her, "That's part one of your plan. It starts today.

"The middle of tomorrow, you meet him and Leo, after Leo's morning session, and you talk to him. Tell him how good he is with Leo. Then say that you're sure that a man as young and strong and kind as he is will find a wonderful woman to have a son with. Like Leo. Say it wistfully like you wish it was really yourself. Whatever he says, you look very sad, and say, 'You will. I know it.' He'll reply.

Whatever he says, you say, 'You'll be gone and I'll miss you.' After that, cut it off, go away."

That's about as far as I got. But I'll have a chance to talk to her some more and coach her through Act II. He is already in love with her. She just has to convince him that his love can win the day, that he can save her from the ogre, and run off with her. That makes him part of our team. Then all that's left to deal with is Yvetta.

A little after eight, as we were finishing dinner, Kaylee called Allison to invite her for dinner, the next night, Thursday. Her uncle Victor was invited as well. Kaylee wasn't about to say it on the phone, but things had taken place that would go a long way toward making her escape much more probable.

As we took our post-prandial stroll through Lech, I noticed a couple of Americans. You can guess at nationalities by appearance and be right a great deal of the time. Certain physiques, facial characteristics, the way people carry themselves and the way they move, their fashion choices, their attitudes. Of course, if you hear them speak, they might as well be wearing flags of their nations stamped on their foreheads. It's not just different languages, or different accents with the same language, it's the way they use language. Brits tend to speak in complete sentences organized in complete paragraphs. I've heard Americans carry on entire conversations with just the word "fuck," its variants, plus "it," "that," "way," and "hey," to give it direction. These were Americans, though not the fucking fuck it, fuck that, fuckadelic, kind. There were three of them, and I would have sworn that the one with the big furry hat with earflaps was the Mormon from New York. But that couldn't be. So it must've been one of his cousins from Utah.

CHAPTER FORTY-EIGHT

BANYA

Wondrous to relate, I saw the land of the Slavs, and while
I was among them, I noticed their wooden bath-houses.
They warm themselves to extreme heat, then undress, and
after anointing themselves with tallow, take young reeds
and lash their bodies. They actually lash themselves so
violently that they barely escape alive. They then drench
themselves with cold water, and thus are revived.

APOSTLE ANDREW, in the year 1113

"Peter the Great attempted to stamp out the banya
as a relic of medieval Russia . . . But, despite heavy
taxes . . . by the end of the eighteenth century, nearly
every palace in St. Petersburg had one.
　　It was called the 'people's first doctor' (vodka was the
second, raw garlic the third)."

ORLANDO FIGES, *NATASHA'S DANCE:*
A CULTURAL HISTORY OF RUSSIA

WE HAD BEEN JUST FUMBLING our way forward. Now something
had happened. Not as a result of anything we had done. Fate had taken a
hand, rang some changes, and cleared the way. Perhaps at the meeting at
the heliport on Wednesday. The Voloshin family's date of departure was
unchanged. But Grigor's destination had changed. He would be going
to Ashgabat, the capital of Turkmenistan, instead of Moscow. Little Leo

would go with him. Kaylee could, too. Or she could go to Moscow. Or even to Wherever, the capital of Do What You Want.

Kaylee had no idea why. Therefore, Allison and I didn't either. It could have been politics. It could have been money. It could have been natural gas. It could have been that God wanted a new girl with that Central Asian feeling.

Whatever the reason, there were security needs. Yvetta and Pavel had gone ahead to prepare. Only Lev and Tomas remained.

There was one day left. Friday. Tomorrow.

I alerted Elizabeth. She did her part. Quickly and efficiently. A helicopter was on standby. A private jet would be waiting in Innsbruck. I didn't have a list Kaylee's favorite foods or Leo's favorite toys. Elizabeth was upset. I told her that for the price she'd be paying to rent the plane, they should be able to improvise, just tell them it was for a young, beautiful, *rich* woman. Everyone knows what they eat, high cost/low calories. Three-year-old boys, even adorable, blond, blue-eyed ones, are pretty generic. Tell them you want a flight attendant with a graduate degree in early childhood education. I was willing to bet the private jet company had one. Or two.

It was crazy. It was high risk. With luck, escape might be possible.

The dinner was surprisingly pleasant.

It had a Russian theme. There was borscht, blini, caviar, *smetana*—sour cream—on the side, a salad with pickled vegetables, veal Orlov, and Borodinsky bread. There were Georgian wines, *medovukha*—something like mead—and vodka to drink. Cliché Russia, but why not? If it had been reversed, an American host would likely serve up cheeseburgers, fries, apple pie, cola, and bourbon. We ate, we drank, we talked about skiing, about Russia and America without being political or even mentioning the names of our gallant leaders.

The two remaining bodyguards, Lev and Tomas, didn't eat with us, but they were around. I didn't ask, but I guessed that Kaylee had been following Allison's instructions, because Lev was now so blatantly besotted that I feared Grigor would spot it, would care, and have him shot. Or whatever they did to a bodyguard who slavered over his master's wife in Russia.

Grigor was being a very expansive and mellow host. As we finished our desserts, he told the me that, in keeping with the Russian theme, we were going to share a great Russian treat. Just the men. Meaning he and I. Excluding Tomas and Lev. He called in the nanny. He told her she could have the night off. There were two young women, Kaylee and Allison, who would be happy to watch over Leo. Women loved sharing childcare together, he declared, like playing with dolls, but better. Everybody else could go home after the table was cleared.

We went downstairs. Disrobed. Then walked outside as the cold air came down from the Arctic and the snow fell. People will tell you it can't snow when it's that cold, but it's not true, it can, and it did. We were behind the house. The hill had been shaved to create two flat areas. The higher and smaller one, next to the house, had a *banya*. A step down, there was a much larger area that had a small pond and a hot tub beside it. The traditional way that a banya works is with heated stones. Left alone, they create dry heat like a sauna. Pour water on them, it's like a steam room. Grigor brought a bottle with him. He complimented me. He said I was a very good skier and quite fit for my age. That I was a good conversationalist and had good taste in women, like that girl.

I said, "She's my niece."

Assuming that I was lying, he said, "I will never understand Americans, leaders in puritanism and pornography. Both. At the same time."

"I don't either," I said. "But it's not like that, with her."

"Rick," he said, "May I call you Rick?"

"You can, but why would you, my name's Victor."

"Small towns, small towns. Do you come from a small town?"

"No. No, I don't. I'm a New York City person."

"I'm a city person, too. St. Petersburg. But you see, in Russia, more than America I think, we have small circles. The higher you go, the smaller they are. Everyone knows everyone and if there's someone you don't know, you do know several people who know that person, and you get to hear everything about everyone."

"Uh-huh."

He got off the wooden bench and went over to a bucket. It had a big ladle in it. He picked it up and poured water over his head, gave a shudder, shook the wet from his hair, and said, "Try it. It's good."

I went over. Did the same. The water was icy cold. It shocked. It was good.

He picked up the bucket and poured what remained over the stones. It whooshed and hissed as it instantly turned to steam. The steam felt good, too. He put the bucket under a faucet and refilled it. "Next year we'll have a plunge bath in here, too."

We sat back on the benches. "Small towns. Here, little villages," he said. "If you listen, everybody hears everything. I heard that Rick Cochrane, from long ago, was back."

It didn't make sense to deny or confirm at that point. I remained silent.

"I am certain that you are that person."

"Would you like to see my passport? Or my credit card?"

"I like you. I really do. Which makes this unfortunate."

"What is unfortunate?"

Sweat was pouring off me. It should have been. Due to the heat and the steam. But that wasn't it. I thought about the physicality of the situation. He was twenty years younger than me and the twenty years between fifty and seventy are decades that mean a lot. He was about twenty pounds heavier. He was much drunker, but I had no idea how that would affect things. It was a Russian Theme night, drunk was its natural state.

Grigor said, "I'm going to call you Rick, OK?"

"Sure. Whatever."

"We are going to do something special now."

"I thought we already were."

"Even more special. A cleansing. Maybe the right word is purification."

CHAPTER FORTY-NINE

GOD IN THE NIGHT

"I'm looking forward to the most fascinating
experience in life, which is dying."

TIMOTHY LEARY

WE LEFT THE BANYA. BACK into the chill of the night and beautiful falling snow. Then into the hot tub. Somehow, God had another bottle of vodka with him. I knew it was another because it was full and the previous time that I'd looked it was nearly empty. Then we climbed into the hot tub. We lay back. We watched the snow falling. He drank. I pretended to drink.

"In the small town in which I live, which isn't really a town. It is a . . . a circle . . . a special small circle . . . like in Dante's *Inferno* . . . and in my circle, there are people who are saying bad things about me. I have to counter that. Partly by doing things that will prove that I am both loyal and valuable. In such situations, it is best to come up with some special gesture, special gift, that has . . . how do I say it? . . . That is attention getting and that is better than substance.

"What I heard was that thirty years ago, when the Soviet Union was collapsing, when my nation was on its *knees*, and the West, especially America, was gloating and taking everything it could and thinking it would have it all, then and forever, in this corner of the world, here, where you would think nothing of importance could possibly take place, there were events that greatly upset our chekists. There was this guy, Rick Cochrane, here, who fucked up several of their people and many plans. Then he disappeared. Pfft! Disappeared. Never found. Sleeper agent they thought. With a great cover. A Laundromat. Why the hell would a deep-cover CIA person set up in St. Anton? They couldn't figure it out. You will tell them, won't you?"

"Grigor, there's nothing to tell. There really isn't. I was never CIA or anything like it."

"You did run a Laundromat, didn't you?"

"Yeah, if you say so. But all we did was laundry."

"Come," he said. "This will be really good. We must plunge into the pond."

"Grigor, there's ice on the pond."

"Don't worry," he said, getting out of the tub.

"I'm not worried," I said. I very much was, but not about the pond.

It had a ladder built into the side. He started going down backward. He reached the ice in one step, then kicked. It was thin and broke apart quite easily. "You see," he said. He stepped back up, turned forward, then jumped in. He went down until he was completely underwater. He popped up with a demented grin, climbed up the ladder, strolled the few steps through the fallen snow to the bubbling tub, and got back in. "Wonderful," he said. "You must do it."

The smart part of me wanted to say, "I'm too old for this shit. I'm getting out of here." The other part of me insisted on saying, "You're not too old. You can still do shit like this." So I climbed out, walked through the snow, looked at the hole in the ice, and jumped. The most dramatic sensation was the noise. My blood beat on the inside of my head like a drum. *Ba-ba, bam, bam! Ka-boom-boom-boom!* I flew back up the ladder, dashed through the snow, and hopped back into the tub. After a moment or two, it all quieted down.

"It was good, wasn't it?"

"Yeah, sure," I said. "It was good."

"I have been studying with Sifu Raja Dubov, he is both a guru and martial arts master."

I said, "Ahh, Sifu Raja Dubov."

He said, "You know him?"

I had no idea at all who he was. With deep, sincere admiration, I said, "Very high esteem."

"Sifu Raja Dubov says we must do three plunges. One for the physical body, one for the spiritual body, and one for the eternal body. Three."

"OK," I said.

He took a swig straight from the bottle, gulp, glug, gulp. Off he went, through the snow, to the edge, leaping in a cannon ball, crack-adoodle-crack, thin ice breaking up, splash! Icy water shooting up. Down he went. Up he bobbed, hauled himself out with the ladder, through the snow, and back in beside me.

Alright. I did it too. Not as dramatically. But I did it. This second was far less violent internally than first. The noise was no longer so great that it was everything. I felt the water and the cold and plunging down and the effort to get back out.

We were both back in the hot tub. He had another slurp and swallow, passed the bottle, and said, "Thirty years they have been looking for you. Thirty years, now I will turn you over."

"What, like a cat dropping a mouse at the door as a gift?"

"Yes!" he said with great delight and a drunkard's merry laugh. "I like that. I like *you*."

"I don't think so," I said.

"Where are you going to go? Naked in the snow? There's Lev to stop you. Pavel is bringing them now. Five, ten minutes, there will be some men here. Who want to ask you questions."

"Fuck you, Grigor. You're not going to kidnap me or torture me or whatever, in the middle of the Lech, the luxury ski resort."

"Come on," he said, "Ready for the third?"

Up he goes, heading for the water. It's time for me to move on. I start getting out of the tub. I'll go inside, grab some clothes, grab Allison, and get the hell out of there. But Grigor comes bouncing out of his ice pond quicker than he went in. He's between me and the escape route. He's smiling. For the wrong reason it turns out. He thinks I'm eager to jump in and says so and how good that is.

OK. In I go. This time it's practically normal. He's standing beside the tub waiting. I stroll back. We both get in the hot water together.

I said, "You won't get away with it."

"There are no witnesses. Why do you think I sent everyone away? You will disappear."

"There's your wife . . ."

"I'm not worried. She obeys."

"There's Allison."

"I like her. I will keep her."

I was in a haze. Of alcohol. Of cold and heat. Of fear. Of the realization that as I had been plotting against God, I had not once stopped to consider that God had been plotting against me. *As flies to wanton boys, are we to the gods, they kill us for their sport.* Loki, who tricks even the gods, just because he likes to, Veles, his Slavic cousin, Hermes, God of Thieves who taught us lies, Eris, goddess of chaos who loves discord and strife, Laverna, goddess of cheaters, liars, and frauds. Isis,

Zeus, Odin, all the old pagan gods told lies, played tricks, took revenge, it must be that the modern Gods do, too, but just won't cop to it. So never trust a fellow named God or a woman called Goddess. Was I Allison's protector or destroyer? Was it time for my own demise? The fellows who were coming, FSB, modern devils in search of answers that would not be true. What to do, what was I to do?

"Sifu Raja Dubov," I said.

"You know him?"

"I know of him. I know the things he teaches," I said.

"How?"

"Russian friends. Who like to fight. In New York. In the mountains to ski with. In Brooklyn to do business."

"Ah!"

"You know what he says," I declared, "he says you must finish on a cold!"

Grigor thought about it for a moment. He said, "You're right!" Which was interesting because I was making it up out of hot tub fumes and vodka waste. He rose. He took the bottle. He swallowed. He put it down. He stepped out of the tub. He strode to the water. As he bent his knees to launch himself, I climbed out of the tub. As he rose in the air, I ran to where he'd been. As he splashed on down, I rose up in the air. I spun around 180 degrees, so that when I landed, standing on his submerged shoulders, I would be facing the ladder and I could grab the metal struts and hold on so that when he tried to push back up I could resist. He pushed. I pressed. He twisted. I pressed harder, working my hands down the ladder, pushing him deeper. He grabbed my ankles. He tried to throw me off. Down. Down, I walked myself down using the ladder for leverage. I felt a burst of bubbles coming up from below. I didn't stop. I pushed. I held on. It was cold. It didn't matter. He tugged at my ankles. Then he stopped. Then it all stopped. Stopped.

CHAPTER FIFTY

EMERGENCY 113

IN AUSTRIA, THE EMERGENCY NUMBER for the police is 113.

I ran inside. I grabbed a robe from the changing room, then charged upstairs. I didn't see Kaylee. I yelled for her. Allison picked her head up, she'd been lying on a big couch with Leo where I couldn't see them. She said, "Shh, you'll wake the boy."

"Where's Kaylee?"

She pointed to where the bedrooms were. I yelled for Kaylee again. She rushed out, straightening clothes, looking disorganized. "Call 113, right now."

"Now?"

"Right now, this second." I saw a phone. An actual landline. I grabbed it. Pushed the buttons, shoved it into her hands. "Tell them there's been an accident. A drowning. Tell them it's an emergency. Get here fast. Very fast. Maybe they can save him."

Lev appeared from the same direction that Kaylee had come from, tucking his shirt in, trying to push his hair back into place. Had Kaylee had sex with him, or been toying with him, and was he all hers now? Was that still part of the equation that I was trying to put together? "You," I said. "I think he drowned. Go try to save him. Go, go, go." He didn't have much English, but he seemed to understand. As he ran out, I barked at Kaylee again, "Tell them it's urgent. Urgent. Come fast."

Allison came up to me. "What happened?"

"He was drinking. A lot," I said. "He had this thing, macho, Russian thing, about jumping into the frozen pond. I tried it once, I thought I was having a heart attack, that my heart was pounding right out of my chest. Scary. Well, I guess it did him. He didn't come up. I tried to get him up, but he's too big, and the water was too cold."

"You did it, didn't you?"

"Accident. I didn't do a thing," I said. "There are some men coming. With Pavel. He went to get them. They want me. We have to delay them, stall them. Until the police get here. We need them to protect us. Me, and you. He wanted to take you, and they may, too."

I went down to get my clothes. I looked out. Lev was pulling God from the water. Nietzsche was laughing of course. He loved that God is dead stuff, even if it was just a pun on a cheesy Russian name. After I grabbed my clothing, I went back upstairs. I asked Kaylee where I could change. She said, "Upstairs." The third floor. That was good. I would be out of sight when Pavel and the others arrived. They'd probably go outside first, expecting me to be there with a living Grigor God Voloshin. Instead, they'd find the dead one with Lev, trying to revive him. That would create some confusion. Which would create time. A few more minutes before they came searching for me. I'd be upstairs, out of sight, dressing. Another minute or two. Maybe more. I waited. My heart was beating hard enough for me to feel it, though not so hard as when I was in the water, anxious to hear the sounds of the police and ambulance sirens, hoping they got there before Pavel came back with the Russian intelligence operatives.

Pavel came before the cops. They ran into the house. They ran downstairs and outside. They came back up. I heard the sounds of their feet rushing up the stairs, barking and yelping, indeed, louder than cats, even though the floors here were much more solid and firm than my own. They surrounded me. Grabbed me. I didn't resist. They shoved me along, down the stairs.

But Lukas and another *bundespolizei* and the EMTs showed up before they could haul me away. The bundespolizei took their guns out. They separated the civilians, Russians over there, in a small group, me, the American, to the other side.

Lukas grabbed me. "What's going on?"

I told him my story. The one in which the cold of the pond had shocked Grigor into drowning. Lukas looked skeptical. Maybe it was the natural response. Maybe because it was me.

Lukas made a phone call. Then he spoke to everyone else. The EMT guys said that the water was as cold as it could get and if Voloshin jumped in, it was likely to cause a heart attack or, even without that, if he was as drunk as the empty bottles indicated—there would be a toxicology report to give some exact measure—he could have been disoriented, not known up from down, tried to yell, swallowed water, all sorts of things, and drowned. They were deliberate, detailed, and thorough, as you'd expect from a Teutonic rescue squad. Even so, Lukas made them repeat it all, as he took notes. It seemed like he was stretching things out.

Then Franz, his father arrived. It was clear that was what Lucas had been waiting for. I guessed that was whom he'd called earlier. They huddled in a corner and consulted.

Then Franz pulled me aside. "What's going on?"

"An accident. He drowned." I didn't go into details. He already had them from his son. "Really," I said. "The coroner will agree. Forensics will agree."

"They better."

"That woman," I indicated Kaylee, though he knew who I was talking about, "is his widow. All she wants to do is go back to America, with her son, to be with her family, to deal with all this. Those guys, the ones who look like Russian thugs, they are Russian thugs. They want to restrain her, rip her off. It would be great if you could get rid of them. Get them out of the way. Then Kaylee, that's her name, and Leo, very nice boy, will go to Innsbruck and get out of your hair."

"My hair?"

"Out of Austria."

"Maybe," he said, open to considering it.

"Then they'll send some money back to pack up their stuff. Clean up this place. Ship things home. *Whatever it costs*. In fact, I have an Amex Black Card, no limits, we could cover it now."

"No," Franz said. "Cash would be better."

"It will be sent. You have my word."

"OK, Rick, Victor, Tony."

"Thank you."

"Don't fucking come back."

"I promise. Not for another thirty years."

We didn't bother with a helicopter. We took two taxis to Innsbruck. It was before dawn. There was no traffic. The drive was only an hour and a half. On the way to the airport, I asked Kaylee if there were any special foods she'd like for herself and Leo on the flight. She indeed had a list. I wrote it down. I phoned it in on the way. When we got on our flight, every item was on board.

CHAPTER FIFTY-ONE

TETERBORO

TETERBORO AIRPORT IS THE NEW York airport you've never been to, probably never heard of, unless you have a private jet.

It's in New Jersey. North of Newark. If there's no traffic, it's twenty minutes to Midtown Manhattan by car. Fourteen minutes by helicopter. It was as comfortable and pampered a flight as I've ever been on. I didn't know, I didn't ask, but I guessed the flight cost about $65,000. The pilot sent our customs and immigration information on ahead. We walked down the steps to the tarmac. Elizabeth was there with a limousine waiting for us. So were a customs and an immigration agent. They smiled at us, waved us along, then the second of the pair stepped up to me and said, "Please come with us, sir."

At immigration you are a stateless person. You have no rights. This was immigration even if there was no building or section of a terminal to mark it. I said, "Go on," to Allison and Kaylee. "I'm sure it's nothing. I'll call you later."

"I'll send lawyers," Elizabeth said.

"Good," I said. It's good for officials to know that someone who plays the game is involved.

As the customs agent waved everyone on, the immigration guy led me to their terminal building. Once inside, we walked through the main waiting area, down a hall, to a small office. He opened the door, and waved me in.

There was a desk and two chairs. There was a folder on the desk. The Mormon was sitting in the chair behind the desk.

With a gesture, the Mormon sent the man who'd brought me in away. As the door behind me closed, he said, "Have a seat."

I said, "What's your name?"

He thought about that for a second, and said, "Arthur James Thornborough."

"Are you a Mormon?"

"No."

"Then what?"

"Casual Methodist, I guess. And you?"

"I once would have said nothing, but I've had encounters with some ancient deities lately."

"Really?"

"I might be insane."

"Interesting. You were traveling on a false passport."

"It was just a ski trip."

He opened his file. He took out the accident scene photos of Mick McMunchun. He laid them out so I could see them.

"Tragic accident," I said.

He took out crime scene photos of Owen Cohen.

"Oh, God," I said, "that's terrible. Who would do such a thing?"

Then he took out a series of photos of the ice pond. It was a whole action sequence. Grigor jumping in. Me jumping after him. Me climbing out. Grigor not climbing out. They were from a very odd angle. I couldn't figure it out. How anyone got up that high.

"A drone?" I asked.

"Yes, very good." Arthur said.

"What now?" I asked.

"Grigor Voloshin," he said, "was a very dangerous person. Did you know he was on his way to Ashgabat?"

"Turkmenistan. Yes."

"Do you know why?"

"Not a clue."

"Nobody said anything about natural gas? Arms? Nationalism for the Russian minority?"

"No. Not a word."

"Would you tell me if they had?"

"Probably. I don't see why not."

"I have you dead to rights with Voloshin's death."

"I think it's already been ruled an accident. I bet the Austrians want to keep it that way. Do you want to send me back there?"

"I have to admit, I still haven't figured out how you did McMunchun."

I shrugged. "Accident. Really."

"And Cohen. I can prove you were in that office."

"I'm sure you can. But not when he died."

"I saw you following him from Brooklyn. But I lost you after you crossed the bridge."

"Maybe I was just going to Manhattan at the same time."

"The thing is, you're very, very good at this."

"At 'this'? What's 'this'?'"

"This"—he tapped the McMunchun photos with his forefinger— "This." Tap. On Owen Cohen. "This." God drowned from the point of view of a drone.

I said, "Oh." What else could I say.

Then he said, "We'd like you to work for us."

"Who's us?"

"It's one of those things, you have to say yes or no before there's an answer."

"What if I say no?"

"Oh, shit. Then you get prosecuted. Probably for Cohen. Certainly for Voloshin."

"I'd really like to know who you are first."

"You know what, I can assure you, we're the good guys."

Maybe it was the tension of the situation getting to me, but I burst out, "You know, I fucking hate that. 'We're the good guys.' The guys we're killing, 'they're the bad guys.' What are we all, six-year-olds? The news talks that way, generals, cops, politicians, presidents. It's like six-year-olds with cap pistols. *Good guys, bad guys.* How about some 'grown-up guys.'"

"Fair enough. We're the grown-up guys. We try to make the best of bad situations. We look for the better of two . . . no, the best of multiple ambiguous choices. Does that suit you better?"

What suited me better was getting out of his office, not being prosecuted in New York or the Arlberg. I said, "Yes." Though I was now agreeing to kill people for an additional organization. Some part of me remembered that such things are wrong. Or, I was making the proper adjustment to a world that had changed. Amoral? Post-moral? Free market economists believe that money is the true measure of value. If people only pay a little for something, it is of little value. If they pay a lot, it is of high value. Madelaine and Elizabeth were paying me $200,000 per corpse, just as a base rate, with significantly more through bonuses and such.

Just out of curiosity, not out of greed, I asked, "Is there money?"

"There would be," he said. "Though I can't say the amounts at this juncture."

Add that on top. In a reality in which the dollar value defined value, murder-for-hire was an act of great value. By the numbers, it was the most valuable thing I'd ever done.

The room was square and bare. The door was closed. No windows at all. No gods, ancient or new, could enter with chaos and lunacies. I said, "OK."

The Mormon, who was actually a casual Methodist, both of us quite godless in any case, given the conspiratorial relationship we were entering into, look pleased. In that pleasant, mild, Men's Wearhouse suit, shirt, and tie manner that he had. With a satisfied smile, but a moderate one, that would never offend, he nodded, and said one simple word, "Good."

Explanations, however limited, were in order.

"We've been embarrassed," he said. "Deeply embarrassed. By oversights. Failures. By our inability to deal with certain difficult problems.

"Let's start with Mick McMunchun, since that's where it starts for you. It looked like we might have another Jeffrey Epstein. Underage girls. Important men. We were keeping tabs on him, just trying to be sure that we got ahead of things before things got ahead of us. We stumbled over Elizabeth Bloom Carter trying to develop a murder-for-hire scheme. Then you came into the picture. Then he was dead."

"It sounds like you were wire-tapping her."

He shrugged.

"I hope you were," I said. "Then you'll have plenty of exculpatory material. I told her over and over again, I was explicit, that my goal was information, or in the case of Kaylee, physical rescue. Never murder for hire."

"We didn't mind."

"That they were willing to pay to have him killed? That I'm in fact innocent of the murder-for-hire scheme?"

"That McMunchun was dead. He was going to be a problem. It might have bothered us that Cohen was dead. But we're pretty sure he'd murdered his partner. We didn't know if he'd go down for that, so his death didn't bother us much either. In the grand scheme of things, some might even think that justice was done. More to the point, we couldn't quite pin that one on you, anyway.

"Then came Voloshin. We wanted to get him. But we couldn't. Worse, if we did, we didn't think we'd get away with it. But *you* did."

"I saw you there, in Lech, didn't I? With that hat?"

"Yes."

"How were you there? You had to be listening in on Elizabeth."

"Yes. Her secure room, the one that nobody can listen in on. One of her builders is one of ours, and the place is wired like the old U.S. Embassy in Moscow was by the Russians when we were foolish enough to use Russian workers to build it. Had to tear it down and rebuild it with stones from Minnesota."

"You know what she wants to do," I paused and didn't actually say murder husbands. "And you're going to let her?"

He sighed. He looked thoughtful. "So far," he said, "her targets have been OK with us." He gave a sort of shrug. Then shifted to a positive spin. "Also, she's opening avenues that we would never have thought of. I suppose that at some point she's going to make bad choices and we'll have to revisit things. But for now . . ."

"Who exactly are you . . . as a group?"

"I can't go into details. I can promise you that if you ever feel a certain specific action or target is a problem, you'll be able to ask about that. You could think about it this way, horizontally you have clearance and a clear view, but vertically, up the chain, you don't. That's how it has to be."

"Who do you want me to kill," I said, getting blunt about it. "The president?"

"Not at the moment," he said with a smile. Like it would never happen. "I'm glad this is working out. We're impressed. You have a knack. A talent. Your country needs it." Then he stood up. He came around the desk. He held out his hand to shake. I stood up, took it, and shook it.

"Here's what I can say," he said, with his mild smile and a real, apparently sincere, but always moderate, warmth. "Welcome to the Deep State."

ACKNOWLEDGMENTS

Thanks to Carl Bromley. I've been with several editors. He's the best of them. He was with this book every step of the way. And has an amusing accent.

The inside of the book—the type, typesetting, design—looks great. In an age in which such things are less than an afterthought, usually as if they had no thought at all, what a surprise. What a delight. Thanks to Emily Considine for that.

To Beste Doğan for the arty, provocative, and apt cover.

To the two Mikes, Lindgren & Barson, to Maya Bradford & Amelia Stymacks for their enthusiasm & support, for promoting and publicizing this book. My gratitude.